The Long Shadow

Of

Hope

By Andrew Spradling

This is a work of fiction. Names, characters, businesses are the product of the author's imagination or are used fictitiously. Interaction by these fictitious characters, teams, and conferences with existing organizations is imaginary and done with the intent of fictional legitimacy. Any resemblance to actual persons living or dead is entirely coincidental.

The Long Shadow Of Hope

A Novel

by Andrew Spradling

LOGAN:
CONGRATULATIONS ON PUTTING
ARKANSAS IN YOUR REARVIEW!
SO PROUD OF YOU! GOOD LUCK
IN YOUR JOB HUNT - MORE
IMPORTANTLY, IN YOUR
HAPPINESS! HAPPY BIRTHDAY
FROM ALL!
LOVE YOU, UNCLE DREW

Andy Spradling

This work is dedicated to the memory of Kelly Spradling Simmons, Jody Jividen, and Mike Cherry, three souls who provided inspiration, and left this world way too soon.

"Hell has three gates: lust, anger, and greed."

- Bhagavad Gita, Hindu Text

Prologue

Across America, it is Game Day. From Maine to Arizona,
Washington state to Miami, players, coaches, administrators, cheerleaders,
band members, fans, politicians, those in the television and radio industry,
campus bookstore workers, apparel bootleggers, tailgaters, hotel workers,
restaurant employees, bartenders, bookies, gamblers, and prostitutes prepare
for college football. Tens of millions participate. Billions of dollars are
spent. Careers are altered with a win or a loss. Futures blossom with the
mere spectacular catch of a leather – now composite -- oblong ball. Others
are ruined with a swipe of a knee, a bad audible under fire, or poor clock
management.

Saturdays in autumn turn hardened bankers into screaming fans.
Doctors, lawyers, and stock brokers dress in similar colors and wear odd
hats in show of support for their alma mater. Their little girls dress as
cheerleaders, their sons wear jerseys and toss miniature footballs in parking
lots. A wide variety of meats – steaks, burgers, ribs, chicken, pork
tenderloin, hot dogs, kielbasa -- are tossed on unique portable grills as dishes
of pastas, casseroles, salads, dips, wraps and wings are uncovered. Coolers
are filled, flasks are topped off. Fans drive recreational vehicles or massive
Sport Utility Vehicles, pitch tents, and brag about the number of cup holders
in their reclining lawn chairs.

No expense is spared. For many, tailgating wreaks of American
decadence as much as stock portfolios, boats, and 6,000 square-foot houses.

It is a way of displaying disposable income. Some travel thousands of miles to away games, live in hotels five or six weekends a season, taste of and experience the nuances of unfamiliar cities and towns -- all with the hope of a warm holiday bowl destination. Some venues pull in over 100,000 fans per game, affecting millions of people. The economic impact nationwide is immeasurable. But that is nothing compared to the euphoria of the home team hitting a pass on third-and-16 late in the game and behind on the scoreboard, a painful sack of a visiting quarterback, or a vicious hit by that prominent linebacker on the state rival's marquee running back.

Americans love college football like Europeans love soccer. Football though has more instant gratification... much more. The game provides offensive beauty, defensive brutality. Fans scream until they're hoarse. Afterwards, when the adrenaline and alcohol wear off – and often that isn't until Sunday morning -- they are drained physically but not emotionally. They know the stars and the substitutes of their teams. Hardcore fans even study the statistics of high school players rumored to be on the recruiting list of their favorite squad. The greatest players are held in highest regard and are immortalized by young fans and empty men.

1

As he often did, the enigmatic Charles Nester sat alone in his Athletic Director's luxury suite perched high in Ludlow Stadium. He relaxed with a cup of coffee and thought about how in five hours, the 75,000 seats around, below, and above him would be filled with euphoric fans craving a Lookout Mountain State University victory. The air outside was crisp, clean, and cool. It felt like autumn. There was but a cloud or two in the blue sky. It would be college football at its finest.

Now though, with just a few dozen workers and student volunteers scurrying about, Nester went through a mental checklist. He had to get in the zone. He ran scenarios through his head -- conversations he would have with the high-dollar contributors to the Black Bears program. And, equally important, the few he would avoid for varying reasons. He studied a list of annual fund donors to memorize the names of donors' spouses, female and male. He would be on... witty, knowledgeable, impressive. He would be well-liked.

That's what University President William S. Everett wanted -- a polished puppet as his athletic director. And Nester was polished from his wire-rimmed glasses right down to his hand-made Berluti shoes. He had admin-speak down to a science. Nester could talk to a reporter for ten minutes without giving a useable quote... a smokescreen with no smoke. A sportswriter would get lost in all Nester's wherefores and thereofs. His face was average with indistinguishable features yet he was not unhandsome. His cheeks were always rosy, but he never perspired. His coarse, reddish-blond hair stayed in place except in the strongest of winds. He could be equally charming speaking with a female tennis coach or a dinner of 2,000 boosters. He bore the burden of the public front, but did so without revealing his feelings or his protective nature.

Behind the scenes though, he held little respect. A yes-man for Dr. Everett, he was despised by Coach Sam Rosemont and his football staff. Nester held equal disdain for Rosemont, but he lacked courage so he continued to play it nice while attempting to use his position as the ultimate upper hand. He failed more than he succeeded. Everett had never allowed Nester to make an important decision or hire on his own, only announce them. Still, Director of Athletics was highest in the administrative pecking order on the athletics side– athletic director over coaches -- and this infuriated Rosemont, who was nearly larger than life to the public. The coach, fourteen years Nester's senior at 58, had grown weary of hiding his feelings towards the A.D.

"Damn it Nester, you don't have the good sense God gave a gnat," Rosemont told him after he'd signed Lookout Mountain State University to a two visit-one return with East Tennessee State, a team Rosemont deemed below the Black Bears in stature.

"Do we have to pay'em when we show, 'Good-deal Charlie?' Can I turn in the game ticket I have to buy on my expenses?"

Rosemont gave everybody a nickname. It was part of his sense of humor. And, part of his cynical nature. He could be cruel when riled and he didn't care who he offended. He was a great contradiction. To the public, Black Bears fans, and the media, he came off as an "Aw shucks" country boy from Left Creek, a hamlet one hour west of Pineknob as a crow flies. Lookout's campus was located on the west side of Pineknob, in the foothills

9

of Lookout Mountain, just southwest, and essentially a suburb of Chattanooga, Tennessee. To the people who worked with Rosemont, there was no love lost. In fact, except for his assistant coaches, most felt he was a prick of epic proportions. He had run off more help from the athletics corridors of Simpson Hall than Richard Nixon did underlings from the White House. Rosemont, though, had a better record than Nixon. His program was successful, and he was shrewd enough to keep that in the forefront. Similar to most American universities, football was the athletics driver. He knew it, and, behind the scenes, he emphatically made sure everybody else did, too... to hell with Title IX.

Rosemont had played his football at LMSU in the early 1960s when the industrial smog of Chattanooga had begun to hover in the atmosphere... a bruising fullback always willing to grind out the toughest yards, especially in the red zone. His strong legs churned like the pistons of an engine. He also had game-winning touchdown catches to his credit as a lethal target out of the backfield... once he had a head of steam -- tacklers beware. Common to those times, he also wrestled and ran track. He was a Hall of Fame icon the town of Pineknob, the 14,000 students on campus, the 150,000 gift-giving alums, many of the 250,000 people of Chattanooga – unless they were fans of the UT-Chattanooga Mocs, and on up the road, big brother University of Tennessee -- embraced as their own. He had blue eyes, tanned skin, and blond hair that had gone gray in his temples and sporadically throughout. He sported what he called "a gut," from too many fundraising dinners, post-game tailgate drop-ins, and late-evening coaches' meeting pizzas. His tired knees and administrative duties kept him from finding a way to be completely fit. But his paunch was just part of his extroverted personality. He was quick to smile and preferred it. He was completely accessible -- except on game day. On Saturdays his keen eyes and adversarial awareness was completely focused.

He was also respected among his peers. Rosemont ascended through the college football ranks like most head coaches, one or two years here, two or three years there. His concentration was in the Southern Conference, Southeastern Conference, the Southwestern Conference, the Atlantic Coast Conference, even the Big 10, and he'd worked as an offensive coordinator for some of the biggest names in college football. His resume read like a road map. From it a sportswriter could connect the dots to determine where Rosemont had worked with those he called friends, where he'd rubbed shoulders with those he now coached against, or where he'd coached or first worked with his current assistants.

The coaching fraternity is often transparent and embraces nepotism -- as long as the boss is winning. His wide receivers coach was Billy Reed, son of one of Rosemont's first bosses, Coach Will Reed, himself an institution at Southern Alabama University. Young Reed had to play two years of junior college ball to prove he could suit up for his daddy, but he was wiry and fast for a white boy. He could make his cuts on a dime, had great hands, and a coach's mentality. He was also extraordinarily slippery returning punts and kickoffs. Coach Reed and Rosemont got him the ball when they could and Billy never made them look bad. For that, and the respect he had for Will Reed, Billy Reed would always have a job with Rosemont if he wanted or needed it.

Besides, Reed was equally colorful on the field and behind the scenes. He had a flair the team's beat writers appreciated. Fair-skinned, while working in the deep South he picked up the habit of wearing a straw hat during practice to keep the sun off his face, ears, and neck, which made him stand out and appear even more colorful. He also interjected his own personality into interviews once he got through the rehearsed coaching clichés. In describing the difference between a Division I and I-AA player, he once told a reporter:

"Bigger, faster, stronger. It's all about inches and what they can become in five years," Reed said, gesturing with his hands as always. "If a fast high school linebacker is 5-10, he's I-AA. If he's 6-1, he might be a pretty good D-I player. But if he's 6-4, he can be a War Daddy. He can knock your jock in the dirt."

Because of Rosemont's offensive brilliance and his winning record, his offensive coordinators became coveted by other universities. Never had one of his coordinators remained for a third season. Many had departed after one. Because of that, he only hired offensive assistants who he felt could eventually be the leaders of his staff. Rosemont liked to delegate responsibility. During practices he would often step off to the side to speak with reporters, donors, fans, or the children they might have in tow. But he always kept one eye on the action. If he didn't like the way an aspect of practice was going, he'd roar like an angry lion.

"You guys are not blocking, damn it," he'd say, stomping back and forth in no particular direction. "You look like a bunch of junior high Sallys. We will not be able to gain a yard if you don't put some ass into it! I want you blowing these guys off the line. Bull your neck, find your man, talk to your teammates, and hit'em! I mean jack'em up! It ain't rocket science, man! It's all about attitude... you've got to want to block!"

Following one of his outbursts, the intensity always peaked for the next series of downs, the rest of the day even. You could hear the vicious collusions of plastic pads and helmets, the grunts of exertion, the shrieks of pain. This was exactly how Rosemont wanted his team practicing all the time, with the burner on high.

"Game preparation, boys… practice like you play," he would say. "Focus through the frenzy."

The defensive coaches were typically more animated during practice, raising the emotions of their players with constant beating down followed by praise. Defensive Coordinator Bud Steel was especially vocal and could motivate his players to the highest level at game time. He could get his players to that place where adrenaline pumps through their veins like a drug, taking control of their emotions and making them feel strong enough to leap over opponents for a sack or explode shoulder pads for a vicious tackle. Steel looked and acted like a square-jawed Marine Drill Sergeant, working his squad of turf warriors. "Attack… get off!" he'd say. "Create a new line of scrimmage! Be disciplined and relentless! Heavy up on the crossface, keep your hips square, make sure your second step splits the crotch of your man!"

To Steel, sports writers were an epidemic. He had a saying that he lived by, "They can't get you hired… but they can get you fired." Only occasionally would he share information about his players or his insights about strategy, and then only with reporters he knew were in Rosemont's good favor.

Rosemont wanted his quarterback on an even emotional keel, but his linemen had to be able to match the emotions of the defense, though it had to be done in a cerebral way. In post practice meetings, he was never shy about reminding Steve Lewis, his offensive line coach, of that fact. Contrary to ancient stereotypes, the modern offensive lineman got it. In fact, offensive linemen were most often the thinkers and highest academic achievers on a college football squad. Digesting their playbook, reads, and adjustments and then translating them to communication and action on the field took extreme dedication and usually about three years to master. It was uncommon for a redshirt freshman to see much action let alone start. A true freshman receiving playing time on the line was the equivalent of superstar status – without the fanfare – and a greater probability that the player would one day be a National Football League (NFL) draft pick.

For the first time in its history, LMSU had multiple -- a half dozen even -- players worthy of high NFL Draft status. In fact, a team that only eight years prior was Division I-AA, albeit National Champions, had on its squad a potential Heisman Trophy finalist and All-American at wide receiver, an All-American at quarterback, an incredible, well-rounded mixture of speed, size, and strength at running back, a left tackle roughly the size of a Lookout Mountain boulder, and a linebacker that had the power to stop that boulder if it ever broke loose. It was high times on campus when summer turned to fall. Everybody, the University, the local merchants, the townspeople, most of whom were fans, looked forward to tailgates and Black Bear victories. University Drive looked like a sea of Navy blue six Saturdays an autumn, and that equated to cash.

With no regard for etiquette, Chap Roberts barged in the open door of Charles Nester's Athletic Director's suite.

"Am I interrupting your pre-game ritual, Charles?" Roberts asked, knowing full well that he was a constant interruption to most people, short of Coach Rosemont.

Chap Roberts gave a couple of million bucks to the Black Bears Quarterback Club annually, far more than any other supporter, and he expected the ass-kissing treatment that went along with it. He'd gotten his start in the insurance business, but now a wide variety of establishments operated under his "Roberts Renderings" umbrella. He, in fact, enjoyed keeping secret just how many "Doing Business As" (DBAs) he had in the region. He'd swoop in like a vulture on any corporation in serious distress and buy it up. Upset with the prices he had to pay for his insurance fliers, he quickly became interested in the printing business. It wasn't long before he was an industry leader. Some of the stories of how he'd bought out all his competition were legendary, in one case waiting in the wings for a father to expire with a contract in hand for the son to sign. Now with a fat contract with the University for any and all print jobs, its insurance and 401K plans, as well as a couple dozen other budgeted areas, Roberts could easily afford a hobby like Black Bears football.

Besides, it gave him a great stage for his second hobby – chasing ladies. A married man in his mid-50s, Roberts was quick to claim God as his Savior but quicker to find a cozy corner of a business, bar, or alumni room to hit on or work up a female conquest. Despite his donation to the quarterback club and another $250,000 to the Big Blue Alumni Association, Roberts paid the $25,000 annual bill for a suite of his own at Ludlow Stadium. While he, like everyone else with the means, used the suite as an opportunity to network, entertain clients, and reward employees, one of his favorite activities was game-day sex. He was about a half hour from this Saturday's attempt when he stopped by to see Nester.

"No, Chap… How are you? Good to see you." said Nester. He cringed at the sight of Roberts. A vice suddenly gripped the muscles in his shoulders and neck. He dropped his feet from the barstool next to the one on which he sat. With a quick, weak handshake he added, assuming Roberts' purpose for the visit, "Is Thompson going to make the ceremony?"

Often, due to their roles with the program, Nester and Roberts worked together on athletic gatherings. But Roberts was Coach Rosemont's best friend, so between that relationship and Roberts' massive ego created by his contributions, there was always an unspoken conflict between him and Nester. Roberts had, and relished in, the upper hand.

Today, the Black Bears were honoring the 1972 13-2 squad. It had been 25 years since quarterback Rob Thompson led Lookout Mountain State University to its first National Collegiate Athletic Association (NCAA) Division I-AA title game, a contest it narrowly lost, 34-31, to Idaho Southern.

"He caught a plane thirty minutes ago," Roberts said. "He should get here just before the coin flip. I'm having someone pick him up and drop him off here to save time."

"Good thinking," Nester said. He cursed himself, wishing he'd been more proactive.

"He really wanted to be here… got a speech ready for the banquet tonight," Roberts said. "That guy keeps coming up with ways to re-invent himself. He'll try to make them think he was a 1,000-yard rusher by the time he's through. Holy shit, they used a sun dial to get his 40-yard dash time."

Nester laughed – maybe a little too loud he thought -- at that illusion. Thompson threw for over 8,000 yards in his career with 50 touchdown passes. While he wasn't exactly a liability in the open field, he wasn't what television commentators would call a burner. He could outrun a weary, overweight, defensive lineman though back when bulk was more important than speed. That 1972 team raised the bar to another level. Over the next seventeen years, LMSU would make it back to nine national title games, winning six. Rosemont won the last three and convinced the administration and Board of Trustees that it was time for Lookout Mountain State University to move on up to Division I-A.

"Well, he rallies the troops," Nester interjected. "Almost half that team gives to the Annual Fund."

"They sure-shit should, too," Roberts said. "Most of those guys didn't pay a dime to be here."

As the two men began to discuss the details of the halftime ceremony and the dinner for the 1972 team, Roberts' mind drifted elsewhere. In a couple of hours, two hours before kickoff to be exact, thirteen "Proposition 48" football players – the players ineligible for their freshman season due to low SAT scores – i.e., non-qualifiers -- would walk into a dozen of Roberts' establishments all over town for six hours of labor.

The work, maybe a bit of sweeping in an establishment already professionally cleaned, would actually take about a half hour. Roberts even provided the transportation. A white, 15-seat van with no identifiable markings, would pick up the players – who as freshmen props were completely on their own at the University other than the guidance of strength coach Pat "Stacks" Osborne – at the sandstone LMSU sign just down from the dorms.

By the time the thirteenth player was dropped at his destination, it was time for the driver, Jim Wheatley, to circle around and pick up the first player out of the van. The players made thirty dollars an hour for their "six hours" of trouble, and would be back in time for the Black Bears' kickoff. Roberts and Rosemont picked Saturdays for the players to work… they didn't have classes and anyone who might care was too busy with game-day

17

obligations or partying to wonder about the props' whereabouts. There were no witnesses on the sites either because the offices were usually empty. The 720 dollars a month for ten months – August to May -- would cover the players' rent and expenses if their parents couldn't afford to house them in the residence halls.

Most couldn't. Most, in fact, were lucky to scrape up tuition for that first semester, much less room and board. The parents that could were giving their sons – and themselves – a chance at the Division I dream and hopes of the NFL. Because it also had a community college, LMSU was one of the few programs of note in the country to take on props. The upside of the arrangement was that LMSU would sometimes gain a blue chip recruit formerly on his way to the Michigans, Ohio States, and Southern Cals of the college football world before stumbling on an academic hurdle in high school.

Many of LMSU's standout players through the past ten seasons had been props… often players who simply hadn't studied hard enough in high school as the pampered athletic stars of their class. Eligibility-wise, the props' freshman year was burned unless they remained on track academically. If they succeeded they could earn back their fourth year. Rosemont stressed it. He genuinely wanted his players to graduate. It was one of the promises he made to them while recruiting. "You'll play for a winner and you'll get your degree," Rosemont would say, appealing simultaneously to the sensibility of the player and the parents – often a single mother – during his home visit. "We play for titles at LMSU."

Of course, back among the ranks of his assistants, nothing was off limits for Rosemont's comedic efforts. "I'd really like to have that kid… he doesn't know the meaning of the word fear. 'Course, there are a lot of words he doesn't know the meaning of..."

Back in the Athletic Director's suite, caterers delivering plump, cold-boiled shrimp, chicken and steak kabobs, vegetable and cheese trays, chili, cold cuts, sandwich fixings - and all the other game-day snacks one would expect for the $25,000 annual bill - interrupted Nester and Roberts' conversation, bringing Roberts' wayward mind back into the room.

"Oh, I'd better get out in the parking lot," Nester said, making a quick study of his watch, anticipating where the Black Bears' other large contributors - and Dr. Everett - would begin to congregate. "Things will go fine tonight."

"Don't forget to mention Pete Jacobs when you're announcing the 1972 team at halftime," Roberts said. "He's been a great contributor and would have been here."

"He's on my list. Is he going to be ok?" Nester asked, of the former defensive back currently battling colon cancer.

"They think they caught it in time," Roberts said. "He's still doing chemo though."

As the two men walked towards the elevator down a navy blue-carpeted hallway, with 2 x 3-foot pictures of LMSU football stars adorning the walls, a shapely, 5-foot-8 blonde woman with a welcoming smile stepped confidently through the opened doors.

"Hi Chap," said Leslie Workman, a 23-year-old Master's of Business Administration student Roberts promised would make some great business connections if she watched today's game from his suite. "Am I late?"

"Right on time," Roberts said, tingling at the sight of her ample breasts filling her navy blue, sleeveless silk blouse. A diminutive but handsome man with a sharp nose, the pair stood eye-to-eye.

"You're going to have a great day, Leslie. Let me show you where we'll be. Do you like mimosas?"

Nester stepped on to the elevator, faced the opened doors -- not yet manned with its game-day attendant -- nervously checked his watch, realized he wasn't moving, then pushed the "G" floor button. As the doors closed, Roberts placed his left hand on the small of Leslie's back, and gently turned her in the direction of "Roberts Printing" luxury suite.

Kickoff was four hours away.

2

In the history of Black Bears football, no quarterback filled the stereotypical bill more than Ben Wright. A 6-foot-4, 225-pound, blond, handsome, straight-A student, Wright was imported from Northwest Ohio. Falling under the radar of the likes of Ohio State and Michigan as a late-bloomer only added to his legend for Lookout Mountain fans when he gained national prominence.

While Nester and Roberts were having their meeting, Wright was into his third hour of watching game film. That, after remaining in the film room until 9:30 the night before, giving him just enough time to be in bed by 10 p.m. He heard the words of his father, Russ Wright, as he had so many times before when he reached to turn out the bedside light of his football dorm room. "The two hours of sleep before midnight are the most important, son," the elder Wright had lovingly repeated so many times throughout Ben's youth.

Like so many successful quarterbacks in the college and pro ranks, Wright's father was a high school football coach. Ben Wright spent his childhood and adolescence around, and then in, high school practices, games, and off-season workouts. Family dinners were not off limits for "chalk talk" for him and his two brothers, as the subtleties of the game would often turn into hour long discussions. Ben's mother, Vickie, knew more ins and outs of the Wing-T and the Triple Option than the better-than-average fan, picking it up as she served and nurtured her football-loving family. The family's post-dinner television was most often film sessions, as Vickie would keep herself busy rustling around cleaning and picking up.

Thus, Wright was a firm believer in preparation. He believed as much in game film as he did his Lord. He would spend as many hours as his academic schedule would allow in the offensive war room of the Black Bears' facilities building, named after Rosemont's coach, Ennis Ivory. Wright rivaled the offensive coaches with film study and was as talented as any of them at analyzing the oppositions' defense. He had an uncanny ability to take what he picked up in the film room and use it on the field. He knew when a free safety would cheat on "trips" (three wide receivers) right, or when a cornerback would get confused on play-option with their tailback, and he would make them pay.

Wright's No. 1 option in Rosemont's variation of the West Coast offense was sophomore wide receiver Danny Smith, an off-the-chart athlete who at 6-foot-5 had world-class speed, a 46-inch vertical leap, and hands so soft he sometimes needed only the four outstretched fingers of his gloved-right hand to pull in a Wright rainbow. He had the ability to break a game wide open, and could bring a crowd to its feet and to a fever pitch as quick as a cutback or a shoulder flinch.

Smith was a young black man from Pineknob with a quick temper, a weakness for an occasional joint, and a propensity for speaking without thinking. The combination of those traits made for a great deal of baggage. While still in high school, but at 18 years of age, Smith was caught with a dime bag of marijuana during a random locker check. Drawing a sympathetic judge who understood what jail time would mean to Smith's future, the athlete received a break in the form of three years of probation.

Prior to his arrest, Smith had his pick of colleges and was leaning towards Alabama over the University of Tennessee and most other Top 25 programs, stating publically at the time he couldn't stand orange or the Volunteers' anthem "Rocky Top," a slap in the face to most Tennesseans. Unfortunately, the scholarship offer from the Crimson Tide and every other top 50 program in the country was pulled after Smith was escorted by police from Pineknob High in handcuffs. Seizing the opportunity, Coach Rosemont first approached Smith's minister about the speedster staying in town, pointing out that he believed Ben Wright would prove to be one of the most outstanding quarterbacks in college football history and would be the perfect QB for Smith. That line cast, and with no other respectable options, Smith took the bait. Rosemont publically welcomed Smith to LMSU, holding a special press conference about the school's good fortune. Black Bears fans hoping for a hometown miracle originally were hurt when Smith had not considered staying put. They were happy now to be getting his talent but distrustful of his motives. Word of any negative activity by Smith brought a flurry of media attention.

"Just keep your nose clean for two years," Rosemont told Smith in his office. "I'll get you the ball and all your dreams will come true. You could play for some NFL teams right now. But if you work, listen to me and Coach Reed, they'll all want you. Just play it smart."

Smith had taken the nation by storm as a freshman. His combination of speed, height, and jumping ability made sub-6-foot cornerbacks of the Southwestern Conference easy targets for the deft touch of Wright's throwing arm. Smith scored 22 touchdowns including a few sweeps, punt and kickoff returns that first year -- *in 12 games* – and became a weekly ESPN highlight reel.

Smith and Wright had the Black Bears off to a 5-0 start this season. The receiver was on pace to break his school and SWC touchdown reception records though he was drawing double-teams from defenses well aware of the dangers he presented.

Despite the high times, Smith hadn't completely put his troubles behind him. In the preseason, an *Atlanta Daily Democrat* writer, Jack Dickson, visited LMSU hoping to update America through the wire services on the former *Parade* High School All-American first teamer. Though he appeared friendly, he got off the plane with an agenda larger than his suitcase.

The story he wrote painted Pineknob as a hick Tennessee town, pointing out that businesses such as a Po' Boy Clothes, a consignment shop, operated across the street from Ludlow Stadium, failing to mention the 10,000 square-foot establishment was across a six-lane, one-way highway. In talking with Smith about an NFL career, he cut and pasted the 20-year-old's quotes to fit his purpose, until his words sounded as though Smith hated Pineknob and would never come back when he was "freed from its grip." The local media of course swarmed. Smith tough-talked his way out of it, with Rosemont's help, saying Dickson twisted his words and took his remarks out of context.

"I didn't say that crap, man, you think I'm crazy?" Smith said, surrounded by print and television media numbering sixteen. "That ain't me, man. Uh, that guy was out to get me. My Momma is here in Pineknob, man. I love it here. I've been watching the Black Bears since I was a kid. I want to give Coach his props for giving me this chance to display my skills and shine. I'll always be back if I'm lucky enough to have a pro football career. Now, does anybody want to talk about LMSU football?"

When the interview ended, Smith walked away with a cocky gate, shoulders thrown back, his chest swelled. Later in his dorm room, one wrinkled, torn Michael Jordan poster on the wall, he lay on his side, knees drawn to his chest, and cried like a child, at times gasping to take in air. Elementary school memories of feeling academically inferior – when the tough talk started – came flooding back like the warm tears falling on his worn blanket. Not reading ready at seven years old, he'd been behind from the start, the hole deepening each year. He wasn't mentally slow, but academically he watched his fellow students surpass him. Thus, he played it off as though he didn't care about school. His defenses got sharper as he grew. But so did his athletic ability. He worked night and day on his skills. He was a natural who also dominated in basketball, baseball and track… basically anything he tried. By the time he was in high school, he'd all but given up academically, taking the most remedial classes, getting by with the lowest possible grade-point-average to remain on the field.

The media always had Smith in its collective thoughts since he remained in Pineknob. Early in the previous season, Rosemont sat with a couple of Black Bears beat writers in his office, following his weekly press conference. One, *The Chattanooga Times'* Rick Bayless, was in his early 50s, a sports bookworm who'd never been married, never spent money on his wardrobe, and was out of touch with the youth of the day. He could recite Mickey Mantle's yearly batting averages, but couldn't distinguish one player from another, black or white. The other sportswriter, *The Chattanooga Daily Register's* Michael Kelly, 30, one day watched Bayless ask every black athlete who walked by him in the facilities building – around 30 players -- if they were Jerome Jones. "Are you Jones? Are you Jones?"

Sadly, all Bayless had to do was ask Sports Information Director Jim Winkler for some assistance.

On another occasion, on media day prior to Wright's sophomore season – Wright had already started the entire previous year as a redshirt freshman and was well known -- Bayless approached Winkler and asked, "You Ben Wright?" Winkler, who was a head shorter than Wright at 5-foot-9 with dark features looked nothing like Wright. He was exasperated.

"Rick, I'm Jim Winkler. I did an internship two summers ago at your paper, remember? I'm the S.I.D. here."

Since that time, despite Winkler's attempts to keep the incident quiet to safeguard Bayless's dignity, the players began asking first Winkler, and then Wright, that question. Winkler would get irate, so the players eventually quit bugging him. Wright, and then his teammates, began using the double meaning of his name for humor. "You Ben Wright?"

"Never been wrong," Wright would say, or "Every time I audible," or "Every time I face a defense." It eventually became a mantra and a battle cry, and Wright's humble demeanor was never compromised by any bravado following what became known as "The Question" and later "The Big Q." His answers on those occasions inspired his teammates and Wright was smart enough to recognize it.

Kelly and Bayless were discussing Smith's most recent three-touchdown effort when Bayless asked Rosemont if the wide receiver was staying out of trouble and off the streets. Rosemont paused, and shaking his head yes said, "Well, you know… that pussy is undefeated."

Rosemont and Kelly burst into laughter.

"What do you mean?" said Bayless, without a change of expression.

"Well, Righteous Rick, and this is all off the record – if you write any of this we're done - I don't think he's doing anything that would get him into trouble," Rosemont said, annoyed the writer missed the joke. "But he probably is out there at night prowling around trying to get some. You know what I mean?"

"Not exactly."

"Co-eds. Female companionship. Sex. You see?"

"Do you endorse that kind of behavior?"

"Endorse? Absolutely not. I'd rather he be in his room studying. That goes for all of my players. But these are twenty-year-old kids. Have you ever tried to stop the wind from blowing? Ever have an urge other than to read a book or run? He's not chasing any more tail than a member of the golf team or the baseball team. But he's probably getting more because he's famous and has the potential for some serious earning power."

"Uh-huh," Bayless said.

"What he does in his spare time doesn't concern me unless he ends up on a police blotter, you know? It's impossible for me to keep track of 110 young adults twenty-four hours a day. We try to keep them busy for about sixteen hours of it. But they've got a lot of energy."

An hour and a half before kickoff, Wright, Smith, and twenty other eager skill players take the field sans shoulder pads, to loosen up and get reps with the football before traditional warm-ups, the coin toss, and kickoff. The players and coaches were all business with a tough, non-conference, East Carolina team coming into Ludlow.

Up above, Chap Roberts learned he'd underestimated Leslie Workman, who sipped her drink seductively but picked Roberts' brain about business while warding off his advances, finally saying to the ever-more-frustrated booster, "This isn't going to happen, Chap. Would you like me to leave so you can call in someone else to screw, or can I stay and meet your other guests?"

Roberts' cell phone rang. Seeing it was Jim Wheatley, he said "Excuse me" and gave a "Hold that thought" one finger motion to Leslie and answered as always.

"Hey. Everyone dropped off?" Roberts asked, into a phone that seemed overly-loud to Workman. She could hear the man's voice on the other end.

"One no-show. The kid from Nashville, Rex Smalls. We waited a bit," Wheatley said.

"Smalls. OK. I'll let him know," Roberts said.

Roberts closed his cell phone and looked longingly at Leslie Workman. He wasn't looking for any lengthy challenges when it came to female conquests, and he found himself respecting this young woman for her toughness and honesty.

"No, please," he said, mustering a charming smile. He picked up his glass casually. "I'd be honored if you stayed. I can see you're going to be a Cracker Jack in the workforce. You call me when you graduate."

The Black Bears were picked to win by three, but with the gap seeming to ever-widen between the talent of Smith and opposing defenses, LMSU fought out a 17 point victory, 31-14. Smith caught two Wright touchdown strikes of 15 and 33 yards in routine manner. But the head-shaker of the day was a punt return in which the speedster seemed trapped to the right, reversed his field away from his teammates' crumbling wall, found a seam, hurdled one defender who blindly attempted to take his legs out, stiff-armed another, then cut back on the last hope over-pursuer for a 79-yard score. The crowd of 75,144 stood on its collective feet and roared with excitement.

Tradition called for the male cheerleaders to stand in the aisles of each home section and military press – that's over their heads and back down to the chest -- their female cheerleading partner once for each point scored *after every touchdown*. The keys to pulling off the stunt were a good grip on the inside of the girls' upper thigh, that the girls didn't weigh more than 110 pounds, that she could keep her body stiff for the length of the presses, and help a little with her lower hand which was placed on the male's shoulder at the base of his neck. It was a feat of incredible strength and endurance for the males – the Black Bears could sometimes put up 48 or 55 points. That could mean 200 or 225 military presses a game. It was a fan favorite and part of the Black Bear atmosphere. The crowd counted the points aloud, as the 100-member band -- including a 24-piece drum section - played to beat all hell. Lookout Mountain State University was 6-0.

There were a few minutes in the third quarter when ECU was driving and looked as though it could overtake LMSU's 17-14 lead, but a safety blitz by Buster Cantley on third down led to a sack of ECU quarterback Rich West, forcing the punt that Smith returned. That slammed the door shut. Wright passed for 319 yards on 21-of-27 attempts, hitting ten different targets, keeping ECU's defense on its heels all day with the help of junior tailback Steve Lake, who rushed for 144 yards and the team's other TD. All those wearing blue believed this was the year for true greatness, when LMSU would enter and remain forever in the ranks of the Top 20.

The game's 1 p.m. start left plenty of time for the party to spill into the evening hours… and it always did. The fans returned to their respective tailgates, or moved on to the local bars and restaurants. The players met with their families and girlfriends outside of Ivory Facilities Building, as did the game's stars, once the media was taken care of. That afternoon, linebacker Jerome Jones led the Black Bears defense with 17 bone-crushing tackles. One particularly wicked hit left ECU tailback Lester Pratt's helmet rolling across the ground. Jones picked it up and without thinking, and looked inside it as though there might be a decapitated head inside. The crowd was euphoric. A humble person, Jones could only smile widely as the media questioned him about the hit and subsequent inquisitive glance into his foe's head gear.

"No. I didn't really think his head was going to be in there," Jones said with a broad smile, "but you never know."

Wright was accommodating to the press, as always spreading the credit, thanking his linemen, and giving the All-America answers. Smith skipped the press conference, leaving the media searching for enlightening observation of his astounding feats of the day. Rosemont filled in the blanks there but gave the typical coaches clichés when it came to looking at the possibility of an undefeated regular season, saying "We're not looking past next week's opponent. We take them one game at a time."

Buster Cantley was a nervous, new, yet positive participant to the proceedings, trying to describe how his blitz worked. In the back of the room stood Roberts… all access was granted to Chap Roberts.

A bit later, Jones, a chiseled, 6-foot-3, 245-pound black man from Southern Georgia, walked out of Ivory with two adoring Prop 48s, Emanuel Bennett and DeJuan Richardson. Both were defensive players who hoped to one day carry the stature of Jones, whose future in pro football seemed secure. Jones was also a mature, respectable student. He had come in as a prop himself and regained his fourth year of eligibility through hard work in the classroom.

By chance, Dwayne Price, a focused associate athletic director whose job was dealing with NCAA compliance, followed the three athletes on the sidewalk that led to Parking Lot A behind the home side of Ludlow Stadium, which was still filled with fans recapping the game, drinking, and eating leftovers. Price, who'd been on the sideline for the clock's final tick, wasn't noticed by the trio, who were making plans for their Saturday night.

"What do you guys want to get into?" asked Bennett.

"I got to get down with some ladies," Richardson said. "Whose crib we going to?"

"That girl Shante said they'd be rockin' all night," Bennett said. "Unless you want to go to a club."

"You sure she's got friends?" Richardson asked. "That girl's got a mean streak in her."

"That's why I like her," Bennett said. "She's a beast. She climbs up on it like a beast."

"I need some food before I do any of that," Jones said. "You guys were eating the whole game weren't you? How many dogs did you slam, Big E?"

"Bro, after the game you had, I'll buy you a dinner…. a steak if you want. I still got some Chap cash," said Richardson, slapping a high-five with Bennett.

"How you still holding on to some of that? Didn't you pay rent?" Bennett asked.

"Man, we got eight brothers living in that crappy house," Richardson said. "My split ain't but $100 a month... another $50 in utilities. I got plenty of cash."

"Shut up about your cash," Jones said. "You can still get mugged around this town. You can get your ass shot flashing it in a club. I ain't getting caught in no bar during the season no how. Besides, these good people out here will feed us."

"Feed you, maybe," Richardson said. "They don't know us."

"Yeah, we're just a couple of brothers from nowheresville," Bennett added.

"You just got to work'em a little bit," Jones said. "These folks are fans, man, and we're a BIG SIX AND ZZZEEERRRROOOO. GOOSE EGG, BABY. They love us. They want to talk about the game."

At that point, Price, smiling from the players' banter -- which he couldn't at times completely understand due to the noise in the parking lot and the radio postgame show blaring over the stadium speakers -- peeled off to the left, cutting between groups of fans as the early October sun began to soften in the western sky. Having only been at his job since July, he didn't know many people outside of his work circle. Many of those were still engaged in post-game duties. Athletic Director Charles Nester, always hoping to sway new employees to his favor before they figured out his boot-licking, fraud act, had asked Price to join him at the dinner for the 1972 team... at the athletic administration table. Nester would be at the head table. But, the more people from the athletic department the better, just not too many, Nester surmised. A good mix of athletics personnel and fundraisers from the Office of Advancement were necessary, and one-on-ones with potential donors was essential. No guests should leave without a moving conversation about Lookout Mountain State University and what it takes to keep it going.

With each step Price took, something from the players' conversation confused him and made him uneasy. His antennae were shooting warning signals to his brain like a hammer striking a 16-penny nail. He replayed it over and over as best he could in muddled rewind as he approached the elevator for the lift to Big Black Bears Hall, used for athletic fundraising events, second floor of the stadium, one level below the VIP suites. "I still got some *what* cash?"... Price asked himself. What did Richardson say? It was so fast and so noisy, and he couldn't see him speak the words from behind. "Got some check cash, jack cash, chat cash, chip cash, ship cash, chick cash." It seemed less and less audible to him as he stepped off the elevator. Each time he replayed it, the blending of possibilities made his memory fuzzier. "Was he talking about drugs? I wouldn't know if he was," Price thought. "Jump cash, junk cash." Whatever Richardson had said, "cash" was a red flag and it was weighing heavy on Price.

Price was a Pennsylvania native who had wrestled at Penn State while earning a degree in political science. He had planned to attend law school but money was tight so he joined the Navy for a four-year stint, hoping he could convince someone there to pick up the tab. He couldn't. He still had law school in his sites though. A perfectionist, Price was meticulously neat and thorough in his job and his life, right down to his high and tight hairstyle. He wrestled at light heavyweight in college, keeping his weight at 180, giving himself three pounds of leeway of which he never had to take advantage. In fact, with his wrestling days behind him, he still wouldn't allow himself to surpass 185 in weight. This kept him taut and his facial features angular, and his eyes and hair were as dark as charcoal.

33

He was single and dated little, none to speak of since arriving in Pineknob. He wasn't opposed to it in theory, but generally wouldn't grant himself the distraction, finding the start-up procedure awkward and annoying. Thus, as the duties of his job dictated, he worked singularly and would leave no stone unturned if he felt there was impropriety under way at LMSU.

3

Back in the "War Room," in Ivory Facilities Building, the room in which Rosemont met with his entire coaching staff, the events of the game were kicked around more conversationally than with the conviction and proof of tomorrow's film study, although, due to their experienced eye, seasoned coaches picked up more from an outing than fans. Assistants were typically watching the players that they coached in their play and stunt calling, and sometimes would have a better idea than the head coach as to why a play or a coverage broke down. Although, Rosemont seemed to have a sixth sense about seeing from the sideline what one would presume was obscured by mammoth blockers and tacklers on the field. It was that ability and his game day intensity that gave Black Bears fans the unforgettable site of their beloved coach verbally ripping into an official, which he did with unbridled conviction.

Saturday night was the only time off for the coaches during the season. They would be back to work at 7 a.m. Sunday morning breaking down film and grading their players' performances, why an offensive lineman missed a block on a certain play, what caused a hole to open on defense. It was all documented… offensive linemen were graded and given effort points. Saturday night was usually the only time the assistants would have with their families all week, other than the time reserved for sleep. If the team was playing on the road, forget it, that free time was taken up by return travel. Younger coaches or student assistants without families could often be found out on the town after games, which was also beneficial in keeping an eye on the players. Rosemont tended to hire God-fearing coaches already married and usually with children. He had four grown kids of his own, two boys, two girls, and he loved seeing his grand kids or other coaches' children around practice and Ivory. But not on game day... or at least not until after the battle.

Though East Carolina was a program that often flirted with the Top 25, Rosemont knew it was a contest his team should have won by the 31-14 margin, thus he was a bit uneasy that ECU had produced well enough to cause some tension on the sidelines in that all important third quarter. The third was historically the Black Bears' knock out time, in no small part due to Rosemont's inspirational halftime speeches. It was failed execution, mental lapses, and a shanked punt that put the Pirates in a position to overtake LMSU, leading to Cantley's heroics.

"Was it Robinson that missed the block on that outside 'backer on second and 10?" Rosemont asked Steve Lewis of their right tackle, Tim Robinson.

"Yep. Put his head down and completely missed him," Lewis said. "Wallace had changed the blocking assignment, but Robinson had the same man."

"That was what play?" asked tight ends coach Nick Blanch.

"34 Dive," Lewis said.

"Probably should have thrown again," Rosemont said. "How many did Wright miss, seven?"

"Six," said quarterbacks coach Trip Cobb. "And three of those were drops."

"Not likely we would have missed two straight," Rosemont said.

"That's what I thought they'd be thinking. And Miller was manhandling that end," Offensive Coordinator Paul Lawson said of tight end Andrew Miller. "I thought we'd have that right side cleared."

"That's when 44 put Robinson's face mask in the turf," said Billy Reed. "Beat him bad on that one. I think he got a rug burn on his forehead."

The comment brought laughter to the room, and while Rosemont wasn't above getting as nasty after wins as he was losses, he was in a good mood. He was a young assistant on the 1972 team, so he had numerous buddies waiting for him. He was usually as quick to laugh at Reed's jokes as anybody, part of the reason he embraced him so.

"They hadn't brought in the nickel back. So they weren't sold on the pass. Just make sure you stress execution on every play," Rosemont said to everybody, though he was looking at Lewis. "No breakdowns. We get through old Lindemood on this road trip and we should slip in to the Top 10. After that, who knows? There may not be six teams in the country better than us. Especially with Smith playing like he is. Did he accelerate on that punt return or what? Looked like me in my heyday."

"Shit, coach, dad told me you couldn't even *finish* a 40-yard dash," Reed said.

"Oh, I could finish 'em all right. The staff just didn't usually wait around that long. They'd be smoking cigarettes out in the parking lot by then. How would your dad know anyway... watch me on film?"

"Yeah, I think he called it a historical documentary," Reed replied, relaxed in the typical banter he shared with his former coach and longtime friend.

Rosemont just shook his head with a big grin.

"All right, we're breaking down film at 7 a.m., grade out reports during lunch, we'll decide on players of the week. Then we'll start on Georgia State. They just beat Texas A&M on a last-second field goal, so we'll have our work cut out for us down there. They're 4-2 but they've won four straight. We got it going the right way. Things are going to start getting crazy around here. We have got to stay focused. No breaks from the routine. Anybody wants to come to this '72 team dinner they're welcome. Bring your wives if you want and if you've got 'em. Great job, guys."

With that Rosemont and his assistants broke from the War Room to get on with their evenings. Few would attend that dinner. Reed would, though he'd cut out quickly after. He saw it as networking. While he too wanted to one day be a head coach, he'd been around enough to know he could just as easily end up in administration or out of the game completely. College football seemed like a paradise, but for many it turned out to be a mirage. A program run correctly was an intense, unending yearly cycle with just a short break in early summer. The season led to recruiting, recruiting to conditioning, conditioning to spring ball, spring ball to "voluntary" summer drills, each phase overlapped the other, though recruiting was really unending, the travel for which was brutal for some assistants. Plus coaches had the constant headaches of injuries, grades, keeping players out of trouble, head coaching changes, and other incidentals that inevitably popped up. It was a wild ride but with beautiful payoffs when the team was winning. Most men just aren't built for it, preferring nine to five and weekends free.

As his assistants exited from either end of the room, Rosemont took the door in the middle, which led to his office. There, kicked back with a Crown Royal and 7UP, waited Chap Roberts.

"Call out for breakfast. I thought you'd never get finished," Roberts belted out.

"It was the radio show and press conference that held me up," Rosemont said. "That's only going to get worse. Winkler told me we've got three national crews coming in here on Tuesday. I'll tell you, we're on a roll right now. You see any of it?"

"You bastard. Yes, I saw the game... started sweating for a minute in the third quarter. Cutting it close, weren't you?"

"Don't get me going on Lawson... I might have to start calling plays."

"Wouldn't be the first time. That's why you wear a headset, isn't it?"

"Yeah... but I like to give them a shot. It's a learning experience for them, too."

"Then shut the hell up. He'll make the right call next time. I'm sure you got him sweating... probably won't sleep tonight. Anyway, I also procured a 20,000 dollar commitment for next year from Dexter Machinery... haven't even told Everett or Nester that breaking news. So, I was working for this place, too."

"You're a Hall of Fame alum, Chap," said Rosemont, with a hint of sarcasm. "Everything else go ok today?"

"One no-show. Smalls," said Roberts. "Everyone else was at the pickup. Clean and neat."

"Good. I'll talk to Smalls. Go ahead and include him. He'll make it up with Stacks," Rosemont said, using as few words as possible, a habit of his on the subject of Roberts' Prop 48 pickup, as if brevity made him less guilty. Stacks Osborne would put the fear of Jesus in Smalls by way of the stadium stairs. "We'd better get up there hadn't we? Let's grab Billy."

4

The party for the 1972 team was under way when Dwayne Price walked through the open, oversized oak doors. The exterior design of the grand room sported floor-to-ceiling windows except for the bit of wall it took to hide the steel that held Ludlow Stadium together. Outside, a magnificent, red sun was setting over Lookout Mountain just to the west. That, the fans below, and Pineknob resting before the explosion of reds, purples, yellows, and oranges provided by all manner of hardwoods in their Autumn splendor made for a majestic view. In the middle of the room, some thirty feet in the air, hung a beautiful antique chandelier which had been imported from France. Price was quite impressed by the scene, and he was gratified to be included in the event. This was the bread and butter of college athletics. Showing respect for your history creates legacies in Admissions.

Price had read a good bit about the 1972 football team as he became familiar with the Black Bears athletics program by looking through and studying old media guides and yearbooks.

The drinks were flowing as he saw old teammates slapping shoulders and laughing, talking about the glory years. The cliché, "The older I get, the better I was" came to mind as he walked close enough to hear some of the banter being exchanged.

From his research, he recognized by name one of two of the '72 teammates talking without a LMSU employee in the group. He ordered a gin and tonic, a rare indulgence for him, before approaching the pair.

"Mr. Hilbert, Dwayne Price," he said, with his hand extended. "I'm the compliance director here. I'll bet you would have liked to have been out there today getting a few licks in on Pratt, huh?"

Bobby Hilbert, a former defensive lineman known for his own bruising style of football, shook Price's hand with his still-strong, thick mitt. He was flattered and impressed with the newcomer's knowledge, smiling broadly then smacking Price's shoulder. He'd been consuming cocktails since pre-kickoff.

"I don't know, he might have been a little too quick for me. They didn't seem to be so fast back in my day. I'm not sure I could've gotten off those monsters on that line either," Hilbert said. He was red-faced from the drink, the heat, and the banter. "Dwayne, this is Anthony DeAutio, our squad's own 'Italian Stallion' at wide receiver. Tony could squeeze through defenders like a wet noodle through your fingers. He could catch it, too."

All three men laughed loudly at the image of DeAutio slipping through a helpless defense as though he were dowsed in olive oil. "Great to meet you, Mr. DeAutio. Glad you are here. Tell me, what business are you in now?"

"Call me Tony, Dwayne," DeAutio said, extending his hand. "Good to meet you as well. I've spent the last 20 years at Goodyear."

"I might have gone to Akron if it hadn't been for Coach Rosemont," Hilbert said. "Buddy, he put LMSU on the map. We were just patsies before he got here."

"Really," Price said.

"Oh yeah. I remember listening on the radio when we knocked off Southern Mississippi. Sam had already scored twice. He blocked a punt and returned it for the game winning score. After that, schools were scared to schedule us."

"Nothing to gain, everything to lose?" Price said.

"Exactly."

There was nothing Chap Roberts wouldn't discuss with Sam Rosemont. They had lived on the same floor, same hall, for two years while at LMSU. Roberts, who had graduated from high school at the age of 16, was a fair miler and two-miler in track, and he ran cross country in the fall at LMSU, earning a partial scholarship for all the miles he logged. Despite an age difference of nearly five years, Roberts was not intimidated by the three-sport star when they met for the first time. Roberts' parents had both died when he was young, and he was hardened by the streets while raised by an older brother. Rosemont was more of a farm kid, so he respected the toughness he sensed in Roberts. But there was something recognizably present in both young men, a similar drive to succeed at any cost, a cutthroat attitude that not only kept them both diligent in their training, but drove them towards each other. As Rosemont climbed the college football ladder moving from city to city, the pair remained close, always getting together when Rosemont was in town and occasionally vacationing together. Roberts never seemed satisfied with his own success. He continued to buy up more and more of Pineknob and its community businesses, expanding first into Chattanooga, then south all the way into Atlanta. When Rosemont returned to LMSU as the head coach, Roberts' stratospheric business successes had him properly placed to begin his run as the No. 1 booster. Rosemont was elated to have him involved, as the blueprint for building a top program became more and more about money.

On the subject of women, Rosemont had heard all the conquest fallout from Roberts before -- many, many times before -- and wasn't above baiting his friend a bit for humor. That was Rosemont's nature, and he never let a conquest attempt by Roberts go without some needling. As they began the walk from Ivory to the Ludlow elevator, it was clear Roberts had spent too much time with the Crown Royal in Rosemont's office on a near-empty stomach. After venting about Leslie Workman's virtue, he began to spell out his attitude on cheating for the hundredth time, saying he felt a "roll in the hay" would do Rosemont some good as well. Of course, he'd been saying that, too, for at least twenty years.

"It would relieve some stress, Sam, I'm telling you," Roberts said. "You don't know how much pent-up frustration you have in you. It comes out on the practice field and during games. You're still a young man. You need to be getting it more than you are."

"Oh, I'd still get hot during games. Even if I was getting laid before, during, and after," Rosemont said, laughing at the image of a halftime rock-star-like conquest. "I'm never going to cheat on Linda. The guilt alone would put me under. *That* would be some stress now. And if she ever caught me… whew. She'd probably cut it off."

"This is exactly when you have to apply my chronology theory," Roberts explained, as they approached the elevator doors with Billy Reed in tow. Reed was like family to Rosemont and allowed in his inner circle. Roberts had long since become comfortable with Reed as well.

"All you have to do is screw someone you screwed before you got married. Linda knows you slept with other women before her, right? I mean, hell, I was there. I've seen the girls and heard the fights. She's ok with it now, isn't she?"

"Somewhat," Rosemont said.

"So now, if you sleep with one of them, all you have to deal with in your own mind is *the timing*. I mean, whoever it is, you've already been in her. It's just a matter of when. That's easier to rationalize. Or, if it's not someone you already slept with, get together with someone you *almost* slept with, who married someone else then got divorced. There's a ton of women out there like that. They save themselves for marriage, five years later they're divorced, and they're out there making up for lost time. Or they figured out their Mr. Right is an asshole, so they decide to cheat away."

"Oh, I see," Rosemont said, exaggerating the expression of consideration, even rubbing his chin with the thumb and index finger of his right hand like a bearded professor, which had Reed bouncing off the elevator walls with laughter. "That's an interesting theory."

"I know you're messing with me, but, man, you are in a primo situation," Roberts pleaded, as only a drunk, habitual cheater could. "Every woman in town knows you and thinks you're some kind of cross between Jimmy Stewart and John Wayne. Sam, you own a restaurant *in a hotel*. Don't you see the beauty in that? It's a license to cheat without risk. Tell'em you need a room there permanently. You bring that place more business than anyone between recruits and fans. Then find someone who has as much to lose as you do, who doesn't have too many friends, and just be smart. No cell phones, no emails, no credit cards, no public lunches, no students."

"Weren't you just talking about a student, Chap?" Reed interjected rhetorically.

"Yes, Billy, you ass, but I'm not Sam Rosemont. I'm not an employee of LMSU. People aren't watching my every move like right when these doors open. It takes a little more work for me to make it happen. And besides, she was a grad student. They're fair game."

"With all your money, Chap," Rosemont said, "I'd think they'd be lying down by the dozen right at your feet... Sugar Daddy to the masses."

Roberts was getting edgy now, as though Rosemont was crossing a forbidden line. Of course, Rosemont had done it many times before. Roberts would never disenfranchise Rosemont. Many of the women he slept with he'd met through the ol' coach. He had ample opportunities through his own businesses but had begun avoiding it, learning the hard way how messy sexual harassment issues can become.

"I work hard making sure people don't know how much money I have," Roberts said, as the trio walked through the doors of Big Black Bears Hall. "You know that. Hell, your salary is in the sports pages every other month. Let's see, three more wins and a bowl game and you'll get another half million bonus won't you? And you've got a balloon payment coming when? Come to think of it, I may just buy that hotel. I'll make sure you have a room close to mine. Top floor. We'll be hall mates again. Better yet, you get that bonus, you can go in on it with me."

Rosemont couldn't help but laugh, though normally when badgering Roberts intentionally he would remain straight-faced.

Nearby, Price concluded his conversation with Hilbert and DeAutio on a high note, discussing the noble legacy the '72 team helped begin. He avoided the company line of pitching an annual fund donation. He wasn't that comfortable with it yet. Moving on, he shook hands with Nester, and as he began to speak with his boss, he noticed Coach Rosemont, Billy Reed, and Chap Roberts entering the room. Roberts was practically joined to Rosemont's hip, his arms flailing about as he spoke.

Sensing that Nester wanted to make a break for Rosemont and Roberts, Price excused himself, saying he'd talk to him later. He walked towards the exit to hit a restroom before the dinner began.

Rosemont now put on a big smile as the 150 or so guests in the room began to take notice of his arrival. He intentionally got louder and mirrored Roberts' animation, as though the two friends' banter was an act for the fans.

"That's a good idea, buddy. That's what I'm talking about... Chap cash," Rosemont said. "The hotel? Man, if I had your money I'd burn mine... I'm making chump change compared to you. Maybe after my *next* balloon payment."

Price gave a nod, a wave, and a courteous "Gentlemen, good game" to the arriving trio as he passed, which Reed and Rosemont returned with a respectful "Dwayne." Roberts ignored him. What Price overheard from Rosemont went through him like lightning. There it was again... "Chap cash." Price's steps immediately slowed as though he was in a daze as the information he was absorbing bounced from his head to his gut and back again.

He sat down on a bench in the large foyer outside Big Black Bear Hall, his eyes darting back and forth. Did he hear that correctly? He knew that he had. But did it mean what he thought it did? Was Richardson, a Proposition 48, talking about having cash from Chap Roberts, LMSU's most giving and most notorious booster? Could Rosemont know about it, or was he just jabbing a friend with one of his nicknames? Or could Chap cash simply be a term within the program, synonymous with high times, having a little bit extra. Thoughts bumped and grinded in the turns of Price's mind like NASCARS. As he imagined what his duty would likely call for, he glimpsed the future and it sickened him. Dread ran through his veins. He shuddered. He'd come from a Division II school where he'd dealt with a few minor infractions, but his experience with his job thus far had been simply NCAA Clearinghouse issues... i.e., making sure athletes had completed their high school work and were actually eligible. This could be so much more than a mere bump in the road. It could be huge scandal, played out on a national stage. And of all times, when the program was having unparalleled success.

As Price tried to gather himself enough to walk into the men's room, a few stragglers for the evening's dinner filed off the elevator. One was Ben Wright, who was receiving adoration from the other guests. When he saw Price, he excused himself from the group.

"Hello, Mr. Price," Wright said.

Price was finally getting to his feet. Wright had only met Price once, but it was a memorable visit. S.I.D. Jim Winkler liked to tell the story that Wright, unlike every other college athlete at LMSU, got the big picture. Winkler would say that Wright understood what every person in every office throughout the University actually did, from the Registrar to the Provost, from University Relations to Compliance. Wright knew most everyone personally, from the librarians to the assistant bursar. Just after Price was settled in his office that summer, Wright popped in for a visit. Having known his predecessor, Wright said he just wanted to say hello. As a sports fan, Price knew Wright. He'd made First-Team All-Southwestern Conference as a sophomore and was obviously destined for an NFL career and greater accomplishments. In learning about Price's background, the two began to discuss the Fellowship of Christian Athletes and the possibility of Price becoming the campus administrative liaison for FCA after he was settled and in to a routine. That's where they left it that day. Price was incredibly impressed with Wright's maturity, intelligence, and humble demeanor. To Price, Wright didn't put on airs or expect special treatment. He could have just as easily been the honor student team manager. Price respected Wright for that, and it made him even more likeable.

"Are you ok?" Wright asked, after getting no reply from Price and noticing that he appeared flushed.

"Oh, hi Ben. Yeah, thanks. Just a little... put out," Price said, still regaining his composure. "Great game today. Their defense didn't seem to know what was going to hit'em next."

"Thanks. It went pretty well," Wright said, with a slight smile. "Hopefully we can keep it up. We're still getting better, I know that."

"Yeah, I can see that. Routes are getting crisper," Price said. "Murvin Rivers seems like he's really improved. Ricky Gates, too. What'd he catch today, three or four balls?"

"Yeah, one of them, I really missed him. He made a great catch. You're right. If we can keep'em from cheating on Danny we'll be tough to beat. Those guys coming along will make the difference... especially for next year. You know Danny will be gone."

"Yeah, kind of figured that. Tough to blame him I guess. Hey, listen, you should get in there. I wanted to tell you though, I called the FCA district rep yesterday about taking the open spot. I had to leave a message. I'm sure he'll get back with me this week."

Price thought about somehow testing Wright on Chap cash, to see if he'd heard it and where its meaning might fall on a non-prop team member. But his instincts stopped him. He decided to think his strategy through a little more first.

"We'll talk about it more later," Price said. "Good luck next week if I don't see you beforehand. Oh, and please call me Dwayne."

"Thanks. Ok, I will."

Wright's entrance brought an even greater buzz than Rosemont's. Nester was at the podium introducing Coach Rosemont, who was sitting between his wife, Linda, and Roberts. Wright was there as part of a student contingency from the school of journalism, not necessarily as an all-conference, future hall of fame quarterback. The student group he joined had a table on the other side of the room. Wright was getting stopped at every table by well-wishers as Rosemont positioned himself in front of the microphone.

"I want to thank everybody for being here today to witness another Black Bears victory. You're a part of the ongoing success of this program. I want to send out a special thanks to the 1972 team, which took LMSU to the top of NCAA Division I-AA, raising the bar for future teams, and giving players something to work towards. It's gentlemen like Rob Thompson, Jackie Franklin, Pete Jacobs, and Bobby Hilbert and the rest of you that made athletes like Ben Wright (motioning with his right hand in Wright's direction, for which the crowd showed its approval with applause and shouts) want to come here and excel on the field and in the classroom. Because of groups like the one here tonight, and leaders like President Everett, Athletic Director Charles Nester, and super boosters like Chap Roberts, I can say that We Play For Titles at LMSU! Enjoy your meal and we'll hear from some of the guys during dessert. Thanks again for all your support. We'll now have a word of prayer from Dr. Everett."

Price reentered and took his spot at the athletic administration table during Rosemont's speech. After the prayer, as he began to pick at a colorful salad, he realized that idle chitchat with his co-workers, their wives and husbands – most of whom he'd met -- was going to be difficult, so why waste the opportunity for some background on Roberts? He had heard most of the fundamental info, he was looking for anything that might help him, though he wasn't sure what it would be.

"Super booster," Price said, to no one in particular when the conversation had stalled. "How many businesses does that man own?"

"I don't think anybody knows but him and his accountant," said Janet Randolph, the administrative assistant of Ivory Facilities Building. "I hear he makes the mint just keeping it all straight and above board for Chap."

"Above board?" said Pat Shell, a local contractor and husband to Assistant Vice President of Operations Mary Shell. "You mean out of jail, don't you?"

"What do you mean, Pat?" Price asked.

"Three different times I had to force the guy to give me a check for work my guys had done instead of cash," Shell said, glancing at his wife to check her level of disapproval. "The guy all but threatened me. I don't do anything for him anymore. But I wouldn't be anyway. I heard that this new R&R Construction is a business of his."

"What's the big deal about cash?"

"In construction it's just a bad practice," Shell said, "if you want to keep your books clean and everything legitimate. If you ever get audited, cash is a big red flag – coming in or going out. Plus, cash on hand makes some people – your own employees -- do things they normally wouldn't. But you're wrong about just he and his accountant knowing, Janet. I guarantee Jim Wheatley knows everything."

"Who is that?" asked Price.

"Wheatley? Second in command," Shell said, "at least on the non-corporate side. Twice, he was the one that tried to pay me. But I knew it was coming from Roberts. The second time I told him to mail me a check or I would report them to the Better Business Bureau. He got pissed."

"Honey!" Mary Shell said.

"Well, mad, then. And not the vocal kind of mad," Shell said. "The calculating kind, you know? I could see his wheels turning."

"Oh, Pat," said Janet Randolph. "Jim stops by our office every Monday. I think he's just the sweetest man in the world. He's from Mobile... got that southern twang like Billy Reed. I love that. 'Hey, Miss Janet. Where can I put this?' "

"Two syllable 'where,' huh? Way-ya can I poot the-is? You sound like Miss Scarlet O'Hara," said Price. "Why does he come by the football office?"

Her brief hesitation was telling.

"Oh... just dropping off proofs, recruiting brochures or questionnaires, invitations, camp fliers. It's always something."

Price had seen Roberts Printing vans all over town and around campus. And he knew of at least two reps that called on the University, one for academics and another for athletics. The chances of someone like this Wheatley making deliveries seemed unlikely to him, but he said nothing.

"You know, we started using R&R here," said Bruce Fellows, Ludlow's Facilities Manager, "just for the renovation to the locker rooms. Course, that was the only project we did this summer other than paint, and we used our own guys for that. Using R&R came down the line, though. First time I wasn't allowed to shop a job. I didn't even know it was his company."

Pat Shell sat back in his chair and crossed his arms, looking around the table with an air of disgruntled satisfaction. Bruce Fellows' brain was obviously churning. Price sensed the whole conversation was getting way too conspicuous.

"Well, he's good for business," Price said, looking around the table at nobody in particular. "I guess there's some give and take."

With that, the ladies moved on to the subject of Roberts' rarely seen wife, Gina.

Pat Shell leaned over to Price and said in a low voice, "He makes himself look good to the public and the press. But there's a whole lot more taking than giving. You can count on that."

The evening ended with nothing else said about Chap Roberts. Talk turned to the 6-0 Black Bears and the chances of going undefeated and what bowl they might go to, followed by Rob Thompson sharing memories of yesteryear.

A high note of the evening was when Wright got up and, standing beside Thompson with a hand on his back, told the crowd, "I've seen the film on this guy. I'm glad he's not around now or I'd be fighting for my job. Mr. Franklin would be giving our tailback a run for his money, too. I've seen some of the hits that Mr. Hilbert and Mr. Jacobs made as well... wouldn't want you guys in our practices either. And God bless Mr. Jacobs in his recovery. You guys paved the road. We're just following your lead. Thank you so much for everything you did here at Lookout Mountain State University!"

Wright's comments brought tears to the eyes of some of the wives of the 1972 team members. His public speaking abilities were rare in a college student but a mere extension of his calm, quick thinking under fire. Rosemont joined the pair of quarterbacks at the podium.

"What a picture. The Black Bears' past and its future in the form of two of its greatest quarterbacks. Thank you all for being here. Don't forget the quarterback club and Big Blue... and we'll keep this thing rolling to the top!"

When the party finally broke it was nearly midnight. Wright had left immediately following his comments, Price soon after. As Price walked to the spot where his three-year-old Honda Accord was parked, the campus and the city itself were still bustling with activity. All Price could think about was what he needed to do to get to the bottom of the Chap Roberts question, and what the answer to that question might bring.

5

Price spent Sunday morning lounging with coffee and the Black Bears-dominated sports page before showering, dressing, and making his way to First Baptist Church of Pineknob. He had visited a number of churches upon moving and his attendance there had been sporadic at best in his four months in town. He was not yet connected and had done little more than fill out a guest card.

He had heard that much of the University's administration attended the town's Southern Baptist offering, but he found the Southern Baptist doctrine too stringent in general for his taste. Besides, he believed that worship should be just that, and not some social club to get attached to. He remembered his departed mother once saying her worship experience was ruined when a socialite and fellow member complimented her dress selection that day.

So on Sunday, much like the rest of his free time, he kept to himself. He returned to his modest two bedroom home. He'd bought the house after accepting the job at LMSU, the practice of all nomadic college employees, especially coaches: buy immediately so if you have to move on, you'll have equity in your dwelling and hopefully the down payment for your next move. He changed out of his church clothes and took a casual five-mile run before enjoying a Sunday dinner of two broiled chicken breasts, wild rice, green beans, and iced tea.

As he ate, he began mapping out a strategy for gaining insight into the possible infraction of Chap Roberts and the football program. He needed to know two bits of information: 1) Was Roberts paying Proposition 48s for work they were not doing? They could have a job since they weren't under scholarship rules. But if they weren't paying taxes, getting Chap cash, that act was certainly illegal, but not necessarily his jurisdiction. If he's paying cash, chances are they're not doing the work. 2) Is Rosemont aware of it?

In Price's eyes, based on the heated table conversations from the previous evening, this could possibly just be the tip of the iceberg. Between the University view books, catalogs, media guides and recruiting material for 16 sports, brochures, tri-folds, invitations, save the date postcards, Roberts could be billing the University millions. Not illegal either, of course, unless there are kickbacks involved. The practice of using just one vendor though would certainly be frowned upon by the Board of Trustees. It was surprising to Price that Roberts wasn't on the LMSU Board. Dr. Everett apparently wasn't part of Roberts' monopoly-like grip on the University, and vice-versa.

Unfortunately for Price, also based on last night's conversation, the wheels of fate were already in motion against him. After dinner had concluded at Big Black Bears Hall, most of the insiders in the group remained for after dinner drinks, coffee, and more conversation. Janet Randolph, ever protective of her boss, Rosemont, tracked the coach down and let him know that Price had initiated some stimulating conversation about his buddy Chap Roberts. Rosemont told Linda he had to attend a late meeting, shared the information with Roberts, then the friends met up with Jim Wheatley to close down Sam Rosemont's Steakhouse, located inside The University Inn.

Allowing his name to be used was a great deal for Rosemont. Originally he granted an already established restaurant the use of his name for 250,000 dollars a year. In exchange he held his coach's radio show there, which usually brought out a couple of hundred hungry fans. He made numerous personal appearances there as well throughout the year. He and Linda could eat there for free anytime they wanted. If he brought in a group, he could pick up their tab for half price. After three years of that arrangement, Rosemont bought in. Same deal except Rosemont no longer had to pay the half price for his guests. And, he began receiving a share of the profits. His partners were more than glad to have him. Fans would flock there year round just for the opportunity to possibly exchange pleasantries with the popular coach.

"Ok, who is he?" asked Wheatley, taking a drink from a bottle of Budweiser.

"He's the new compliance guy," Rosemont said. "Seems like a straight-shooter. I don't know if we could get him on board. What could he know, though?"

"Probably nothing. Could have just been curiosity," said Roberts, flipping to Price's picture in the football media guide and sliding it across the table to Wheatley. "Remember, we walked by him when we came into the dinner. We'd better watch him, Jim. Don't worry about him, Coach. We'll find out what he's up to."

"Indeed, we'd better," Rosemont agreed, as two just-off-the-clock waitresses, dressed in well-filled navy blue golf shirts with black skirts, approached their table. One was carrying a bucket of longnecks.

"Hi Coach Rosemont," said the first, in a friendly, but not flirty, tone. "Nice game today."

"Hello Jennifer," Rosemont said. "Thank you, sweetie. It was a tough one. Hi Betsy. You girls work hard tonight?"

"Oh, we were slammed from the fourth quarter until about thirty minutes ago," Betsy said. "Backed out the door."

"Did you make good money?" asked Roberts, who was a familiar face to the girls even if they didn't know him by name. Roberts was always interested in where the cash was going in town.

"I cleared about 155 dollars," said Betsy.

"I didn't do quite as well," said Jennifer. "But good enough. So, you guys want to have a beer with us?"

Rosemont looked around the empty restaurant. The wait staff could only remain to socialize as long as the kitchen help was closing up. The manager was busy with his two cashiers. An assistant manager was checking out the stations of the remaining wait staff. These women, non-students in their mid-20s, looked pretty nice considering they'd been busting it for the past seven or eight hours delivering food items such as Rosemont's signature 24-ounce porterhouse.

"Jim here still has to make the rounds," Roberts said, sensing Rosemont's approval of the situation. Maybe his little talk had helped. "But Coach and I will join you. Hi, I'm Chap Roberts."

"Yeah, I'll have one," Rosemont said, with his trademark grin. "That sounds like fun."

Roberts walked with Wheatley to the door, giving him some instructions. Part of Roberts' diverse holdings included three bars. Either he or Wheatley usually checked in on all three on a Saturday. Tonight though, Roberts wanted Wheatley to tail his boss if he and Rosemont left with the girls. The bars, which typically stayed open past the time law allowed – at least 3 a.m. -- could wait till later.

57

When Roberts returned, the beer began to flow. At the end of the third bucket, he suggested the party move on to one of the girls' apartments. With a quick, post-work buzz on, the girls agreed. "I've got some beer and wine at my place," Jennifer Newton said. The girls had shared a ride to work. Being as discrete as possible walking out, Rosemont jumped in Roberts' Mercedes XL-3, and followed the girls.

Roberts had also sensed the alignment of Coach Rosemont and Jennifer Newton as the evening progressed. Once in the apartment, drink in hand, Roberts initiated his purpose. He stepped close to Betsy Parrish, looked into her un-anticipating eyes and kissed her with the tenderness and affection of a man who hadn't kissed a woman in years. When they broke the embrace, Roberts looked around the room and asked, "Is that a balcony?" When it was confirmed, he took Betsy by the hand and asked her if she wanted to get some air.

"That would be great," she said, picking up a glass of just-poured chardonnay. She willingly followed Roberts to the sliding glass door.

"Can I take this blanket?" Roberts asked Jennifer. "Might get chilly out there."

"I doubt it," said Jennifer, with a laugh. "But sure."

Rosemont was somewhat uncomfortable with Roberts' abruptness, but the whole scene in general wasn't totally new to him, just distant. He was still weighing if he should go through with what he thought was about to happen. He had rationalized on the way over that this girl was at least somewhat unconnected to the daily business of football. Then he thought about the radio show, all the times that Jennifer had waited on him and Linda, how uncomfortable he would be if she ever waited on them again… which was bound to happen.

"Coach, I can tell you're having second thoughts about being here," Jennifer said.

"No, that's not true. Well, maybe a little."

"I have to tell you, I've imagined this before," Jennifer said. "I think you're a sweet man. Before you make up your mind, come in here to my bedroom, relax, and give me five minutes to take a shower."

Rosemont followed her into the bedroom, after she dismissed herself, he took off his navy blue sports coat and hung it over a chair. He wore khaki slacks and a pale blue dress shirt. He kicked off his burgundy loafers and slid them under the bed with his heel. He sat back, took a drink of his beer and checked his watch: 12:32 a.m. Linda would already be asleep, and it was common for him to work until 2 or 3 a.m. if need be during the season. Rosemont thought back to the conversation early in the evening in the elevator with Chap and Billy. He laughed. One of the only aspects of Rosemont's personal life Chap didn't know about was his extra-marital affairs as a younger coach, especially during bowl weeks. Except for the bonus of four to six weeks of additional practice, some head coaches treated bowl games as well-earned vacations. The parties started upon arrival and continued through the postgame, with local dignitaries acting as hosts and doing everything to impress the visiting organizations, including providing plenty of events with well-stocked bars and making sure there were numerous single, good-looking women at the functions. Once, at a particularly tantalizing party in the deep south, one with plenty of southern belles sporting plunging necklines, obviously proud of their cleavage, a boss of Rosemont's who had his betrothed with him as an escort turned to him and said, "I don't know who the first coach was to bring his wife to a bowl game, but he damn-sure screwed it up for everybody from then on." That statement was only partially true. On an assistant coach's pay and with four kids at home, Linda never made it to the bowl games early in Rosemont's career. He lived with the guilt of his conquests by keeping it internal, sharing the stories with no one.

Outside on the balcony, Roberts was about to make good use of a cushioned wicker sofa. The flirtation of two willing participants had begun at the bar and immediately continued at the apartment. Betsy, a 5-foot-3 brunette, was just Roberts' type. She was chatty – would never let a conversation die – and she was quick to laugh. It was a pleasant laugh, he thought. He didn't know if she was really as in to him as she seemed – touching his arms and shoulders throughout the evening as they spoke -- or if her behavior was the result of alcohol. But his only worry at that moment was the stability of the lawn furniture. He was inside her, though she still wore her black skirt. He pulled her shirt over her head, then, as she shook her hair to re-adjust what the shirt had put out of place, he unhooked her bra. As the lacey black garment fell slack her nipples hardened in the chill of the October night. The moonlight showed goosebumps on her ivory skin. They both paused for an instant and smiled at the obvious sensation, then Roberts began to kiss and caress her. He was in no hurry, and that turned her on.

As promised, Jennifer stepped out of her bathroom five minutes after she entered. Nearly 5-foot-8, her blond, mid-length hair was wet, and she wore only a short, silk, multi-colored robe which was clinging to her still-damp, athletic-looking body. She sat down on the bed at Rosemont's feet.

"Coach, I know you don't know me that well," she said in a sincere tone. "I'm not one of these girls out running around with a bunch of partiers or co-workers. Those guys bore me. I work days at First National Bank. I'm just working at the Inn to save enough money to finish my degree in finance. I'm telling you this because I can be discreet, I don't want anything from you or have any long term expectations, and, like I said before, I've always thought that you are a sweet and handsome man."

Then she whispered in a tantalizing voice, "And don't worry, I'm also on the pill."

"That's good honey," Rosemont said, "cause I'm still shootin' live ammo."

With that Jennifer smiled, untied the belt of her robe, then leaned over and began slithering up Rosemont's body until they were face to face. "So, you think you want to stay?" Enamored, he never said a word. He only smiled. Rosemont had always been the aggressor in his sexual encounters, especially with Linda. It was that or do without. He'd never experienced this self-confidence, this purpose in a woman. This was new. But he wasn't thinking about that or anything else. All he could do was look at this sensuous being, the motion of her hips, the arc of her back, and how those movements made her firm, round breasts rise under his strong but awkward hands. When she began to climax, her hands went from his shoulders to his hands, which were still on her breasts. She put his hands on her shoulders, then grabbed his wrists for leverage. He got the message and pulled her more tightly to him. She gasped with excitement as they finished together. She smiled and fell to Rosemont's side, her head and still-wet, mid-length hair resting on his shoulder.

Holding her with one arm, Rosemont waited for the blood to return to his brain before he spoke.

"I'm floored, Jennifer," he said. "That blew my mind."

"I loved that," she answered playfully. "Did you?"

"Oh, I can't tell you how much. You are unbelievably beautiful in action."

"Thank you, Coach," she said. "You're pretty incredible yourself."

Outside the window, through a mere slit in the curtain, Jim Wheatley did his best to capture the sex on film. Chap Roberts had learned early on that an ace in the hole went a long way, even if you hoped you never had to pull it.

Rosemont and Jennifer returned from the bedroom to find Roberts and Betsy on the couch having a nightcap. Rosemont had a light-hearted air about him that removed

any awkwardness from the moment. "Catch any of the late scores you two?"

"No, Coach, Chap here wouldn't let me near the remote."

After a bit more small talk, Rosemont suggested he and Chap get on the road.

"Betsy, Jennifer, thank you so much for the hospitality," Rosemont said. "We'll have to do it again sometime."

"Yes, soon," Roberts added.

With the good nights said, the old friends made their way back to Chap's car.

"How'd that work out for you?" Roberts asked, looking over with a grin as he drove.

"That was an amazing experience," Rosemont said. "I wasn't just out of a sexual routine, I couldn't even remember what the routine was. That was something. She's got some skills now, although I may have just been used as a piece of exercise equipment. But she seems like a good girl, too. Someone I can trust."

"Let me suggest one thing," Roberts said. "Since your car is still at Ivory, take 10 minutes to go inside and wash that thing off and put on some clean drawers. Many a husband got caught due to dirty laundry."

"Taken care of, my man," Rosemont said. "What about you?"

"Gina doesn't do our laundry," he said. "She doesn't care what I do anyway."

Sunday morning for Rosemont was back to the routine of the season, although he was feeling the lack of sleep. He walked in to Ivory at 7 a.m., made sure all his coaches were getting after it, then he went in to his office, leaned back in his leather chair, and thought about the events of the last ten hours. Walking into his bedroom at 2:30 a.m. the night before, he felt extraordinary guilt… safe in his chair the next morning, not so much. He shook his head with a quiet "whew" thinking about Jennifer's sensuous nature, as though he still couldn't believe what had happened, then popped in a tape of Georgia State-Texas A&M, so his guys would have some "points to ponder" after lunch.

Roberts slept in till eight, took Gina to breakfast, and by 11 a.m. was in the best and most productive of his three watering holes, The Lookout, making sure his in-house bookie was on the phone covering NFL games for their clients. Saturday had been a big day, as upsets dominated the college football national roundup. The Lookout alone cleared $23,450 despite 33 straight-line winners on LMSU, who was giving ten points at home. It wasn't great money, but it was cash. And cash-on-hand was always necessary for Roberts. Most bookies hedge their bets, offsetting a potential bad day by placing a few big bets of their own the same way as their customers. They still make enough money on the margins, customers must bet $110 to win $100, to make it worth it. Because so many gamblers will bet every college game on the parlay card, and every over-under, just to come out a little bit ahead. For some, gambling is recreation. Others let it take hold of their world like a cancer, bankruptcy sometimes the final prognosis. But the amount of money that changes hands each week of football season in America is immeasurable.

Back at his dining room table, following his Sunday afternoon meal, Price jotted five items on a note. 1) How many businesses does Roberts own? 2) What was the total amount of University payouts to what number of those businesses? 3) What is Wheatley's Monday delivery to Ivory? 4) Where were the Props living? 5) Why did his compliance predecessor leave?

He knew he had his work cut out for him. It would be an uphill climb. He would have to show some discretion, and think steps ahead as though he was playing chess. Already maxed out with his regular duties, he knew it would be a busy week. He smiled. It was the first time since moving to Pineknob he was truly excited about his job.

6

Dwayne Price's plan of attack called for diligent surveillance of Ivory Facilities Building and an excuse to be there if Jim Wheatley made his weekly delivery. The excuse was easy enough. Getting athletes through Clearinghouse was often a year-round battle. The problem was, he didn't know Wheatley and couldn't presume he'd be driving a vehicle related to Roberts Printing. He didn't want to start asking more questions about Chap Roberts' operations after it turned into a bashing session on Saturday night. His instincts told him that it had gone a bit past conversational. He just hoped that Janet Randolph had simply forgotten about or ignored the implications that were tossed around.

As the compliance director, he had a bit of free rein to snoop among University Departments, much like the Internal Revenue Service during an audit. The courtesy he enjoyed did not extend to the outside world. He wanted to know how many businesses Roberts owned so he could in turn find out how many were being paid for goods and services by the University. The IRS would be a great place to go for help if he had the authority. He thought the Tennessee Secretary of State's Office might help him, which is where all business licenses are currently applied for and processed. Normally, Price could just bring the infraction to the light of day in-house, have it discussed openly, then self-report, file a report with the NCAA, college athletics' governing board. The NCAA could then do the investigating, find the guilty, impose the penalties. The harshest penalties could be, for example, no postseason games, no competing for conference titles, a loss of scholarships for anywhere from two to ten years. In a case like this, ties would likely have to be severed with the booster – Roberts -- and more important to the program, his contributions. Losing two million dollars from the quarterback club would be a serious blow… over a third of the annual budget. It was because of the severe nature of the possible infractions, the willingness to cheat, and the enormous amount of money, that Price decided to investigate on his own first. By contrast, a local business misusing an LMSU image in a four-inch ad was reason enough to self-report, and expected by the NCAA.

Once on campus Monday, he checked all his incoming business, made sure nothing was immediately pressing, answered a few emails, then set about the business of surveillance. He had a meeting with Nester at 3 p.m., but he could prepare for that while he waited for Wheatley. He gathered some files, and printed out a list of this year's Proposition 48s… thirteen names. He forwarded his calls to his cell phone, grabbed his laptop, and headed for the door.

His office was part of a four-associate athletic director area that had a shared secretary. The title of secretary was changing in society in name and awareness, due to political correctness, to administrative assistant. The office AA was Amber Duffy, a young woman who in Price's mind was a joy: always friendly, always on time, never engaging in what Price called "fem-speak," that is, overly enthusiastic, high-toned, "okey-dokey" use of the language. In other words, Amber didn't have a phone voice. She was always herself… a rare, and Price thought, appealing, quality. Though Price had never asked, he guessed that she was around 27 or 28 years old. He would be 30 in a few months. She was certainly attractive, but in a natural, wholesome way. Her skin was olive, her eyes and hair brown, she had distinguished cheekbones and a sleek jaw line that led to a delicate-looking neck.

"Amber, I'm off to do some research," Price said. "I'll probably go straight to lunch from there. I'll be back before my three o'clock with Charles."

"OK, Dwayne," she said. "Anything I can do for you while you're out?"

"No, I don't think so," he said. He then got an impulse to ask her about his predecessor. "Um, Amber... how well did you know Max Milovich?"

"Not too well," Duffy said. "I was still in the Sports Information Office when he left though. He seemed nice enough. He wasn't unfriendly, but I never really got to know him."

"Do you know why he left?"

"I heard that he just wanted to get out of higher ed," she said. "He took a job in the private sector."

"I see... wanted a real job."

"I know this though, it was sudden. I remember that," Amber continued. "It stood out because, well, you know how it is around here, any college I guess. Most employment changes come after commencement... in summer. This happened last fall. Charles Nester had to scramble a bit doing both jobs. That was talked about."

"It was all about money," said Bruce Fellows, who as Facilities Manager shared one of the four offices, as he filled his cup from the office coffee pot. "Took an insurance job for over three times what he was making. Oh and, don't feel bad for Nester. He didn't kill himself doing both jobs... believe me."

"Do you know what company it was, Bruce?" Price asked.

"Oh, yeah. Ridgecrest," he said. "Sound familiar?"

It did. Ridgecrest provided the insurance and benefits package for all University employees. "Every pay stub," said Price.

"It's a good company," Fellows said. "Fingers into everything… finance, 401Ks, investment of the annual fund – all of it. Our stadium insurance is with them, too. I think everything we do, including the students' insurance."

"Man, that must be a bill," Price said. "You ever see Max anymore?"

"No. Not since he left," Fellows said. "He loved football, too. He played on the team here, from what I heard. He was always tailgating. But I could just be missing him. It's easy to do with that crowd."

By now Price had followed Fellows back into his office.

"Did you think it was odd when he left… in the fall and all? Price asked, his voice a bit lower.

"Well, I guess it was a big decision for him. Right before he put in his two weeks, I remember he got, um, kind of introverted."

"How do you mean?"

"Well, he quit joking around, started shutting his door all the time. Didn't hang out at the coffee machine, you know? When he told us he was leaving, I thought, 'Ok, I get it' about the way he was acting. Changing jobs affects people differently. Some people just move on… no big deal, it's just a job. For others, it's a life-altering decision."

"Hey, well thanks, Bruce," Price said, looking at his watch. "I've got to get moving."

"Interesting, but not uncommon," Price thought to himself about Milovich after telling Amber Duffy good-bye and heading out to his car.

"Max probably got recruited through the regular channels. That kind of networking goes on all the time. Staff and Admin pay at LMSU wasn't the greatest. He likely knew or met someone over there at Ridgecrest who obviously thought he'd be an asset."

The University was a sprawling campus which took up about 20,000 acres and ten Pineknob blocks… two wide by eight deep. Price moved his car from his own spot down to Ludlow Stadium lot A, which was used for overflow commuter student parking during the week. There were plenty of spots available as he positioned himself to watch the traffic into the main pedestrian entrance of Ivory Facilities Building. He thought this would be a crap shot…in fact he could have already missed Wheatley. But, he'd give it a go. He could get lucky.

There was more traffic in and out of Ivory than Price expected mid-morning on a Monday: three different slick-dressed salesmen, a weight equipment serviceman, two older couples, probably visiting or dropping off donations, a female ad rep from one of the Chattanooga newspapers.

As those visitors came and went, Price used his phone to find out what he had to do to get a list of Roberts' businesses. After a number of calls, and being switched around the Secretary of State's licensing department multiple times, he finally spoke with a supervisor with access to the information he was looking for. But the voice wasn't immediately forthcoming with help.

"I understand this isn't a normal request," Price said. "But I need you to please understand this. I am the Director of NCAA Compliance for Lookout Mountain State University. I am working on a preliminary report. I know that you don't have to help me. But the NCAA will likely be around in a few weeks or a month for the same information. You will have to give it now, or give it later."

"Ok, sir," said the voice on the other end of the line. "You'll have to give me a little time though. You say Roberts Printing or R&R Construction are two of the businesses? Got it. Give me your number and I'll call you back when I find something."

Just as Price gave his thanks and hung up two vehicles pulled up to the closest spots to the sidewalk leading into Ivory: a Ford Taurus and a white van. Both contained men. The Ford's passenger was obviously another salesman of some sort. He had the look: expensive dark suit, starched shirt, gelled hair, carried a brief case... he was definitely selling something. The guy driving the van though might be him. When he got out, Price saw an unkempt man who obviously spent a lot of time in a vehicle. His pants were wrinkled, well-worn khakis. He wore brown loafers, and a blue windbreaker covered the open collar of a brown shirt. He was in his mid to late 40s, wiry – almost too thin – though tough-looking with dark, tired eyes. He combed his dark brown hair straight back. It looked to be held in place by its own grease, and he needed a haircut. All he carried was a large manila envelope.

"That's got to be him," Price said out loud, as he put down his phone and picked up a document for assistant coach Nick Blanch, who was the team recruiting coordinator as well as its tight ends coach. Price gave Wheatley a few seconds to get in the door then headed for Ivory himself.

Ivory's hallway ran all the way through the building, parallel to the street in front of it, and parallel to the end zone behind it. On the right, behind a large glass wall was the main office which included Rosemont's office, the windows of which overlooked the field and stadium, the war room, the offices of Paul Lawson and Bud Steel, the offensive and defensive coordinators, respectively, and in the front of all that, Janet Randolph's desk with a waiting area and room for the boxes that often came in via the express mail services. To the left were a couple of hallways that led to more coaches' offices, with another film room for the players.

Price smiled and waved at Janet after he was through the door and into the hallway. His eyes though quickly darted from her, over her desk, then to Wheatley. His destination was to the second left hallway, to the offices of the position coaches. Sensing he was being too obvious – he would normally always pop in, say hi, and meet any visitor – Price stopped, turned and backtracked a few steps, then opened the door to Janet's area.

"Morning, Janet. "How are you?

"Hello, Dwayne," she replied.

"Fun time the other night," Price said.

"Yes, it was. Hey, say hi to Jim Wheatley."

Price pushed the door all the way open, propping it with his right foot, and extended his right hand. The hair raised on the back of his neck, sending a tingling sensation across his shoulders and down his spine, he thought mostly from being correct in his guess. "Hello, sir, Dwayne Price," he said, looking into Wheatley's cold eyes.

"Pleasure, Mr. Price," said Wheatley, slightly pulling their exchange and leaning in, bringing their faces a bit closer. Price, the larger of the two by four inches and 20 pounds, squared his shoulders and straightened his back before releasing Wheatley's callused hand.

"I'm just dropping off to Nick, Janet," Price said, waving a couple of documents. As he did, glancing at the desk and seeing the envelope again, he noticed "31" written small in pencil in one corner... but the numeral three was backwards. "See you later. Good to meet you, sir."

"Likewise," Wheatley said, the comment laced with his southern drawl.

71

The coaches were apparently all in offensive and defensive meetings, so Price set the two Clearinghouse documents on Blanch's desk, wrote a quick note, and was back into the hallway in a short two minutes. He nearly bumped into an older gentleman as he turned the corner quickly. Price recognized him to be Coach Ennis Ivory. He was a slight man, rail thin, and the lines in his face made deep grooves. His hair was silver, though some wild strands made it seem he'd bypassed his comb that morning.

"Coach, how are you? My name is Dwayne Price. I'm the new compliance director here."

"Hello, son. Nice to meet you," Ivory said, giving Price a one-pump handshake with no more regard than a man desperately searching for a bathroom. "I'm looking for Miss Janet. I've got to make my donation for my parking spot. I've been talking my way on to the lot thus far and I think the guards are on to me."

"This building is named after you and you have to pay for parking?"

"Well, son… that name on the building is kind of like that curly tail on a pig. It looks really cute, but it don't get you no more meat!"

Price's laughter echoed in the open space of the building's high-ceilings and empty hallway.

"Hey, since I've got you here, can I ask you a question?"

"I believe you just did."

"What was Sam Rosemont like as a player?"

"Slow as molasses but tough as barn wood," Ivory said. "He'd do anything to win."

"Is that right?"

"Don't tell him about the barn wood part though. His head is already too big."

"Oh, I won't. Thank you, sir. It was nice to meet you. Janet's office is right down there."

In the parking lot, Price again saw Wheatley, this time climbing back into the white van. Wheatley shot Price a look of distain, cranked the ignition, pulled the gear shift into drive, and quickly exited parking lot A.

What had Price learned? The envelope could have been anything… but it was obvious Wheatley knew who he was and didn't care for him. He grabbed a pen and scratched the backwards 31 on a legal pad, tossed it on to his passenger seat, and leaned on his steering wheel with both arms. The sky was overcast and a fall wind blew, but it was a rationalization that gave Price a second chill as he glanced back over at the notebook. The feeling of dread he experienced Saturday night came back.

"You dumb ass," he said out loud. "That was a 13 written, not 31… 13 props." Price then thought, the envelope *had* to be this week's payment. She said he visits every Monday. What else could it be? I need to know their workout schedules… and when they actually work. Or do they actually work? I just need to see some of them – one of them – with an envelope full of cash."

Mondays in Coach Rosemont's Black Bears camp was more of a day of healing, learning, and for the redshirt freshmen and non-two-deep players (first team, second team), a night of fun. After double meetings to learn the next opponent's tendencies, a light, half speed practice, the non-essential players would play their own version of "Monday Night Football." With no expectations or pressure from the coaches, but under their supervision, those who weren't yet contributing were allowed to just have some fun with football, like they were kids again playing in that empty neighborhood lot.

Rosemont realized long ago how tough the first couple of years of college can be on a recruit. Redshirting players is supposed to give them a year to get acclimated, to grow and prepare. But for some, even though they practice with the team, they have difficulty feeling they are a part of the program. That, coupled with the fact that each player was a pampered high school star, gives some players a feeling of emptiness they've never experienced. If the player is a far from home, that feeling multiplies.

Once, years ago, early into a new football season, Rosemont was driving home late from the stadium and he saw one of his redshirt freshmen, a thin but broad-shouldered, 6-foot-3 defensive end named Chuck Bowen, suitcase in hand, walking to the bus station. Rosemont pulled off the road and parked.

"I just don't like it here, Coach," he said, tears welling up in his eyes. "I don't fit in. Classes are tough. And, well, I miss my family."

"Are you using a tutor?" Rosemont asked him, sensitive to the emptiness and struggles he was feeling.

"No. I... I guess I was too embarrassed to set it up."

"Listen, Chuck. Everybody needs some help now and then. Hear me? Everybody. College isn't easy. That's why getting a degree means so much."

"I know. I realize that now."

"I can tell you're not afraid of hard work. I've seen that in you," Rosemont went on. "So, let's make a deal. You give it two more weeks. We'll get you a tutor. I want you to schedule a meeting with the professors of the classes you're having trouble in. Just tell them hello, that you're going to work harder, and ask what you might do to help your situation. And then you go at it hard night and day like it's a job. You work it overtime. If you still want to go home after two weeks, I'll buy you your plane ticket. No hard feelings. Ok, Chuck?"

"Ok, Coach. It's a deal."

Behind the scenes, Rosemont pulled aside one of his veteran defensive players at the time, Jacob Williams, and asked him to ease into a mentoring situation with Bowen. A little success in the classroom, a big brother-like figure slightly doting on him, and the experience of homecoming, which was scheduled for that second week, would likely be enough. That, and a few kind words from his position coach and Rosemont.

Long story short, Bowen went on to be a two-time all-conference player and a Division I-AA All-America. He had 19 sacks as a senior, breaking the LMSU season record. As Bowen matured, he and Rosemont developed a close relationship based on respect that they continued to enjoy. It was one of the privileges of coaching and one of the rewards of sticking it out as a player.

It was because of players like Bowen that Rosemont started his version of Monday Night Football. It helped the newcomers with the feelings of not yet being integral cogs in the program. The players used it as a chance to show their moves, blow off some steam, and shine. On Monday nights, there was always a lot of banter between players, "talking smack," and laughing, and everyone in the program remained to watch. The Props couldn't participate, but they showed up as well. It was the players on the field that they would be competing against the following years. Rosemont would walk around the sidelines and talk with all the players as the game went on, and he would go up into the stands and talk with the fans.

Price would be there that evening as well, with the many fans so eaten up with Black Bears football they wanted to see the redshirts competing. If any of the props flashed envelops of money, Price wanted to be there to see it. He sat in the thick of the crowd, even brought binoculars.

While Price sat through his tedious weekly meeting with Charles Nester about the business of compliance and Lookout Mountain State University, Jim Wheatley caught up with Chap Roberts at The Lookout, and reported the events of the morning. The pair sat in the back corner booth of the near-empty bar, close to the office in which Roberts' bookie did business. On the table was one of the bar's portable phones, Roberts' cell, and some paper work he was going over before Wheatley showed.

"I believe he's stumbled on to something," Wheatley said, after swallowing a drink of a Budweiser. "I think he was checking me out. I'm not 100 percent sure, but he may have been sitting in his car when I pulled up to drop off the guys' money."

"How could he know?" Roberts asked. "What could have tipped him? Are you sure he wasn't just doing what he does? He has business in the building."

"Could be. It just seemed like there was something... he was fishing," Wheatley said. He then backed up to answer his boss's previous two questions, a habit of Roberts' that pissed Wheatley and his southern sensibility off profusely.

"As for how he found out, Chap, it could be any number of ways. I mean – damn - you've got it set up where dirt-poor Mississippi niggers could be out buying rounds of drinks for their friends, or buying blunts for the weekend, or hell, sending cashier's checks home to their mommas for that matter... if they had enough sense. I mean, Christ Chap, Price could have seen one of them boys in the damned bank."

Roberts watched Wheatley with a look of distain over the fury of his comments, as his most-essential employee lit a Marlboro Red and took a long, much-needed draw. He turned his head to the side and exhaled, the smoke hovering in the nearby atmosphere like a cloud.

"All I'm saying is, this is a dangerous game you're playing, Chap. It's messy. Too many people know. We already bought off that damned Milovich. Is this something we're gonna have to do every year?"

"You're right," Roberts said, gathering his paper work and putting it in a file folder. "All right, we need to tighten it up then. I'll talk to Sam and have him tell those boys to be smart and shut up. You need to go in. Find out what he knows."

Roberts handed Wheatley a swipe card that would get him into the Athletic Administration Building, a wing built off of the LMSU basketball arena, a four minute walk from Ludlow. Rosemont had provided the card through proper channels a long time ago… all access. Roberts could enter anywhere Rosemont was allowed on campus.

Roberts looked at his watch. It was nearly 5 p.m. The players would be breaking from practice to get their dinner in the dining hall before the young players' weekly game. He would pay his good friend a visit during his dinner break.

7

While Chap Roberts and Jim Wheatley hashed out a theory about Dwayne Price, who was still concluding his meeting with Charles Nester, Janet Randolph innocently went about the business of distributing envelops to the Proposition 48s. In the season routine, it was during the players' 2 -5 p.m. practices that the props received their weight and agility training from strength coach Stacks Osborne. The nickname 'Stacks' came from Rosemont, and alluded to the stacks of weights setting around the rubberized floor of Ivory's cavernous workout facility, prior to the program purchasing weight trees to hang the massive steel discs on.

The props on Mondays, workouts completed and showered, were to see "Ms. Janet" before exiting Ivory. Only once, seven years ago, did Coach Sam Rosemont give her that instruction. He didn't say what was in the bank-sized envelops, and he never mentioned it again. Wheatley always placed just four crisp bills in the envelops totaling $180, so essentially anything could have been in there… tickets, coupons, anything… making sure they safely found their way into the players' hands was just part of her routine. She also gave game tickets to players, and expense checks to coaches.

That day, she'd given out 12 of the 13 prop envelops, and was waiting on Rex Smalls, who was running the stadium stairs a painfully excruciating 24 times – twice for each of his teammates he stood up Saturday -- when Roberts popped in to see Coach Rosemont.

Rosemont was meeting with Sports Information Director Jim Winkler about the additional media coverage the Black Bears were starting to receive due to their 6-0 record. "We're going to keep the player access to Monday, Tuesday, and Wednesday," Rosemont said to Winkler, as Roberts appeared in the coach's open door.

"Fox Sports was hoping to get Wright and Smith on Thursday, maybe Jerome Jones, too," Winkler said.

"If it were just Wright I would think about it," Rosemont said. "He could handle the break in routine. But I don't want anybody – including assistant coaches – getting out of what they normally do. We're not going to change what we do and how we do it for the media. Ok?"

"You're the boss," Winkler said. "If Fox can get here on Wednesday, could you say something to Smith about doing the interview? It would be great exposure for him."

"Maybe it would, depending on what he said. I'll talk to him, but you tell them he's not going to talk about anything related to the *Daily Democrat* thing. In fact, it would be the perfect time to start pushing him for the Heisman Trophy. I know he'll be the dark horse, but just getting an invitation to New York would be huge for LMSU."

"All right, sure… 15 touchdowns on the season, 12 catches and 256.5 all-purpose yards a game, I'll buy it," Winkler said, getting up from his chair, then turning his head as Roberts walked in. "We should do a mailing… maybe start a website for him. I'll get on that. It's not in the budget, of course. Hey, here's the answer. Chap, would you like to chair – and finance – the first-time and thus historic Danny Smith for Heisman campaign?"

"You bet, kid," Roberts said, shaking Winkler's hand. "Be glad to. Tell you what. I'll donate the postcards if your office will design it."

"Good deal. We'll whip up something simple. I'll shoot it over there tomorrow as soon as Coach approves it," said Winkler. "See you gentlemen later. Have the juice up tomorrow, Coach... big day."

"Oh... I'll be ready," Rosemont said, as Winkler headed down the hallway to Janet Randolph's post. Then he turned his attention to Roberts, who was mixing a drink. "What's on your mind, my friend?"

"You want one?" Roberts asked, holding up his rocks glass. "Let me re-phrase that. Have a drink, Coach."

"Ok, lay one on me, Bartender Bob," Rosemont said, clapping his hands together and rubbing his palms in exaggerated anticipation.

"Know who Wheatley met here today?" Roberts said, handing Rosemont a Jack Daniels and Diet Coke.

"Who?"

"Dwayne Price. Kind of handy, don't you think?"

"I'll admit that sounds like more than just a coincidence," said Rosemont, "but he is in and out of here all the time."

"Wheatley definitely thinks he's on to something. He's going in to check it out tonight or tomorrow night."

"Tell him to wait till tomorrow night," Rosemont said, stepping up to the window that overlooks the field. "There's a lot of activity tonight. Winkler and some of his interns will be here for the freshman game later."

"Ok, done," Roberts said. "Are we really going to do this thing with Smith?"

"Chap, this guy has a chance to be one of the greatest ever," Rosemont said. "And I'm talking in the NFL. He's still learning... just a pup. But he's got more natural talent than any player I've ever seen. There aren't five individuals better in the country."

"He's got a bit of an image problem," Roberts said.

"That shouldn't hurt with the Heisman people… might hurt his draft status. I'll talk with him… get him thinking about it," Rosemont said. He laughed and shook his head. "Plus, it'll piss Nester off something fierce."

"That it will. Ok. Now, here's the really important question," Roberts said, craning his neck to see over the back of Rosemont's empty chair, checking the door for possible eavesdroppers. "When are we going to hook back up with those sweet things from the Inn? Have you talked to her yet?"

"No, I haven't talked to her," Rosemont said, with an intentional frown. "Don't plan to."

"Coach…, Coach. You don't want to talk to her… your sweet little Jennifer? You haven't been thinking about her?"

"No, I haven't."

"You haven't been thinking about that little wiggle… that sweet smile?"

"Nope."

"You haven't thought about that tight little package rubbing up on you?"

Finally Rosemont began to chuckle over Roberts' interrogation, and the non-official subject.

"Yeah, I thought so," Roberts said. "She's got you squirming in your chair all day long doesn't she? Huh? You want to go back, don't you, get your face between those firm young breasts?"

Rosemont cleared his throat.

"Yeah, I don't think that would be the wisest thing right now," Rosemont said. "Did you hear? We're number 12 AP, 13 Coaches' Poll. Probably not the best time to be chasing split tail."

"Oh, you got it all wrong, Coach," Roberts continued. "Now is the *best* time. To the victor goes the spoils. Come on, think about it... if you just screw this girl once she'll think you're an asshole. Show her you're not a one-night-stand jerk. She likes you."

"Chap, I don't have time for that stuff. Man, we're in the middle of a football campaign."

"Oh, heck. Georgia State? Honestly, what do you think their chances of beating you are... 1 in 20? You've got Jack Lindemood's number and you know it. He's been chasing you ever since college. I'm just glad the gamblers don't know what I know."

It was true. Jack Lindemood was the quarterback and punter on that Southern Mississippi team that fell to LMSU so long ago. Nearly 35 years had gone by, but a matter of inches, Rosemont's hand reaching to block a punt solidly, his ability to stretch a foot out and catch himself rather than fall so he could pick up the football and run with it, made all the difference. It was psychological warfare. Rosemont was Lindemood's Mohammad Ali, and "Lindy" was Joe Frazier, waking up in a cold sweat at night, thinking of how things could have been... should have been, eventually twisting it enough until he believed there was some kind of conspiracy against him. Southern Mississippi had a chance to win the national title that year, but the Black Bears' upset knocked them out of top five.

In the late 1970s, when the NCAA changed the rules concerning the way in which offensive linemen blocked – from elbows out to essentially allowing a legal hold between the armpits – it was Rosemont, the former fullback, who already had a wide open passing offensive devised, not Lindemood, the All-America quarterback. Rosemont was considered an innovator, Lindemood a follower. Rosemont treated him with respect, but when they shook hands and looked into each others' eyes, both knew that Rosemont was the winner.

"Georgia State's a great team," Rosemont said. "We're going to have our hands full."

"Bullshit! Don't feed me your coach-speak. Tell you what. While you're working the crowd at the freshman game in a little while, I'll run over and see if they're working," Roberts said. "Fair enough? Wouldn't hurt to grab a late bite would it? Having a little diversion will help your focus… a little left brain, right brain."

"I don't know. We'll see," Rosemont said, shaking his head at Chap's persistence.

The high-energy freshman game went on as always. Rosemont had his assistant coaches out there monitoring the action and keeping it clean. With so much trash talking, an occasional fight would break out – just like in practice. The players were vying for future playing time and they knew it. Most of the veterans were on hand. Rosemont would send any player in academic dire straights on to a team study hall. Ben Wright was out in the mix, helping the quarterbacks of both teams. Danny Smith was on the sidelines with a group of eight or nine players – one of many groups -- who were watching the scrimmage with dying enthusiasm. One player in Smith's area, third string defensive back Jason Means, a white junior with marginal talent who would likely never see regular playing time, approached the wide receiver, who at 6-5 was a head taller than Means.

"Hey Danny, you want to get out of here and try to find a number to twist up?" Means asked, his meaning of smoking marijuana not lost on Smith.

"You got any?" Smith asked.

"No. You?"

"No, I haven't had any for a few weeks. Hit one Saturday," Smith said. "Man, I'm broke though. I don't have four quarters. What about you?"

"Let's go," Means said. "We'll figure something out."

Rosemont wasn't too far away when he saw Smith and Means turn to leave.

"You guys going home?" a smiling Rosemont said loudly from about 60 feet.

"Yeah, Coach," Smith said, still walking. "I got swimming at eight tomorrow. I gotta get some sleep."

"Hold on a minute, please," Rosemont said, with a little more intent, closing the distance between them. "Danny, I want you in my office tomorrow at 1:30, ok? I want you to do some interviews this week."

"Aw, Coach… I can't stand talking to those people."

"Well, you need to get used to it… it's a necessary evil. It can hurt you or it can help you. You be there in my office. We'll talk about it."

"Ok, Coach. Yes sir."

"What about me, Coach, you need me too?" Means asked.

"Not this time, Jason. You just show up for your 2:45 meeting."

"Thanks, Coach," Means said, as the pair began walking up the ramp that led out of Ludlow Stadium and in to the October night.

"So what you thinking?" Smith asked.

"I've got a buddy who's in tight with some pawn shop guy," Means said. "I just give him something, and he'll give me a few joints, maybe a dime bag if it's something good."

"Give him something. What you talkin' about?"

"You know... goods. Something he can sell... a radio, picture frame, mirror, kid's bike, anything. Hell a good lawn mower will get us a half pound."

"Man, I don't know. That's stealing," Smith said.

"Oh, not really. We'll walk down the alley over on Ninth Street. Those folks throw out gold, bro. You want to get high, don't you?"

"Yeah, all right. Let's get moving."

The residential start of the Ninth Street alley was only a few blocks away. On either side of the one-lane, graveled path were the back yards of large, two and three-story brick houses, most of which at the time were worth well over $750,000, and some of the most affluent homes in Pineknob.

"If we don't see anything out here near the trash, we'll take a look at a back porch or two," Means said. "Look for a screened in job or an add-on sun room. No one ever locks those."

"Man, you know I'm on parole," Smith said. "I can't get caught doing this shit."

"Keep quiet," Means said, lowering his own voice. "I'll do it. You just watch my back. It's not breaking and entering if we step on a porch. Look, that house up there. No lights. The people are probably still out. Let's see what they've got."

Smith could see his breath in the mid-October evening. Through a thin windbreaker he was aware of both the falling temperature and his uneasy nerves. He looked at the two houses on either side of the Means' home of choice. The unlikely duo really couldn't be seen due to trees and manicured shrubbery from either home. So Smith, who'd smoked pot recreationally since his early teens, followed Means through the gate he opened and in to the back yard lit only by a waning Tennessee moon. He shut it behind him, a habit enforced by his mother at their own tiny, fenced-in yard. Once to the house, the pair could see the gleam of a small compact disc/radio outfit on a table between two wooden rocking chairs.

"I'll check the door," Means said, walking around the corner of the screened-in porch. "Locked … but just with a hook."

Means took a Swiss Army Knife from his jeans pocket and cut a slit in the screen and with the blade flipped up the primitive hooking device. As Means stepped through the door the pair could suddenly hear the engine and tires on gravel of a car driving down the alley from the direction in which they'd come. The lights were now visible as well, as it moved closer. Smith followed Means on to the half-walled, screened in porch, and shut the door behind him. Both young men crouched down as the car approached. They could see the markings of a police car. Dread shot through Smith. He could feel his heart pounding in his chest. How did he get here? If he were caught, Rosemont would have to suspend him if not kick him off the team. What NFL team would want him then? He's pissing away millions of dollars for what, a joint? The cruiser's spotlight slowly swept across the long back yard. Smith could hear the dispatcher's voice from the two-way radio. The pair ducked lower as the beam of light approached the porch. Smith's neck tingled with anticipation. For an instant, he thought about running. But he held firm, a muscle not so much as twitching. The light disappeared into the next yard and the cruiser moved on down the alley as steadily as it appeared.

"Probably just a routine check," Means said with a nervous laugh, unplugging the small stereo unit and wrapping the cord around it.

"Yeah, taking care of the rich white folks," Smith added. "Let's get the hell out of here."

An hour later, in Means' low-rent apartment, the substitute flipped the last quarter of Monday Night Football on, lit a joint he'd just rolled from a dime bag of Tennessee skunk weed, and he and Smith laughed at their daring as the buzz began creeping through their bodies.

"You want a beer or something, man?" Means asked, walking into the nearby kitchen door.

"Yeah, I'll take an ice water, if you don't mind," Smith said. "That joint is drying me out."

"Hemp tends to do that," Means said with a laugh, handing the superstar his drink in a large plastic cup. "That's pretty good stuff, yeah?"

"No doubt. I feel good... it always makes me want to stretch out my aching muscles. Sometimes, I won't even realize I'm high, then I'll look down and I'll be doing a hurdle stretch or something. The brothers be lookin' at me like I'm nuts. 'Nigger, what you doing? You going to a track meet?' It's all good though. I feel right."

"Well, you're cool here. Crash here if you want. My roommate practically lives with his girlfriend. Did I hear you tell Coach you've got an 8 o'clock class?"

"Man, I ain't going to that class," Smith said. "I've went once in two months. This is my last semester of college. This time next year I'll be in there – in *the league*. I'll be waving good-bye to this place."

"You'll be there, Danny, no doubt," said Means. He was a business major that would use his enterprising nature to one day be a success in corporate America. "Who's going to take care of your money? You can't trust just anybody."

"I hear you, man. Believe me, people are already lining up with their hands out. I won't get crazy with it. We had nothing. I just want to take care of my momma."

"I hear you. That's cool."

"This couch is feeling good to me," Smith said. "It's too cold to walk back to the dorm tonight. I'll tell you what. It feels good to feel good."

Both players laughed at Smith's stoned philosophic tone, but in truth it was his first unguarded moment in a month. The world class athlete kicked off his black, high-top Nikes, pulled a blanket up to his chin, and fell asleep to Stephen Davis and the Washington Redskins defeating the visiting Dallas Cowboys, 21-16.

In his travels that evening, Chap Roberts found the girls' team split. Betsy Parrish was hard at work when he arrived at The Inn. Jennifer Newton, he found out, worked only three nights a week at best: Thursday, Friday, and Saturday, to minimize the effects of work on her day job. Roberts read in Betsy's reaction to him sitting at the bar that he was welcome, so he ordered a double Crown and 7UP and made a few phone calls while watching a little Monday Night Football. The favored Redskins had covered the spread of three – barely – but the tight line had bettors going both ways which made for only an average night in Roberts' empire.

In one of her passes through the bar, Roberts asked for and acquired Jennifer's phone number from Betsy, then called Sam Rosemont's cell phone.

"What say, Chief?" Rosemont answered, with a familiarity he would display with few. "Are you already doing the deed?"

"No. Watching your buddy Barry Switzer get stomped by the Redskins. Your other friend has the night off," Roberts said. "Here's the number: 555-1039."

"Tarkington-Csonka... got it," Rosemont said, using his pro football jersey visualization method of memorizing phone numbers. "Not that I'm going to use it."

"Betsy said Jennifer likes to watch Monday Night Football," Roberts said. "That's all I'm going to say. You're a big boy."

"Thanks, pal, appreciate you letting me make up my own mind. Are you staying at The Inn? I might run over."

"Don't come here. *My* business is taking me elsewhere. Just call her."

"Alright. We're getting ready to break here.... gotta go."

As Rosemont and his assistants pulled the freshmen and seldom-used players into a group, about 150 fans began to file out through the stadium exits. One of them was Dwayne Price, who had no luck spotting any evidence of cash payoffs that evening. He thought to himself Tuesday was another day, and he still had other leads to follow. The most important of which was the names of Roberts' other businesses. With that thought in mind, Price went home for the evening.

Rosemont had something more powerful guiding him, something he really wasn't even aware of. It wasn't just his libido. He wasn't above needing a little ego massage either. Despite being the leader of 120 young men and a staff of ten willful men, being a successful coach supported by thousands of contributors, being heralded in the press, he still needed his manhood stroked. He needed... and that was awakened Saturday night.

Back in his office he called home to Linda, who would be preparing for bed and not expecting him… not during the season.

"I'll be home around one, baby," Rosemont said. "I'm going to meet with the guys and watch a little more film."

"Ok, Sam. Be careful," Linda said. "I love you."

"I love you too, Hon. Good night."

Rosemont called his coaches together to recap the day, give some instruction for Tuesday, a brief lecture about Georgia State's tendencies, a re-emphasis of the need for their own consistency with no mental breakdowns, and he dismissed, which struck Billy Reed as odd. He watched Rosemont get up and leave the war room after five minutes of what would normally be at least an hour long meeting. Most of the coaches went back to their respective offices anyway, the habit of preparation well-ingrained.

Rosemont showered and departed. In his loaded Toyota Camry, one of three demos provided to him and Linda, he called Jennifer and asked if he could stop by.

"Sure, Coach," she said. "I'd love to see you."

Jennifer met him at the door of her ground floor apartment. She didn't expect to hear from Sam Rosemont again, though she truly wanted to. His call filled her with excitement and passion. As he closed the door behind him they embraced, her arms around Rosemont's neck, his tightly around the small of her back. She was wearing a pair of semi-tight gym shorts and a form-fitting tank top. Her hair was pulled back in a pony-tail but was loose enough to have strands falling to the sides of her face. To Rosemont, her look was so unpretentious it was charming. And her firm breasts against his chest were driving him crazy.

"I've only got an hour or so, but I wanted to see you," Rosemont said, almost awkwardly at first. Then he slid his hands down to her backside and smiled with more confidence.

"I'm glad you called," she said, taking him by the arm and leading him into her apartment. "I haven't stopped thinking about you."

"Neither have I, darling," Rosemont said, "neither have I."

"How about something to drink. You've been working."

"Ok, how about an ice water."

"No beer?"

"Let me tell you, Jennifer. I don't need alcohol to want to make love to you."

"Coach, that's sweet," she said, putting ice in a glass and filling it.

"That really wasn't me the other night as far as pounding a bunch of beer," Rosemont said. "Well, what we did either."

"I know. Sit down and relax. The game is about over. Wasn't too exciting."

"Yeah, I heard. Both those teams are down."

Rosemont got comfortable on Jennifer's couch and took a long drink of water as she sat down on her knees facing him.

"I know that wasn't your style. But I appreciated it. I thought it was fun."

"You take me back somewhere I haven't been for a long time," Rosemont said, touching her cheek with the backs of his fingers. He thought of Linda. The Linda of 35 years ago, the young woman, full of humor and passion, the woman that he fell in love with. Somehow, Jennifer *did* take him there. He leaned in and the two kissed softly at first, and then with purpose.

Rosemont's hands caressed her smooth, naked thighs, right up to her panty line. He then lifted the bottom of her gold tank top, running his hands up her warm sides. Bra-less, he felt the soft sides of her breasts. His excitement grew both mentally and physically. She smiled solemnly and raised her arms as Rosemont pulled the cotton garment over her head, displaying her perfectly shaped breasts.

"You should be proud," Rosemont said with a disbelieving shake of his head, as he began to lean her back onto the couch to kiss them. With her legs folded under her, she needed to re-adjust.

"Let's go check out the bedroom," she said, with a playful laugh.

"I'm right behind you."

Topless and with an air of confident sexuality, she stood, and took the normally gruff coach by the hand. She led him for the second time in 48 hours into her bed.

8

Back in his office mid-morning Tuesday, Dwayne Price received a call that opened his eyes to what he was getting himself into. A nervous anxiety engulfed him as he spoke with the licensing supervisor, Tim Little, at the Tennessee Secretary of State's office.

"Yes, Mr. Price, it took me awhile, but I eventually found out what the problem was. Those two businesses you mentioned – Roberts Printing and R&R Construction were DBAs for a company called Roberts Renderings. And let me tell you, there's a bunch more," Little said. "I printed out a list. Want me to fax it to you?"

"How many more names?" Price asked.

"Looks to be a … 10, 15, 23 total," Little said.

"Wow. Yeah – yes, please -- just fax it. I can't thank you enough for your help. I may be back in touch."

Price hung up the phone and a minute later walked out to the shared fax machine not far from Amber Duffy's desk.

"I could have brought that to you, Dwayne," Amber said.

"Aw, I've been waiting for it. Needed to stretch my legs anyway," he said. "But thanks. Amber, who could I talk to in the Business Office… oh, wait, Jane pays the bills, right? What's her last name?"

"Jane Haynes."

"Haynes, right," Price said, distracted as the fax page finished its run with an annoying beep. "Wow. Unbelievable."

Reading the list intently as he walked away, he mumbled "thanks" to Amber.

"Do you want the fax receipt?" she asked.

"No, just throw it away, please," Price said.

Doing business under the Roberts Renderings umbrella was a number of recognizable names around the University, around town, and even regionally:

Roberts Printing

PayDirt Uniforms,

T's & Trophies

Ridgecrest Insurance and Financial Services

Roberts Fuels

Lookout Ford and Chevrolet

Liberty Fuels

R& R Brick & Block

R&R Construction

R&R Linen Service

Clear Glass Replacement and Cleaning

Pineknob ABC Store

Pineknob Computer Outlet

Pineknob Concrete

Pineknob Fitness Center and Equipment

Pineknob Heating & Cooling

Pineknob Manpower

Pineknob Party Store

Pineknob Plumbing and Hardware

Pineknob Real Estate and Rentals

Mountain View Steak and Seafood

The Lookout

The Bear Claw

Chappy's Bar and Grill

LMSU's business office was in the Administration Building, a majestic-looking, three-story sandstone building centrally located on campus. The sun had burned off all of the morning dew when Price walked over to see Jane Haynes. In the higher education game, Datatel was the software system of choice for administrative bookkeeping: not only bill paying, but all information pertaining to students: registration, payment, financial aid, grades, and transcripts. When Datatel went down occasionally it crippled the University, making it ever more dependent of its Institutional Technology (IT) or computer department. Datatel access was limited to specific offices.

For Price's need that day, Jane Haynes was the perfect person to have to deal with because she was that one soul on campus everyone tried to avoid. In other words, he wouldn't have to stand in line for her services. Places of business always seem to have one of the sort in their employ. Not unpleasant, Haynes loved to talk and would share stories about her parents, kids, and now grandkids as though the listener had intentionally tuned in to the soap opera and that they were already privy to the preceding years of delicate information. To top that, she was a woman who tried to present herself as someone 20 years younger. Pushing 55, she wore tight, skimpy, revealing clothes... short skirts, open blouses with spaghetti strap tank tops. In the winter, she had the same look only add V-neck or button up sweaters. To her credit, she had remained thin if not fit, but her hair, makeup, and fashion sense didn't correspond with her age. To her discredit, she wasn't smart enough to figure out that people avoided her like the plague. If you had to deal with Jane Haynes, you knew you must endure a painful story or two, and 15 minutes minimum.

Price was about to become her best friend. She wore a fairly short jeans skirt – jeans were normally forbidden for LMSU administration and staff -- with hose and brown cowboy boots, a white tank with a chocolate brown sweater. He was hit with the aroma of her nauseating perfume in the hallway before he walked into her office late morning Tuesday.

"Jane, I've got an important favor to ask you. I need to know how much money the University paid the businesses on this list last year. And if it's something that you can do easily, maybe the last 10 years as well."

"Oh, well, that's not too difficult," she said. "It'll take, oh, about an hour... maybe a little more. Is there something wrong?"

"No, it's just research," Price said. "Mr. Nester asked me to figure out how to cut some costs. You know how that is... never ending."

"Tell me about it," she said, as if "cutting costs" were a cue. Price cringed at being absent-minded enough to give her a topic to tee off on. "Last weekend I had to drive down to Florida to my parents' house, and get my father set up at the hospital down there for a procedure he was having on Monday. He was having some places checked for skin cancer. You remember I had to take him a couple of months ago and have some moles removed... well this was due to that. But you would not believe what they were going to charge for this little bit of outpatient work. I swear, I don't know how anybody does it anymore, do you?"

"It's crazy, that's for sure. He has insurance though doesn't he?"

"Yeah, but Lord, just the cost of their prescriptions is enough money for most people to live off of."

"It's not easy. I feel for them. Well, listen, I'll sure appreciate…"

"Hey, how is Amber doing over there?" Haynes asked, interrupting Price's cut off sentence.

"Oh, she's doing fine," Price said. "Hard worker… she does a great job."

"That's not what I mean, Dwayne. How *is* she? You know, when you started working here, I thought you two might spark."

"Oh," Price said, smiling, almost embarrassed with Haynes' true meaning. "No, nothing like that. So, to answer your question, I guess I don't know how she's doing."

"Well, you should find out. Probably do you both some good. Don't work too hard. Life is too short."

"That's a good thought, I guess," Price said. "So, here's the list. When can I…"

"I'll give you a buzz when I've got it finished," Haynes said. "Or just swing back by after lunch."

"Ok, thank you, Jane. I really appreciate it."

"No problem. You just think about what I said about Amber. Ok?"

"All right, I will," Price said.

As Price walked back to his own building, he thought about what Jane had said concerning Amber Duffy. If he had ever considered asking her out, he dismissed it quickly using the excuse of not believing in dating someone he worked with. But she was extremely attractive, beautiful in his eyes, with a temperament that he found especially pleasant. What was he waiting for?

Was he that... mechanical? He laughed briefly as he walked. Who would have thought a Jane Haynes suggestion would have sparked such thoughts?

As he walked through the office door, Amber was on the phone helping someone who had dialed the wrong extension. Suddenly, he found that her smile was intoxicating as she glanced up and met his eyes when he entered. He carried that thought to his desk. When he set down and opened the file he'd started for this case – Props – he realized he could have also asked Jane Haynes to check for the Props' addresses in town. Actually, probably better that he didn't, Price thought to himself.

"I can get that from anybody," he said out loud, absent-mindedly.

"Did you say something to me, Dwayne?" Amber Duffy asked, appearing in Price's door, leaning slightly on her right hand and forearm, which rested on the door frame, accentuating her slender build, and the contrast of her breasts. She wore a black and white patterned skirt that hit her just above the knees, and a black, short-sleeved, form-fitting sweater. "She's a vision," he thought.

"Oh, I was just talking to myself," he said. "I just forgot to take something across the way there before."

"Is there something you'd like me to do?" Amber asked.

"No, I'll take care of it," he said. "I was wondering though, I mean, I don't really know much about you. We work here together and all, and I don't..."

"What are you wanting to know?" she asked, laughing at his boyish awkwardness, not anticipating his intentions.

"I guess I'm wondering if you're going out with anybody right now," he blurted out quickly, looking up at her with hope, yet relieved to have said the words.

"Oh," she replied. Her eyes widened. Now she was the one caught off guard by the personal nature of the questioned. "No, I'm not right now."

"That surprises me."

"Does it? Why?"

"Well, um, I can't think of a woman around here who is as pleasant, and also as... beautiful," Price said. "I think you're a special girl."

"That must be why my social calendar is so full," she said.

Her smile intensified Price's sudden eagerness. At the same time he felt he was speaking in tongues. He'd never been so openly honest with a woman.

"Well, we should do something about that. How about Saturday?"

"I could do something Saturday."

"Ok. It's a date then," Price said. "We'll work out the details later."

"That sounds good," she said. Suddenly there was an uncomfortable instant, as if, "how do I now break away from this moment and get back to normal business?" Luckily it was nearly noon.

"If it's ok, I'm going to go ahead and grab a bite," Amber said. The two had never lunched together.

"Oh, sure, go ahead," Price said. "I'll go later. I had breakfast."

A bit later, Price took the list of 13 Proposition 48s to the Registrar's Office and requested the local addresses from an assistant there. He then stopped by the Business Office. Jane Haynes was out, but she left an envelope on her desk with his name on it. He shuddered with excitement when he picked it up, enjoying the investigative aspects of this infraction. He didn't consider at that moment the dread he'd felt previously, when he considered the consequences of being the whistle blower.

He walked outside with the envelope and sat on a nearby bench. He briefly closed his eyes to absorb the pleasant warmth of the sun. It was pushing into the high 60s. He opened the flap and began to analyze its contents, as chattering college students passed by. Of the 23 businesses on the list, LMSU had made payments to 18 the previous year. The highest was Ridgecrest Insurance at just over $4 million. Roberts Printing was next at $1.8 million. Individually, the rest didn't seem too out of the ordinary, just a little high. $1.2 million to PayDirt for all sports uniforms, warm-up suits, travel wear, multiple styles of T-shirts and sweatshirts, some for resale of course, plaques and awards; $1 million to Computer Outlet for computers, upgrades, and software; $800,000 for fuel; $400,000 for replacement concrete; $250,000 for upgrades in fitness equipment; $150,000 for liquor and beer; $40,000 for linens; the list went on and on. In all, just over $11 million in payments went back to Roberts Renderings in the past year, which was roughly 1/8 of the University's annual budget. The total for 10 years prior wasn't nearly as intrusive -- $3.9 million the first year of the list – but as Roberts added businesses to his empire, the services to the University nearly tripled through the years.

"That guy is one enterprising S.O.B.," Price thought. "Gives two and a half million and looks like gold, but charges eleven. Sweet deal."

As Price returned the information to its envelope, he saw Ben Wright among the numerous groups of students walking up and down the sidewalk. Price motioned for him in his wave.

"Hey, I just wanted to let you know I got that return call from the FCA office. I'm in," he said, after Wright had excused himself from his friends.

"That's great news," Wright said. "When can we get started?"

"I'm supposed to meet with him next Monday night formally, get a breakdown of the duties and expectations. Then we should be able to have our first campus meeting later in the week."

"That's great, Dwayne," Wright said. "I've been talking with some guys who could really use the guidance. Can you get hold of me next week?"

"Why don't you just stop by my office next Tuesday on your way to practice. If we're ready to have a meeting, I'll have some fliers printed up. Could you take a few to the Ivory and the dorms, maybe recruit a few others to help you?"

"Yeah, that's no problem at all," Wright said. "That sounds good then. I'll see you Tuesday."

"Ok, Ben, thanks. Good luck again for Saturday."

"Thanks."

While Price was digesting his revelation about Chap Roberts on that campus bench, Coach Rosemont was welcoming his star receiver, Danny Smith, into a seat in his office.

"Danny, we've been talking around here about starting a real push to get you to New York to the Heisman Trophy ceremony," Rosemont said. "Now, your numbers may be enough to get you there anyway. But anything that is done out of the S.I.D. office couldn't hurt. I need to know if you're willing to help the cause by playing nice with the media. And I mean starting today."

"Coach, you know I'll do whatever you want," Smith said. "The main thing is, I just want to get drafted."

"I understand that, Danny," Rosemont said. "And you will. But this will help that, too. If you make it to New York, everyone in the world will know who you are. Now, there aren't too many Heisman voters out there -- only two in Tennessee. But we've got national sports crews coming in here today. Everybody is going to see what they televise. You can show them the Danny Smith that we all love, or you can be difficult."

"What about the other guys?" Smith said. "We're not just winning because of me. And Ben is a junior."

"Have you ever heard the saying, 'A rising tide lifts all ships?' "

"No."

"Well, you are a perfect example of that. If you make it to New York... if they consider someone from Lookout Mountain State University for the Heisman, that will make it that much easier for Ben to make it next year. And it will make the program stronger. Think about what a help it will be with recruiting. There will be high school guys out there who'll see that they can be considered one of the best in the country when they come here. They're already seeing you in the highlights every week. They're out there saying 'I want to be like Danny Smith.' Now I appreciate what you're saying about Wright, but he'll be here next year. Are you going to be here next year?"

"No sir," Smith said, sitting back and seriously considering what Rosemont was asking.

"Think about this. Because of you, more scouts are going to look at Ben, Jerome, Steve, even the younger receivers. Now, the season is half over. We've got five on the schedule and hopefully a good bowl game left. The scouts are already coming in here. You've got to show that you'll play ball. And I don't just mean football. If you make it to New York, that could mean that you'll be a top three Draft pick. The difference between three and 23 could be millions of dollars for you and your family."

"I'll do it, Coach," Smith said. "You just tell me what to do."

Smith was the perfect example of why college athletes needed media training and Rosemont planned to implement just such a program in the future. But that ship had sailed for Smith. Promoting him for the Heisman, in a way, was Plan B of Damage Control 101... "Get them focused on something else."

"Main thing, Danny, take two seconds to think about what you're going to say... after every question... take a breath, slow down. I have to do that. And I don't say exactly what I want to. I never have. If you give them anything controversial... anything juicy, man, they're going to run with it. You know that by now. Talk about your teammates, about Ben's arm, or how the younger guys are coming along. Show them you're a team player. Tell them you'd be honored to even be considered for the Heisman, see? Be humble. You may be the greatest receiver ever, but if you say it out loud, they're not going to like you. They'll say you're cocky and big-headed. So, do what?"

"Slow down and think after every question," Smith said, though with little conviction. Rosemont picked up on it.

"You may not believe this Danny. The NFL teams that really want you, they'll call everybody to get a sense of who you are... what kind of person you are. They'll call these local beat writers. Was he cooperative? Is he a nice guy? They'll turn over rocks... you understand? It's a huge investment they're making... and there's enough talent out there to where some teams won't take a chance on a troublemaker."

"Ok, Coach, I get it."

"Now, go ahead and get your practice gear on, shy of your pads and jersey. You got a decent-looking T-shirt to wear under your pads?

"Not really."

"I'll call Ray to give you a new LMSU shirt of some kind," Rosemont said. "Pick it up at the equipment window downstairs."

With that understanding hopefully accomplished, Coach Rosemont took the lead in the promotion of Danny Smith for the Heisman Trophy campaign. He'd been mentioned on some watch lists prior to that but considered a long shot at best… quarterbacks and tailbacks were the normal fodder. Six years prior, in 1991, Michigan's Desmond Howard had won as a wide receiver. Four years before that, Notre Dame's Tim Brown took the Trophy. Historically, that was a flurry for the position. Prior to Brown, it had been 37 years since a non-quarterback/running back had won – Notre Dame end Leon Hart in 1949. This year, the frontrunner was another Michigan athlete, defensive back Charles Woodson, also a part-time receiver, but a special teams dynamo. He returned punts and kickoffs with incredible speed and grace. If he took the prize in New York, it would be epic.

Rosemont had already shared the plan to push Smith with Wright, and Wright was on board. Next would be offensive coordinator Paul Lawson… future play calling would have to be factored in as well. Rosemont hadn't sent the idea up the line to Nester or Dr. Everett, because he had a sense they would disapprove. The coach's experience and charisma would get some additional votes for Smith, as would Wright's humble praise.

The question Rosemont was asking himself was if Smith would help or hurt himself… and if he could stay out of trouble for two months. After he watched Smith and Means walk off together the night before he had strong suspicions. He made a mental note to make sure he passed down the line that Smith would not be chosen for "random" drug tests anytime soon.

9

Wednesday looked to be a glorious day in Pineknob, Tennessee. The Danny Smith for Heisman push was under way. Smith, Rosemont, Wright, Steve Lake and Jerome Jones were all going to be on national sports telecasts – and that fact was publicized in the local and regional papers with the normal daily splash of LMSU updates and features. The team was 6-0 and three days away from an important showdown with Southwestern Conference rival Georgia State. It was high times in Pineknob.

That morning though, word broke of the untimely death of a former player. Ron Bennett, an LMSU Hall of Fame offensive lineman, passed away at his Chattanooga home Tuesday evening due to heart failure. He was 38. He left behind a beautiful wife, Christy, his college sweetheart, and two young sons.

Stories like Ron's were becoming all too common. People talked about the tragedy of his death but out of respect, not about the real reasons. Yes, he'd kept his weight on, and that contributed. A hulking man, Bennett was 6-foot-8 and weighed 320-pounds. As a left tackle he was the key to the Black Bears pass protection on offense. He was the island to the left, protecting his quarterback's blind side. He earned first-team All-Conference honors three times, and was Division I-AA All-American as a senior. He even made it to the NFL, but he didn't earn his pension. Devastating knee injuries ended each of his first three campaigns. After the third, he gave it up. He was physically broken down at 26, and addicted to pain medication. He ate Darvons like candy. Worse yet, throughout his career, he not only used, but abused, the juice… eight years of chemical enhancement.

Steroids may not have been as prevalent in college football as many fans assumed, but there was a moderate percentage, maybe 10 to 15 players out of 100, who were users. What did they hope to gain? Faster strength increases in the weight room, and to physically grow in pounds and muscle, to have more quickness, and more "pop" when they played.

Non-users willing to work consistently in the weight room could become as strong as those using steroids. All players lose size and strength through the season. Though most players continue their basic lifting every day or at least three days a week, it's impossible to devote the time that they did through the winter, spring and summer. Bumps and bruises to the players who stay healthy contribute as well. More time is spent in the training room and on the practice field. So through the season, they do their best to maintain what they've achieved. Since non-users gained their strength through hard work only, they experienced less of a fall off. This was part of the problem of steroids in college football.

Bennett came to Pineknob with massive physical potential but little strength. He could barely bench press 200 pounds as a freshman, so as expected, he was redshirted. By the time he was a senior, he could close-grip 505 pounds *when he was on the juice*. A typical cycle ran 12 weeks, then off for eight. Of course, this was not under a doctor's supervision. Steroids affected each player differently. There were the common side effects: acne, reddish-purple skin tone, shrinking and inconsistently performing penis, mood swings, rage, and aggression.

For some, and this included Bennett in a big way, going off a cycle brought depression. The weight room is where you earn your identity among your teammates. A football season goes by like lightning. Players get sucked in one end and shot out the other. It's a blur. But the weight room is constant, for four or five years. Gains are measured and displayed on information boards. Leaders are coveted. Record-holders praised. Testosterone is raging as iron is thrust about. For a player coming off a cycle, one who could bench 475 on Monday would suddenly have a 40 to 70 pound drop off by Saturday. During the off cycle, Bennett would be embarrassed – humiliated -- in the weight room. At night, he'd lay awake thinking about the need to get back on… to get those shots in the ass. Bennett eventually became a dealer, providing steroids to his willing teammates… those who could pay, of course. Diana Balls -- or D-Balls – was the flavor of the era. By the time he was a senior, he would only cycle off for 12 or 14 days, his judgment completely clouded. Emotionally, he was a train wreck. Physically, his arteries and heart valves were already out of whack. By the time he retired from football three years later, the damage was irreversible. But no one knew it.

Today there are coolers full of legal supplements for players to drink… When Bennett was using, there was only the illegal version. Coaches didn't encourage use, but they, like the players, usually knew who was using and who wasn't. Many players, plucked from a lower middle class existence, wouldn't have the money if they wanted to buy in. With weight work keeping metabolism cranked up 24 hours a day, players were always hungry. Some players wouldn't have money to buy a loaf of bread and some peanut butter and jelly. They'd leave the football training table at 7 p.m. and be starving at midnight. Once he started dealing, Bennett had that covered. He always had money for late night food. The habit of wanting something late continued through his life after football, so he stayed large as he grew soft and his strength decreased.

Due to the timing, the news of Bennett's death didn't make the morning papers, but the word began to spread fast through the morning, and it hit the wire services by 8. The football office was called shortly after 8:30 a.m. and Rosemont issued a statement on behalf of the Black Bears program, though he was an assistant coach at North Carolina when Bennett played:

It is with great sadness that we learn of the untimely death of one of our own, Ron Bennett. His contribution to the Lookout Mountain State University program is immeasurable. As a Hall of Fame athlete, he is one who helped make the Black Bears grow and become what it is today. The image of number 77 protecting at all cost will forever be ingrained in the history of LMSU football. We ask God to be with Ron and his family on this tragic day. Our thoughts and prayers are with Ron's family.

Rosemont and his staff would take the time to pay respects at the visitation on Thursday evening, but Bennett's funeral arrangements were planned for the same time the team buses would be pulling out for Georgia State on Friday. So other than being the buzz of the day on campus and around Pineknob, including talk of a memorial fund in Bennett's name for his family, it was business as usual in the LMSU football office.

In addition to the list of Chap Roberts' businesses, Dwayne Price now had the local addresses of the Proposition 48 players. He thought to himself on Wednesday how best to use the latter information as he went about the normal business of his office. He had rationalized that due to night classes and their daily workouts, Saturday mornings would be a logical and safer time to have these players do their work. So Price decided he would take some time on Thursday to check some of the players' housing and scout a good stakeout location for Saturday. It was then he hoped to follow a player to a Roberts-owned establishment.

Jim Wheatley's services, it turned out, were needed for more pressing matters on Tuesday evening, so Roberts' right-hand-man hadn't gone in to the University to find what he could about what Price might be up to. Instead, he was sent out to collect on a large gambling debt that had gone delinquent. The hunt for this multiple loser took longer than expected. Wheatley found the mark in a sex-for-drugs trade with a local part-time prostitute hooked on crack cocaine. Normally less diplomatic, Wheatley allowed the mark to get what he came for before he roughed him up. Of course, he snapped a few pictures of him in the act just in case, boldly sneaking into the girl's house which had been left wide open. Despite this mark's lowly social activities and inability to gamble he had a well-paying job. Roberts always stressed to Wheatley that it's smart to have the goods on someone with income.

Wheatley went in Wednesday evening, dressed as facilities personnel, not difficult to do since the University ordered the shirts and hats from Paydirt Uniforms. The swipe card assured his entrance, but he would have to pick the lock of the outer office door to reach Price's office. The only camera surveillance was at the other end of the building, which, along with the interior entrance into the basketball arena, housed the University's ticket office. Through time and Rosemont's counsel, Wheatley knew that facilities only had two men working at night for the entire campus, and security was only deployed as needed. Short of a breech or break-in that had set off an alarm, University security would likely be showing its face around the five residence halls and in the parking lots where commuting students would be walking to and from evening classes. Security's evening staff was inadequate to even do those jobs properly.

When he reached the heavy wooden, fire-proof, office door, Wheatley went down on one knee to rake the tumblers, an art he'd mastered while still in his teens. He always carried miniature burglar aids – a pick and a torque tool – in his wallet or jacket pocket. They were especially handy when he was collecting gambling debts. Weekend losers didn't usually answer their doors on Monday or Tuesday if they were low on cash or planning to skip out on a debt.

Less than a minute passed before Wheatley found his way safely into the lobby of the four offices. He shut the door to Price's office and began looking through the papers on top of Price's tidy desk... one small stack. Next he pilfered through the drawers. No files, or evidence of anything associated with props being paid or Roberts. Wheatley then turned on the computer. He used an administrative override to get by Price's pass word – a trick Roberts' paid the assistant manager of I.T. for -- then went straight to his email. Nothing suspicious in his inbox, and likewise nothing related in his stored, sent, or deleted files, though checking took some time. Wheatley noted with disdain that Price had no personal correspondence at all, fitting of his all-business personality. A check of Word revealed no files or documents related either.

Wheatley next focused on Price's phone. An interoffice system, which at the push of a button displayed the last 30 calls placed, received, or missed. Most were interoffice calls, signified by only four digits. Wheatley wrote down the 12 that were not so he could check them the next day. He then leaned back in Price's chair and thought what else is there? He saw the trash can and checked through it. Nothing. As he looked around again, he asked aloud, "No fax?" Maybe in the outer office. As he reached for the knob he heard a voice in the hallway through the outer door. As he continued to watch, he saw two males walking towards the ticket office end of the building. They didn't wear facilities or security uniforms so Wheatley again felt safe. "Probably a couple of fags," he said under his breath as he looked around the outer office. He quickly filtered through the trash by the shared fax. Wasn't a lot there, one from the Tennessee Secretary of State's office. "Odd, but who knows?" Wheatley thought. "Two days old." He folded that paper and stuck it in his pocket. Wheatley made a quick look around the receptionist's desk, aware that someone could see him through the small window if passing by. He then opened the door slowly, listened, popped his head out and checked both ways, and exited in the direction he came from, away from the ticket office surveillance. He walked quickly off of campus and across the street. He hadn't parked on a University lot, just in case security did come by. One thing Rosemont hadn't provided Roberts for himself or Wheatley was a faculty/staff parking pass, though Roberts had parking lot A privileges on game day due to his donations.

Wheatley exhaled when he reached his van, although entering an empty LMSU building certainly wasn't the most dangerous task he performed in a given week. He carried a snub-nosed .38 in his jacket pocket, but he was sure going in that, if confronted, he could talk his way out of the situation.

As he turned the key to start the van he thought that if Price was investigating, he must be carrying any documents he might have with him. "Next step, find out where the prick lives," he thought.

Wheatley looked over his left shoulder, pulled into the quiet Pineknob street, and headed for The Lookout, where Chap Roberts would likely be.

Thanks to ESPN, college football – and gambling – was nearly an every night affair. The bar would have a few baseball fans as well as the Florida Marlins and Cleveland Indians were kicking off the World Series.

Roberts was at his regular table, all business, working the phone when Wheatley entered. He ordered a beer from the female bartender, Josie Albert, and left a couple of dollars on the bar. Josie was a single, 27-year-old woman whom the regulars loved. She had a fun time behind the bar, but nipped trouble in the bud before it had a chance to start. Roberts liked her because she didn't alienate female patrons, and she had a slew of her own friends that made their way in to see her as well, which was good for business. The oblong room wasn't huge but it had eight televisions scattered about, and mounted in the corners, three behind the bar. There was always a steady flow of business.

Wheatley slid into the seat opposite Roberts.

"What did you find out?" Roberts asked.

"Nothing conclusive," Wheatley said. "If he's started a file, he's carrying it with him. I did find this."

Wheatley took the fax receipt from his pocket, unfolded it, and handed it to Roberts.

"Uh, yeah, from the Secretary of State's office? He's definitely checking me out. What else could it be? That's the only place other than the IRS and my files you could find out what all I own."

"Oh it *could* be something else," Wheatley said. "It was in that outer office. But I don't think it is. He's keeping it quiet though. He hadn't called Nester, Everett, Rosemont, or Indiana. That's where the NCAA's headquarters is, right, Indianapolis?"

"Yeah. That's right. Well, we need to know what he's carrying and what and when he's going to do something with it. We need to start watching him at home."

"Let me grab a phonebook out of the office," Wheatley said.

"He's not going to be in the book. He just moved here this summer."

"You think Sam would know?"

"Probably not. He's not much on chit chat. Doesn't sound like this guy Price would be either. They'd have records at school in the business office. The swipe card doesn't get us in that building though. You're going to have to follow him... go in his house if you see him carrying his work."

"We could just ask him... or we could kill him," Wheatley said, as both men laughed. "We confronted Milovich. At the time, that was pretty bold."

"Yeah and he's ended up being the biggest leech on the payroll. If Price is on to us, he's going to want to be sure. You don't start a stink like this unless you're sure you're right. What in the hell tipped him off?"

"A recipient no doubt," said Wheatley.

Roberts looked at his watch... 11:45 p.m. "I wonder if Sam is still at the office?"

Sam Rosemont had just planted himself on the couch beside Jennifer Newton for a short chat before what he hoped to be another glorious sexual encounter when he felt the vibration of his cell phone. He looked at the ID and considered not picking up, but under the current circumstances he thought better of it.

"What's up, pal?" Rosemont said, standing and walking a bit to give himself some buffer space.

"Did you put Lindemood to bed for the night?"

"Yep. Sure did."

"Does that mean you're at Ms. Newton's?"

"Yep. Sure does."

"Coach… you're on an every-other-night pace. Your dick must not know how to act. I'm jealous myself."

"He's happy to be back in the game," Rosemont said, with a laugh. "What can I do for you?"

"Listen, do you know where our new friend lives?"

"No. Not a clue."

"We came up empty on the office visit. We need to get a look at what he's carrying."

"I don't need to know that."

"Yeah, you're right. Dip your wick."

"Wait a minute. Are you talking about an address?"

"Yeah."

"What about Ridgecrest? Wouldn't that be on file up there?"

Roberts went silent.

"Oh, yeah, takes the country boy to solve the big problems. I believe you even know the owner, you sorry sack of shit."

Roberts laughed.

"We'll talk tomorrow. I'm flying to Atlanta but I'll see you Friday night at the hotel."

Rosemont sat back down beside Jennifer, then slid his right hand across her stomach and the soft fabric of her gray sweater as he pulled her tightly to him.

"Sorry about that," he said.

"Oh, that's ok, Coach," she said. "Just don't let it happen again."

They looked at each other and smiled.

"I won't."

The lovers kissed passionately, Rosemont's hands running freely over Newton's body. He was about to get what he came for. What he still didn't realize was how much he needed at home what he was getting here. He felt empowered by the love he was getting now.

10

"I don't like – the President and I don't like – this Heisman campaign for Smith," Charles Nester said. After he said it he looked down at his shoes, nervously pulled at a button on his jacket, and began to squirm in his stance.

It was ill-advised for Nester to have the conversation with Coach Sam Rosemont at any time, especially without Dr. Everett by his side, but walking in 30 minutes before practice on Thursday was equivalent to blasphemy. Nester's ignorance, Ron Bennett's visitation, and Dwayne Price acting truly spontaneous in the name of romance, made this particular Thursday unlike any other in Pineknob.

In the weekly breakdown of college football, this was the day players started recharging their batteries. Monday they get the game plan, Tuesday and Wednesday they work it out on the field with hard-hitting practices, Thursday they review at half-speed with no hitting. The repetition of reviewing the opposition's tendencies was of extreme importance, and an aspect of preparation Rosemont did not take lightly. The coach needed to know all the players were well-versed in their duties.

Attempting to establish his position on the institutional ladder, crossing Rosemont, was a huge mistake.

"We believe placing Smith above all the other players just isn't what college athletics is supposed to be about," Nester said, weakly. "You've got the marijuana charge in his recent past. If he were a better student it would be one thing, but …"

"Hold it right there," Rosemont interrupted. "Is Smith eligible according to the rules set forth by the NCAA?"

"Yes."

"Then don't bring his grades or his ability as a student into this discussion. What you don't know is the players voted on it. And it was a landslide," Rosemont lied. "We'll do the same thing for Wright next year. This is an unprecedented time in our history and we have to take advantage of it. This may not happen again."

"That doesn't excuse the fact that you didn't get it approved," Nester said, trying to remain emboldened.

"Do you realize that every time they show Smith on ESPN, the best high school receivers in the country decide that LMSU is the place for them? We've got kids from Watch Lists emailing us about coming here. That has never happened. We're 6-0 and hopefully with a little luck about to crack the Top 10. If Danny gets to go to New York it will be more of the same, multiplied by 10. You can't buy that kind of exposure. Now is this really about holding one player higher than another or is it about me?"

"President Everett and I feel you should have asked before starting this campaign on your own," Nester said.

"Let me tell you something, Cryin' Charlie. This is my program! Do I make money? Yes. Does anybody else? No. Basketball breaks even at best. Have I broken the rules? No. So you do not reserve the right to walk in here and tell me how to run my program. Just sit back on your pansy-ass and take the credit. You got it? Keep your mouth shut... people will only *think* you're stupid."

"I don't appreciate this tone, Sam. You do understand I am the Athletic Director?"

"Yeah? So go help women's soccer. Don't you ever walk in here five minutes before practice with this kind of shit. Next time, schedule a meeting. Now get out of here. I've got to get ready for work."

When Nester left his office Rosemont leaned back in his chair and smiled. There were times – games for example – when he truly lost control of his emotions and he stomped the sidelines untamed. Bullying someone like Nester though was not one of those times. He could turn it on and off like a faucet. Rosemont grabbed a Life Saver mint out of a glass jar on his desk, opened it, popped it in his mouth and shook his head laughing. "That putz."

Nester remained composed as he walked out of the football offices and past Janet Randolph's desk, but once through the exterior doors he was fuming. Typical of such situations, he internalized his humiliation, frustration, and anger as he walked back to his office. He didn't have in his bag of tricks the moxie or fortitude to put Rosemont in his place, and that ate at him as well. By the time he reported to the president later that day that Rosemont showed no remorse concerning starting the unauthorized Heisman campaign, he was completely composed.

In that building, Dwayne Price was losing his focus. Amber Duffy, a vision in a navy skirt, matching shoes, and a white, no frills, button-up blouse, had infiltrated his mind. Setting up a date so early in the week had left the office encounters a little awkward, though breaking that ice had at the same time opened up a little more playful banter occasionally between the two.

About the time Rosemont was chewing Nester out, Price made a snap decision and he was waiting for the right moment to put it into action. Of his co-workers in the other three offices, Bruce Fellows typically liked to be in or around the stadium during practice, in case Rosemont had a request of some sort. It was also important because fans, or opposing coaches disguised as fans, sometimes made their way into the stands to watch practice. Price knew as well that Mary Shell had a meeting across campus. That left only Marcus Robinson, campus historian and photographer, in his office. Robinson, though, was working on his master's degree, so, when his door was shut you could presume he was napping, working on his research, or looking at "fleshy" photos of female students. When he shut his door, it usually remained so for a couple of hours at least.

The next time Price saw Duffy on her feet, he asked her to come in his office.

"Hey, Amber, I've been thinking," he began, "Since we're going out on Saturday, it seems kind of silly to put off... umm, breaking the ice a bit. So I was wondering, if you didn't have any plans this evening, maybe we could get a bite together after work. What do you think?"

"Well, it's a good idea," she said. "I usually go to the gym after work when I can."

"Oh, well, I usually run, too," Price said. "What if we did it afterwards? Real casual... sweaty even?"

"I don't think you'd want to see me after my workout. If you did, you wouldn't want to see me Saturday."

"That couldn't happen. You could never look bad to me. Do you work out here or where?"

"Over at University Drive."

"Ok. How about I pick you up at 6:30?"

"Well, all right. Quarter till though."

"Will you be in sweat clothes? I don't want you to get cold."

"I've got sweats to cover up with. I usually go home that way."

"All right. That sounds good. I'll be there."

For the first time since his college days, Price was beside himself with excitement. When 5 o'clock came he headed for the door with only Amber Duffy on his mind. He discreetly told her he'd see her soon, then, like a teenager, he patiently leaned against the warm bricks of the building for her. They became better acquainted on the walk to their cars. Nearby, Jim Wheatley waited in a used Chap Roberts demo to observe and follow Price.

"Huh. No notebook or briefcase," Wheatley noted. "Maybe we're wrong about this guy."

Wheatley followed Price to his home and once parked, wrote 173 Monterey Drive on a small spiral note pad he kept on him at all times. Price reemerged from his house at 5:40 for a four-mile run, which he completed in a respectable 25 minutes... 25:13 to be exact. He grabbed a felt-tip pen and scribbled it on a chart on the side of his refrigerator as he began to stretch, drinking water between lunges. Wheatley drew hard on a Marlboro and continued watching as Price finished the stretches then dropped for pushups and crunches on his living room floor.

At least partially true to his word, Price took off his sweaty running clothes, washed the salt off his face, and put on a dry T-shirt, underwear, sweat pants and jacket, running shoes and headed back out of the house to pick up Amber. Wheatley continued his pursuit. When Price pulled into University Drive Health Club's parking lot, Amber had already returned her own gym bag to the trunk of her silver BMW coup, a gift from her father.

"Sweet ride," Price said through his open window. "Should we leave mine?"

"It'll be ok. I don't want you in my car if you're really sweaty… I've got brothers," she said. She smiled as she walked around to his passenger side, opened the door and slid into the seat. "Besides, yours is warm. So where are we heading?"

"You want to grab something at an Applebees-TGIF-type place? There's a good game on."

"Oh, yeah? Who's playing?"

"Penn State at Pitt."

"What's so good about that matchup?" she said. She laughed, knowing Price's devotion to his alma mater. "I *guess* it will be ok."

"I'm glad we're doing this," Price said, pulling his Honda back into the street. Wheatley resumed his drive as well.

"Me too," she said. "I was hoping you'd ask me out… just not to a Penn State telecast."

"Who's your team?"

"The Black Bears, come on, are you kidding? We rock."

"That's true," Price said, for an instant reminded of the unpleasant task likely in his future. "This will be a big game Saturday."

"Saturday will be no problem. Mark my word."

"Ok, we'll see. Are you going down there?"

"You know, I thought about it. But my friend that I would usually do that with, she and her husband are flying down to the Keys for a long weekend. So I was looking forward to a quiet 'catch-up' weekend. Are you going? You're not required to go?"

"No, not required. I'm not going. I've got some business to take care of Saturday morning. Otherwise, I'm just looking forward to seeing you. Had I been going, that probably wouldn't have worked out."

After he parked, Price hustled around and opened Amber's car door, something she didn't expect but appreciated. They walked comfortably together as they were led by a hostess to a table in the bar of the Pineknob Applebees. Both ordered water to begin their meal, and Southwest Eggrolls for an appetizer.

As the Panthers of Pitt kicked off, Price thought about his new FCA obligation, looked around the room for students, then proclaimed his need for a beer. "Do you mind?" he asked Amber.

"Of course not. I'll probably have something in a while, too. I just want to cool down a bit more."

"Oh, how was your workout?"

"Great. I did 30 minutes on a stair climber, then some light barbell work."

"Really? Wow, wouldn't have thought that."

"What, the weights? Hey, I'm strong," she said, tilting her head with a stoic look and pointing at Price. "Don't ever cross me."

"Oh, I won't. Don't worry."

The playful banter continued through the evening. Amber Duffy eventually had a couple of glasses of chardonnay and Price enjoyed three, slow-paced beers. Outside, Wheatley lit another smoke, then took a drink of George Dickel from a pint bottle he had in a brown paper bag under his driver's seat. He watched them from the parking lot, calling Chap Roberts at one point. Roberts was in Atlanta for some Ridgecrest business and was taking his reps from that area out for a meal.

"Right now this guy has his mind on a chick," Wheatley reported. "He's definitely not thinking about our issue. I probably should have gone back to his office tonight."

"Right… but the swipe is with me," Roberts said. "We should have considered that the other night. Sounds like you might as well call it a night."

"I'm going to hang. I've got my camera. I don't think this loser is going to get laid, but if he does, I'd like to have the pictures of this girl he's with."

"Really. Good looking, huh. And you've never seen her before?"

"No. But she must work there too. They walked out together earlier."

"Yeah, get some shots," Roberts said, always interested in an attractive female. "We'll find out who she is. You'll make the rounds later, too, right?"

"All right. Later."

A few blocks away at Parker Funeral Home, Rosemont was one of the first to pay his respects to the family of Ron Bennett. The coach had to get on to the University Inn for his 7 p.m. radio show. Most of his assistant coaches were with Rosemont, as was Ben Wright, the players' usual ambassador. There were a couple of hundred who went through the doors that evening, but only a handful knew the depths in which Bennett abused his body with steroids. One was Max Milovich, a teammate of Bennett's and LMSU's former compliance director.

There was a large painting on an easel Bennett's parents had commissioned during his playing days with number 77 upright in pass protection, battling a defensive end. The painting truly summed up Bennett's career, save for the drug abuse. There were a few whispered comments among former teammates about the use and selling of D-Balls, but the saddened congregation as a whole viewed the tragic death as an overworked heart finally giving out.

The Inn was hopping with fans when Rosemont arrived. That was to be expected with a 6-0 record and such high hopes. The show was MC'd by Bill Randolph, the University's longtime radio announcer. He was not related to Janet Randolph, though it often came up in football conversation. The questions were flowing and Rosemont was his usual colorful self. He got an even bigger rush when he found out that his favorite waitress, Jennifer Newton, was going to serve the "talent" table as the show progressed.

"These waitresses down here at the University Inn do an incredible job," Rosemont said at one point. "If you haven't been here in a while, they alone are worth the stop. Throw in the best meal in town and there's no reason not to be here. In fact, why don't we give away a free dinner to our next caller, Billy."

"Ok, Coach. Let's take another question from our 'Inn' crowd while that call comes in at 12-SCORE," Randolph said. "This is Ira, Coach."

"Coach, I read that Georgia State is a really strong team and that their middle linebacker, Steve Freely, bench presses over 400 pounds. Are we going to be able to block this guy?"

"That's a great question, Ira the Inquisitive," Rosemont said, knowing the fans loved getting a nickname label from him. "Georgia State does have a bunch of good athletes, so we'll have our work cut out for us. If you look at Freely, he is a strong kid and can probably bench what you say. But he's listed at 6-1, 215. So he's probably actually 5-11 ½, 200. He's what we coaches would call 'light in the butt.' He might be really strong, but a bigger guy will be able to put him on his back. That's where getting a hat on the guy on every play is important. If Freely has a big game - and he could if he's able to run around… well, freely - it's because no one blocked him. Believe me, we plan on blocking him."

As Rosemont was finishing his answer, Linda Rosemont made her way into the room along with Randolph's wife, Victoria. Linda didn't always come to the radio show, but she often made a point to when the team had a road game. Rosemont was so busy that day, he hadn't thought about that tendency or considered that she would make an appearance. He was hit with a truck load of guilt and a feeling of being caught, which was an entirely new experience for him. Suddenly his face was a hot iron and his stomach housed a twister.

"Oh goodness, look here. We're now being joined by the first ladies of Black Bears football, Linda Rosemont and Victoria Randolph," Rosemont said. The fans in the room gave the two familiar faces a round of applause, which overshadowed Rosemont's social clumsiness. Linda, looking dignified yet cute in jeans, tennis shoes, and a Black Bear navy golf shirt pulled over a navy turtleneck, gently threw her hand to the crowd with a modest smile. Victoria was equally casual, in a Black Bears sweatshirt. They sat down in empty chairs at the end of the talent table, out of the way.

The show went on and conversation continued to flow, but Rosemont was in a surreal moment – almost an out of body experience -- as he watched Jennifer Newton glide over with a smile and ask Linda and Victoria what she could bring them to drink. Jennifer was smart and discreet and did nothing – and had done nothing - physically to give away what had been going on between her and Rosemont since Saturday.

Rosemont though, looked at his petite – almost fragile - wife with reemerging love, and realized he'd been neglectful. He realized too that he needed to make an effort at home to bring the couple back together. He felt drained. Thankfully, the show was almost over. Only a few more minutes of air time remained.

The four would have dinner together as Rosemont gave Randolph some insights on both the Black Bears and Georgia State to share to his radio audience on Saturday. That was also part of the season routine. Randolph's insightful "Coachisms" gave his telecasts a special flavor.

Every time Rosemont looked at Jennifer Newton, it reminded him to show Linda some affection. At one point Rosemont leaned and whispered in her ear, "Since I'm leaving tomorrow, I think we should go home and have a little 'Mommy and Daddy time,' " referring back to the days when their children were still young and constantly underfoot, causing the act of love-making to be more about endurance and finding a time slot than spontaneity.

"Sam!" Linda said. She was at first perplexed by his forwardness, but after giving it some thought she responded, "I think that's a great idea."

The couple followed through. Coach Sam Rosemont made love to his wife tenderly that night. He nearly cried as the familiarity of her – her scent, her arms, her breasts, the way the couple fit perfectly together – came flooding back to his senses. That night the couple fell asleep holding each other. Rosemont looked up at the ceiling and in his mind asked the Lord for forgiveness.

Back in Applebees parking lot, through his open window with his Nikon and a 220 millimeter lens, Wheatley took a half dozen shots of a radiant, happy, Amber Duffy with Dwayne Price, then he headed for Mountain View Steak and Seafood. With or without Roberts in town it was good to give the managers a friendly reminder that Wheatley the Watchdog - as Rosemont called him - was always on duty. After a sirloin steak sandwich and a couple of tall drafts, Wheatley would hit Chappy's Bar and Grill, the Bear Claw, and The Lookout in ascending order. He liked to be at The Lookout when Josie Albert was closing by herself. He knew she was quite capable, but an occasional horny drunk could make it uneasy for her. It was also wide open for a quick robbery if anybody had the balls. Most local criminals knew better than to cross Chap Roberts. Besides, Wheatley thought, Josie Albert was nice to look at. It was nearly his only human sentiment.

Sitting with Amber Duffy in his Honda, Dwayne Price cursed himself for not thinking to pick his date up at what he learned that evening to be her condo. Her good sense to buy rather than rent made him respect her even more. Now that the date was over, it seemed insensitive to drop her off at her car. They'd had a great time together. As the conversation dwindled and the moment of truth came, he looked deeply into her brown eyes, leaned, and kissed her quickly, drew back, and slowly kissed her again with passion. Her warm lips returned it equally. With his left hand he touched her cheek softly as their lips parted, her tongue and taste sending tingling sensations through his body.

When the unexpected show of affection ended, Price jumped out and opened her door. He waited while she opened the door to her car, kissed her one more time, then watched her drive away in her BMW. He couldn't believe his good fortune.

11

All roads out of the Pineknob-Chattanooga area had scenery worthy of calendars: rolling hills and rugged mountains splashed with blazing reds and oranges an artist would find difficult to duplicate. It was idealistic country. Geographically, Georgia State was a 'tweener trips for the Black Bears. Thanks to Chap Roberts they could easily fly to any road game, but if the journey was only a few hours, Rosemont preferred the players have time to reflect and see the countryside. Each year, the Black Bears' roster was filled with mostly city kids. The players, dressed in Black Bears travel sweat suits, could quietly chat, study, review the game plan, or watch a movie. On this trip Rosemont chose *Hoosiers*. It was basketball, but inspirational nonetheless, and an iconic sports movie in Rosemont's mind.

Once the team arrived, they would have a late afternoon walk through at the opposition's stadium, and a good meal. That night, the group would see *The Game*, starring Michael Douglass and Sean Penn, in the theatre. Rosemont knew his players would be focused on Saturday, but he still reminded them in his parting words on Friday night… focus and execution. Having the best talent didn't matter if a team failed to execute, had multiple penalties, or a few turnovers. He wanted them on an emotional even keel, unaware of the crowd noise, focused to the point of "crystal clear clarity of purpose."

The day had gone quickly in Pineknob. There was a new kinship between Dwayne Price and Amber Duffy and her smiles in the office that day had him distracted. It had really been since his college days that he'd felt so enamored with a girl. After his stint in the Navy he began to think of himself as a permanent bachelor, his intensity for his work and his level of fitness leaving little time for a woman. Somehow the sensibility of Jane Haynes' message on Tuesday awoke something in him that had not only been asleep but had nearly died.

That wasn't the case for Amber Duffy. She was far too attractive to walk among men and women without notice. She had been in love in college to a student two years her senior, but he went on to medical school at the University of South Carolina and he eventually broke it off for a fellow resident there. That rejection hurt her deeply. Feeling betrayed, she became untrusting of men she wasn't familiar with. Since that time she'd never really connected with anyone. Her college friends were all getting married and starting to have children. Men at her health club would ask her out but more often than not they were just looking for a quick score, and she wasn't a sex-on-the-first-date type of woman... or third for that matter. She was a traditional girl. Her mother kept telling her to find a man at church, but she found those pickings slim as well. She was overqualified for her job, but it had been convenient for her to work at her own university, so she was a girl seeking more when Price walked into her life. Suddenly she felt she had part of what she was looking for. She'd seen Price in a different light Thursday. She understood his approach to work. Price in fact reminded her of her own father. As the day wore on, Price couldn't help but to ask what Amber was doing that evening.

"I'm driving back home to watch my youngest brother play in a high school football game," Amber said. "It's a big game."

"Oh, yeah?"

"They're six and two, so if they win tonight they have a good chance of making the playoffs. Their last game is against a patsy."

"How many brothers and sisters do you have?" Price asked.

"I'm the oldest of four. I have a brother and sister – Grant and Sarah -- between Heath and me. Why don't you come with me? It's about an hour and 10 minute drive back to McMinnville. My mother always tries to get me to stay over. You'll be my excuse to get back. When's the last time you went to a high school football game?"

"High school."

"Well, there you go. You'll love it. Warren County High School has atmosphere exceeded only by the Black Bears. I'll even give you time to run home and put on some jeans if you want and grab a coat. It'll be cold by the end of the game."

"All right, I'll tag along. If you're sure you don't mind."

"Mind? You just can't make fun of my singing in the car. I tend to rock out on road trips. I'll pick you up at your house at quarter till six. We'll be cutting it close, but it should be ok."

That evening, Amber Duffy led Dwayne Price back to a time in his own life where all that was important was family, friends, and high school football. Where neighbors stood and cheered side by side for a common cause. He had his dinner from the concession stand, and he thought those two hot dogs with chili, slaw, mustard, and ketchup were the best ever. He met Amber's parents, all three of her siblings, her sister's husband, and at least a dozen other couples from the McMinnville community – population 11,194 -- including the mayor. He especially enjoyed the Pioneers band at halftime, something he never appreciated in his own high school days.

Warren County earned a hard-fought victory that night, which made Amber and her entire family ecstatic.

The couple returned to Pineknob at about 11:30. After a passionate kiss at her car door, Price asked if she'd like to come in, even though he planned to be out by seven in the morning.

"I should get home," she said. "I like to get a really good workout in, plus do a little cleaning, before noon on Saturday. Normally I watch the game with some friends of mine, like I said, but they're out of town."

"Did you hear they changed the kickoff to four o'clock for TV?"

"I did," she said. "Do you want to come over to my place and watch the game before we go out?"

"Yes. That would be fantastic," Price said without hesitation. "I might miss the kickoff though. I'm not exactly sure when I'll be finished in the morning."

"Oh, yeah… what are you doing again?

"Just a little investigating. It shouldn't interfere with the plan. I'm looking forward to it. I've had a blast these last two days Amber. Tonight was great. I never, in all of my life, thought that I would meet the mayor of McMinnville, Tennessee."

"Yes, well, you're now a privileged soul," she said. She teased him by patting his chest indifferently. "Ok, I'll be looking for you tomorrow around game time."

"I'll see you then. Thanks, and good night."

"Good night."

The next morning – 6 a.m. wakeup by alarm clock -- came quickly. Price admitted to himself that all his extracurricular activity with Amber had him feeling as though he was falling behind on sleep. Still he smiled and thought about how lounging at her place today for the game made it worth it. He had that early relationship feeling when one soul connects with another. His heart was soaring, his mind raced with thoughts of Amber, his libido suddenly had a pulse of its own as well as a sense of purpose.

Despite the last-minute change of plans to attend the football game with Amber on Friday, Price had remembered to bring home his Chap Cash file in a black, leather, hard-cover notebook. In that file were the addresses of the Proposition 48 players. To be safe, Price picked DeJuan Richardson to watch rather than a random player. Price didn't have any answers. All the props may not be involved. All he really knew was what Richardson had said following the game last Saturday, and what he believed to be Wheatley delivering the last payment. Over a hot cup of coffee on the cold, still-pitch-black Saturday morning, Price thought to himself how he really didn't want to be the whistle blower. He thought about how disappointed Amber, and thousands of people just like her all over the region, even the state, would be. But he reminded himself that Chap Roberts, and likely Sam Rosemont, were blatantly breaking the rules, pure and simple. And, there may be more behind Roberts billing the University over $10 million a year.

Price pulled on a coat and walked out into the cold morning. He started his car, then felt the dry, toothy sensation in his ears and head as he scraped the frost off his windshield. Richardson's rental unit was a two-story house just a few minutes-walk from the LMSU campus. Price parked half a block up and across the street from his house, closer to where some businesses took over the residential housing. He didn't want to seem conspicuous to other people in the area, especially since a few blocks back from Richardson's rental was the beginning of the only bad section of town. It wasn't a big area but still prevalent when it came to drug crimes or the rare Pineknob murder. It was called the Depot District for the old train station that many years ago thrived when people still traveled by train. Amtrak had long since stopped running through this part of the country, instead using a route east of Chattanooga. The depot itself was a dilapidated structure that the homeless used for shelter until run out by the local police.

Price sat and thought of Amber as he waited for a sign of Richardson. At 10 minutes till nine, he emerged from the front door wearing a red and black high school letterman's jacket and a blue and white LMSU toboggan. Price watched him walk towards campus from across the street. Richardson then crossed to Price's side. The compliance director started his car, and allowed Richardson to almost leave his line of sight. He pulled out and into the sporadic early morning traffic. When he passed Richardson he could see up ahead of him a group of students congregating at LMSU's bricked entrance, a stretch of campus that, once through, allowed a few acres of green grass on either side before a visitor or student reached the first parking lots and buildings.

"That must be the rest of them," Price said out loud, "at the pickup point."

Price drove past the entrance and found an open slot on the street about eight cars up and parked. He had recognized some of the other players as he passed by them, and could now watch them from his side view mirror. Their meeting place couldn't be more conspicuous, he thought to himself.

At precisely 9 a.m. a white van pulled to the curb in front of the young men. All 13 LMSU Proposition 48 players climbed into the van. When it passed him, Price could see that Jim Wheatley was the driver. Traffic was still fairly light so Price let the van get a couple of hundred yards down the road before he cautiously began to tail it. No more than a minute and a half went by before the van pulled into the parking lot of Liberty Fuels, a distribution center. Price pulled off the road two lots up and watched Wheatley unlock the front door and walk in with one player. A minute later he was back under the steering wheel of the van and driving. Pineknob Heating & Cooling was next, followed by Pineknob Real Estate and Rentals. Wheatley then dropped two off at Pineknob Computer Outlet, and continued right on down the line.

With one player remaining in the van, Price turned off the road because Wheatley was obviously heading to Chappy's Bar and Grill, which was a roadhouse off the beaten path outside of town. He would most likely arouse Wheatley's suspicions by then if he hadn't already. Besides, Price now knew the route. He circled around town and back to within sight of Liberty Fuels. Sure enough, five minutes later, Wheatley pulled back into that lot. He gathered the player, locked the door, and moved on to Pineknob Heating & Cooling. So there it was, as illogical as it seemed. "Why go through this pretense?" Price thought. He followed for a few stops, then drove back to school and parked where he could get a good look at the drop off.

Within minutes of his estimate, Wheatley returned with the 13 future Black Bears players. In what he could only define minutes later as a moment of triumph, Price stepped out of his car, both arms resting on the roof, as Wheatley pulled out from the drop off to continue his day. Wheatley saw him and slowed to a crawl as he passed, the two men exchanging icy stares. Realizing he'd been followed and its implications, Wheatley struck his dash board with his right hand and let out a growl of anger as he left the scene.

Later that day, Ben Wright, Danny Smith, and Steve Lake kept Georgia State's best weapon – its crowd – completely out of the game. LMSU's offense relied on quarterback audibles at the line. Wright was a surgeon, dissecting the opposition, changing plays based on coverages, or potential blitzes. Lake scored on a 70-yard run straight up the middle when Wright correctly identified a safety blitz. The line adjusted perfectly. "You Ben Wright?" Lake asked him in an end zone celebration. "Never been wrong, baby," Wright answered in heat-of-the-moment bravado. For Wright, the football leaving the grip of his fingers for a 35-yard strike, or any pass, was humbling perfection. Inside, an uplifting joy surged while he remained all business to onlookers. Wright was at the top of his game, and on that day a better quarterback anywhere would be hard to find.

Smith again made the opposition's defensive backs look like high-schoolers, catching 13 passes for 212 yards and three touchdowns. The play of the game was his again, but it wasn't a punt return, nor did he even have the ball. On this play, he and Murvin Rivers were wide right. Smith took off, drawing the defense. Wright hit Rivers in the flat. The receiver accelerated to his full head of steam when he reached Smith's first block. As Rivers streaked down the sideline at a scorching pace, Smith *passed* him as though he were standing still, made a second great block on the last would-be tackler, and Rivers coasted into the end zone for an 83-yard TD.

In the living room of her tastefully-decorated condo, a Black Bears T-shirt and jeans-clad Amber Duffy looked at Dwayne Price with wide eyes of disbelief as the replay showed Smith's incredible ability to accelerate, the ESPN II commentators accentuating what a team player he was.

"Aww, he couldn't even play special teams for Penn State," Price said.

Amber playfully hit him with a couch pillow.

Smith's Heisman Trophy and NFL stock soared on that day. Final score: 41-10. Lookout Mountain State University was 7-0 and moving into the Top 10 in the nation.

The team's bus ride home was all about the elation of a key victory. The players chattered and talked smack. Coach Rosemont listened to the happy voices behind him and thought briefly about his post-game handshake with Jack Lindemood. His old friend wouldn't even look him in the eye, embarrassed by the whipping the Black Bears had just put on them in front of his home crowd. Rosemont took a sip of Pepsi and laughed.

"Ok, give me a few minutes and I'll be ready to leave," Amber said. "You can freshen up over there if you like, or soak your head in the sink after your vehemently cruel remarks about my Black Bears."

"Oh, forgive me, please," he said. "I will never disparage your team again."

As they left her condo for dinner and a movie, Price loved the fact that, after excusing herself for five minutes, a quick change into a thin sweater and boots, and she was ready to go.

"You look extraordinary," Price said.

As she thanked him she blushed slightly, but was also confident in her appearance.

At The Eagle's Nest, a small, reservation-only restaurant perched high over Pineknob, the couple gazed into each other's eyes by firelight, sipping wine. She had a pasta and shrimp alfredo dish that she found to be delicious, playfully sharing a bite or two with Price, who also found great satisfaction in a 9-ounce fillet prepared medium-rare with sautéed onions and mushrooms, and a side of steamed vegetables.

Later, Price sat in the dark theatre with deep pleasure as he lightly touched the tips of Amber's fingers with his as they held hands and watched *Playing God*, with David Duchovny, Timothy Hutton, and Angelina Jolie. Their only other valid choice that evening without driving across Chattanooga was *Seven Years in Tibet*. They went with the former for the action and Price's input, though Amber admitted she'd enjoy watching Brad Pitt for two and a half hours. As his mind wondered back to his job and the current issue, the significance of their movie's title wasn't lost on him. He thought about Chap Roberts. It wasn't so much about the way he was steamrolling his way to excessive wealth, but how he was callously breaking the rules. He pushed it out of his mind and put his arm around Amber.

The couple had spent three consecutive evenings together, and when he took her home later, Price didn't want to leave her. He stood at her partially opened door and kissed her good night, his hands touching her bare thin sides as her arms went up and around his neck, raising the fabric of her blue sweater. She was so fit that under her smooth skin he could feel her ribs. He was ready to go to the next step, and he hoped she was too. Their kisses gained force, as she backed through her condo door. His hands now went behind her and down to the small of her back. He pulled her close to him. She could feel his firmness on her belly. Her desire was equally stirred. She looked at him longingly and whispered, "Not yet. I want to, but not yet."

"This isn't going to be easy," he said. "You're a vision. I don't want to leave."

"I don't want you to. But... "

"I know. It's hard."

"It seems to be," she said, looking into his eyes with a warm, knowing, smile. "No, it's too soon. But thank you so much for tonight. I had a great time."

"No, thank you, Amber. I can't remember ever feeling this way."

12

The news spread quickly that a Lookout Mountain State University employee had been murdered. But not as fast as the bullets that pierced Dwayne Price's chest.

By 1:45 a.m. Sunday, investigators were at Price's home, and had come up with a preliminary report that the murder was drug related. It was determined that the crime was either the robbery of a heavy user, or a deal gone bad. Loose cocaine was found in a compartment of Price's coffee table, as well as on the table itself and later in Price's blood and nasal passages. Neighbors had heard two shots, but, somehow, nobody saw anything. Though, admittedly, none ran out into the street looking for the shooter after hearing gunfire. Price had been hit twice. Two slugs entered the right side of the victim's chest. By the way he'd fallen in his living room, it looked as though the murderer could have been sitting on Price's couch, more evidence that – along with no forced entry – the shooter had been welcomed in.

"Looks like a double cross on a drug sale," said State Police Investigator Robert Mills to a couple of Pineknob cops. "Or he was selling to somebody who decided he wanted the whole shebang. Did anybody know this guy?"

"Neighbors didn't seem to know him too well, but there were no complaints of high traffic or parties or any of that," said Pineknob officer Rick Street. "They just knew he worked at LMSU, he ran pretty much daily, and he kept everything clean. He's only been here since mid-summer."

"Have university officials been called?" Mills asked.

"Everyone with the team just got back from the Georgia State trip about a half hour ago. We informed Coach Rosemont, and he gave us the cell phone of Charles Nester, the Athletic Director. Nester is this Price's boss," said Street. "They haven't reached him yet though. Rosemont said he thought Nester would be spending the night down there. President Everett is down there overnight as well, apparently."

At the taped-off outer perimeter of the crime scene, Amber Duffy pulled up in her BMW. She made initial comments to a female officer there, who then brought her to Detective Mills.

"Ma'am, can we help you?" he asked.

"I got a call from Jane Haynes, who I work with and who lives around here somewhere. I work with Dwayne as well," she said. "I just don't believe it."

"Your name is?"

"Amber Duffy."

"Was he seeing anybody that you knew of, Miss Duffy?" Mills asked.

"Well, yes," she said, as she began to cry. "We'd been seeing each other the last few days. This just can't be."

"Did you ever see him use drugs, or did you ever use drugs with him?" Mills asked.

"No. Never. Absolutely not. I don't believe he did drugs."

"They often hide it well, ma'am," Mills said. "What about suspicious characters. Every see him talking with anybody that looked to be of that nature?"

"Never."

"You worked together?"

"I'm his -- was his -- administrative assistant."

"Ma'am?"

"His secretary."

"What about phone calls. Ever hear anything suspicious?"

"Nothing that would make me think he was ever doing or dealing drugs. He kept an open door, too."

"Well, this can be a white collar drug. You'd be surprised at by the people actually doing it around you."

"I never saw any signs, either."

"Signs?"

"Signs, yes. Excessive sniffing, rubbing of the nostrils, H-cubed."

"H-cubed?"

"Hyper, happy, and horny."

"That's good. Let me write that down," Mills said with cold sarcasm. "You seem to know a lot about it."

"I'm only six years removed from being a college student. I've seen people on coke. The sensation has been described to me."

"Who said it was cocaine?"

"Come on. White collar drug?"

"Did he have any family that you knew of, Miss Duffy."

"No. His parents had passed. He was an only child," she said, starting to cry again, thinking of how he enjoyed meeting her family. "Can I see him?"

"No. Crime scene. Are you familiar with his home? Would you know if anything else was missing?"

"No. I picked him up here yesterday, but we were in a hurry to get to a football game. He was at my place today. He just dropped me off two hours ago. That's why I – I just don't believe this."

"What time was that?"

"It was 11:45 or so. We'd gone to a movie at 9:10. But we'd been together since four. We watched the game together at my place and had dinner up at The Eagle's Nest."

"Did you notice anybody suspicious then, or was he approached by anybody?"

"No. We never talked to anybody."

"I see. You can leave your address and phone number with the officer there, if you don't mind. Here's my card if you think of anything else you feel might be useful. Are you going to be all right going home?"

Amber looked at her car, at the front door of Price's house, and then back at Mills a bit dazed, the flashing lights of the nearby police cruisers illuminating her face in blue every other instant. She felt lost and was hurting deeply. "I suppose I'll be fine."

"Don't forget you have my card. If you think of anything else that might help us, don't hesitate to call. Thank you for your help. And... I am sorry."

When Charles Nester got the word the next morning about the death of his compliance director, he was as surprised and shocked as he was disappointed. He would have never predicted such behavior out of Dwayne Price, and expected him to be a part of his team for a long time. William Everett didn't know Price as well as Nester, but he was less skeptical, having seen drugs and alcohol wield its powers on numerous employees over time.

"You never know how the devil might infiltrate a soul," Everett said, as the two administrators traveled back to Pineknob that Sunday, their wives in the back seat of Nester's Lincoln Towncar. "I've seen good, hardworking, brilliant men lose themselves to alcohol… to where they couldn't control it. Sneaking it into work in their socks… keeping it in their desk drawers. I knew a lawyer who lost his practice over cocaine, and one doctor who got hooked on pills. Educated people think they're above addiction… pedigree dictates it. You just never actually know what is happening with a person. God rest his soul."

"Price was a veteran though," Nester said. "And he was fit… a serious runner."

"You just never know, Charles. I guess now you're going to have to assume his duties until you find a replacement," Everett said looking over at him. "Is there anybody you can think of that would be a viable candidate for that job?"

"No, not off the top of my head. That's the one position that really calls for an outsider," Nester said. "You don't want it to be 'one of the boys.' "

"Right. Well, don't waste any time. Of course, I'm sure it will take till January at the earliest."

"I would imagine."

"I'll put out an internal statement when we get back. I'm not sure we make a public statement on this one," Everett said. "Who knows what the press will do with it anyway. Maybe we should have security check around, find out if anybody bought anything from him on campus."

"Ok. I'll take care of it. That could make everybody look bad."

143

"Well, no. But it could make *you* look bad. … Just kidding," said Everett, in unconvincing fashion. "You're right. If it's something parents of potential students hear of and cling to, it could certainly be a detriment to the university as a whole."

"Right. Of course, I don't know how many students would volunteer the information that began with the statement 'I bought cocaine from X.' "

"No. It will be hearsay at best... let them be anonymous. And keep it quiet. We want to be discreet. I swear, professors sleeping with students and drugs are two of the worst things that can happen to a university. At least it's not a safety issue."

"It was for Dwayne," Nester said, as his mind flashed to the 9 mm Smith & Wesson in his trunk, his travel "peacemaker."

"Touché."

"For that matter, it still could be," Nester continued. "What if he had student customers? It could have been a student or students that killed him. We're just assuming its some element from town… or out of town. It could have originated on campus."

"That's more than a valid point, Charles," Everett said. "I guess we just find out what we can with security. They can relay it on to the police. I would think the police will do some investigating on campus as well."

Back in Pineknob, Coach Sam Rosemont met with Chap Roberts for Sunday brunch at the University Inn. Since the team's final open date of the season was scheduled for the upcoming week, Rosemont gave his staff Sunday off. The team had Monday off as well, so the players could heal and catch up on their studies. Film study on LMSU's next opponent would also begin on Monday.

The old friends talked first about LMSU's victory of the previous evening, as well-wishers streamed by to congratulate the personable coach. As always, Rosemont engaged all of them, listening intently to their references to specific play calls or a broken down defensive coverage. He rarely cut a fan short... occasionally on the coach's show if the person had consumed one too many. Roberts would grow impatient with the interruptions if he were with anybody else, but with Rosemont he appreciated it, listening and absorbing the information from the commoners for his own professional use.

Once the crowd cleared and hot omelets arrived at the table, Rosemont's tone became more hushed.

"I guess our little problem took care of itself," he said.

"Yeah, I heard about that," Roberts said, watching Rosemont stir two packets of Sweet-n-Low into a small bowl of grits.

"Really? How?"

"Heard it on the radio this morning," Roberts said. "They were all over it. Anyway, I guess he had it coming."

"Had it coming? What the hell are you talking about?"

"I'm talking about his side game -- the drug business."

"I don't know if I'm buying that," Rosemont mumbled with a mouthful of egg.

"Sounds like the evidence was there," Roberts said.

"Still, 'had it coming' seems a little strong."

"Sam, think about it. In this guy's front, his job, he's sneaking around digging in other people's business," Roberts said. "He probably had some bullshit sense of entitlement. If he took that attitude into the drug business, somebody probably made him pay for it. That's all I'm saying."

"He didn't seem to me to be the kind of person to do that stuff," Rosemont said. "That guy was in shape. Military background and all…"

"Military background? Sam, don't be naïve. I appreciate the military as a whole, and am glad it's there and in place – it's why America is great - but don't think individually they're not above using or abusing drugs and alcohol. They go to work every day just like the rest of us unless they're deployed."

"I know that," Rosemont said.

"These days, everyone's eating some kind of pills like candy. This guy probably had a little taste for the coke, then thought he could start making some good cash from it. I mean, he only works at a place where 14,000 young adults live or visit every day. That's a pusher's paradise."

"It all just seems really neat," Rosemont said, leaning in. "Look at me. Swear to me that you or that hound Wheatley had nothing to do with this."

"Damn it! Are you kidding me?" Roberts whispered. "Sam, you've known me for almost 40 years. I'm ambitious, sure, but I would *never* do something like that. What's my motivation, to hang around your facilities building? No offense, but it ain't that nice. I can't believe you."

Roberts leaned back away from Rosemont, who stared at his old friend, sizing him up. Chap's greatest fear was impotency: both sexually and in business. Rosemont knew that and had seen and heard it manifest itself when Chap was drunk. Chap was a hedonist, but Rosemont didn't believe he was a murderer. After a long five seconds, Rosemont's boyish grin returned.

"I'm sorry, Chap. But I had to ask. You understand, don't you? People are murdered for less every day. You know that. I had to be sure."

"Yeah? You're a piece of shit, Coach. Don't let anybody ever tell you different. But I'm going to let you slide this time. If…"

"Oh, man, what now?"

"If you'll tell me what it's like to have a team in the Top 10 of all America?"

Rosemont sat back in his chair and smiled broadly.

13

LMSU quarterback Ben Wright had taken a few licks in the win on Saturday. He had a typical outstanding effort, but was battered and bruised for it. He'd been sacked four times, and took another six hits after getting rid of the football. No real injuries there, but his body was stiff all over and he had a minor ankle sprain he'd suffered a few weeks prior that required treatment, so after an early breakfast in the residence hall cafeteria and a chapel service he made his way to Ivory Facilities Building, where the talk was the murder of Dwayne Price.

Wright hadn't heard the news prior to his arrival and was shocked to find out. His intelligence went well beyond the average person's, but he had no experience with death. He'd never even known anyone who had died, except for a great-grandmother when he was a just a young child.

"They're saying he was murdered over drugs?" Wright asked Bart Hill, LMSU's head trainer. "And that he might have been a drug dealer?"

"Looks that way," Hill said. "I heard there was definitely a supply in his house that got lifted. Apparently he let somebody get too close and they turned on him."

Wright was too disturbed to even continue the conversation. He sat in silence as they alternated first ice then a stimulator on his ankle. He didn't buy the story and his mind was already working past what he believed to be a gross mistake on the part of the police, or a cover-up of some sort. His mind was racing with other scenarios. And that was without throwing in the fact that Price had accepted the role of advisor to the campus branch of

Fellowship of Christian Athletes. Investigators didn't likely even know about that important fact.

Wright knew he had to do something, and it had to begin with a trip to the police. The open week gave him some free time, and he wasn't about to let something so important just fade away.

He was uneasy when walked into the Pineknob Police Department, simply because, unlike the classroom or the playing field, he was walking blind and unprepared into a situation he was not familiar with. Had the Tennessee State Police Depot not been housed in the same building, Wright would have actually been in the wrong location.

"I would like to speak to whoever is in charge of the Dwayne Price murder investigation please," Wright said, his mere presence bringing knowing stares from staff employees as well as uniformed officers around the large, open room of cubicles.

"That would be Robert Mills," she said. "He's in the north wing. Have a seat and I'll call him for you.

"Thank you."

Robert Mills of course knew who Ben Wright was, and walked to him in the public lobby of the barracks. The holding areas for criminals were in the back of the building. Mills had yet to sleep after spending most of the night at Price's house.

"Hi Ben. Robert Mills," he said, shaking Wright's hand. "What can I do for you today?"

"Detective Mills. Is it Detective?"

"Yes."

"I just heard about Dwayne Price about an hour ago. Of course, I guess this is just a rumor, but I heard it was over drugs? I just don't believe it."

"Well, the investigation is ongoing, but it will probably be in the paper tomorrow. Yes, we found a large stash of cocaine. And that looked to be just half of what was there."

"I just don't buy it, sir," Wright said. "I've talked with Dwayne half dozen times since he's been here. Did you know he was becoming our campus FCA advisor?"

"I'm sorry, FCA?"

"Fellowship of Christian Athletes."

"Really? No, I didn't know that," Mills said, giving the notion sincere thought. "I'm not writing it off. But think about it. That's a perfect front for a drug dealer. You would be shocked at the people who get mixed up in the buying and selling of cocaine. It has brought down so many professionals and elected officials."

"Could it not have been planted or something? I saw Dwayne twice in the last week. Last Saturday he kind of looked... uh, shook up. You know? Perplexed."

"Did he say why?"

"No."

"That could have been due to the pressure of his dual life."

"Or it could have been due to his job..."

Both men looked towards the end of the room as Amber Duffy walked through the front door, looking sullen and tired, but otherwise terribly attractive. She saw Wright -- whom she'd known casually since he arrived on campus as a naïve 18-year-old due to her previous post in the Sports Information Office -- speaking with Mills and walked over to them.

"Hi Amber," Wright said with a smile, in a familiar tone.

"Hi Ben. Detective Mills. Am I interrupting?"

"Hello, Miss Duffy," Mills said, respectfully. "You two know each other, I presume. Well Mr. Wright here and I were just discussing the case. He doesn't believe our findings."

"I don't believe them either," Duffy said quickly, almost harshly. "That's why I came down. I've been thinking about it – and him -- all night."

"Did you come up with something else?" Mills asked.

"Well, he was coming over to watch the game Saturday but he said he might be late because he was investigating something that morning."

"Did he say what?"

"No. Just that. But it seemed really important."

"It could have been a drug deal, and he just said it was an investigation to make it sound work-related. Or he could have been uneasy due to who he was dealing with that day. Those concerns would now seem obvious."

"Or he could have been showing the professional integrity he always did," Duffy said, angered by the tone Mills was starting to take. "You don't know him, sir. I may not have known him long, but I know through working with him that he had a high standard of ethics and he stuck to them personally."

"Really? And the two of you had started dating? Do you know it could be considered a form of sexual harassment for a supervisor to date an

151

employee he had professional influence over? You think he didn't know that?"

"Well, thankfully, he didn't take time to think about it I suppose. It was more spontaneous than that."

"I'm not saying he harassed you, Miss Duffy, I'm just trying to get you to look at the case from a different perspective. The evidence was there."

"The evidence could have been planted," Wright interjected. "To do exactly what it has done… encourage you to look no further."

"It was in his bloodstream, too. He'd used. Now I don't mean to be callous, but I don't think somebody would go to that trouble over an NCAA compliance director. Why would they?"

"Exactly. Why would they? It's your job to find out why. You see that it's a possibility?" Wright asked.

"I'm not saying that," Mills said.

"I don't mean to be disrespectful, and I don't know what Dwayne was looking in to. But think about it," Wright said, almost pleading. "College athletics is a multi-billion dollar business. He could have found out about something going on."

"Do you know about anything going on illegally in the athletic department?"

"Well, no."

"What about any violation of the rules?"

"I don't know of anything," Wright said. "But, I kind of keep my head down and plow through *my* job. I don't allow myself a lot of time for chit chat."

"Well, the investigation is not closed," Mills said. "I'm still looking for the murderer. If I come across something that disputes my findings, I certainly won't ignore it. But, because of that, please, neither of you say anything to anybody about our conversation. It's best for now that the murderer or murderers think they've succeeded if it was a plant. But personally, I think the shooter is back in Detroit or Miami by now. Thanks for coming in, both of you."

Mills turned and walked away, leaving Amber Duffy and Ben Wright standing alone in the precinct foyer.

"I didn't know you and Dwayne had started dating," Wright said.

"Our first date was Thursday night," she said. "He just seemed to open up all the sudden. He was always all business in the office."

"He was a good guy. I understand why he'd want to go out with you," Wright said. "Look, maybe we could help Mills."

"I don't know, Ben. Your plate is kind of full, isn't it? And if we're right, and we start meddling, that could bring it to us."

"Well, at least we know the stakes. I'll bet Dwayne never knew that whatever he stumbled into could cost him his life."

Amber looked up at the young quarterback with solemn, sad, brown eyes, the pain of Price's death still a new wound for her.

"I'm sorry," he said. He hugged her. "Just think about it though. Something is going on and we might be the only people who care enough to see it through. I mean, Dwayne was murdered. That's just not right. We can't just walk away."

Wright led Amber to the door and held it open for her. The afternoon sky had gone gray, and it was cold and windy as they reached the sidewalk.

"Look, this is an off week. I'm going to look into this somehow. I could sure use your help," Wright said. He noticed a small café across the street. "You want to grab a coffee or something and talk about it?"

Amber gave it a bit of thought.

"Ok. I'll help you as best I can."

"That's all I ask. I just want to get Mills going in the right direction. We owe Dwayne that."

As Amber and Wright crossed the street through a break in mild Sunday traffic, Jim Wheatley slid into his familiar spot in The Lookout, across from Chap Roberts. The only difference in Wheatley's normal demeanor was a cocky air of satisfaction.

"Everything is going as planned," Wheatley said. "The next thing the cops will hear when they check their rats is that local coke prices will likely go up due to a disruption of the normal channels of distribution. That might cause a little desperation on the street."

"Seems like an iron clad case," said Roberts, looking around the room as he pulled a white business envelope -- which contained $10,000 in cash – from his jacket pocket, and slid it across the table. "Well done. Any trouble?"

"None," Wheatley said, with a slight shake of his head. His stare turned cold as he thought about the ambush and execution of Dwayne Price.

After staring each other down in the street on Saturday morning, Wheatley had gotten emotional… in fact when he saw Price standing there on the curb his blood was boiling. He was about to shoot him down on the spot. But after an instant he got a grip on his emotions and realized he had to be smart. He had to keep an eye on Price. He switched vehicles, from the van to a less-conspicuous demo, then he drove to Price's neighborhood.

He watched as Price reemerged from his house to run. Wheatley took that as affirmation that Price had compartmentalized his worlds... that he wasn't going to do anything with his newfound information until Monday. Made sense... who would answer at the NCAA office on Saturday? He watched as Price returned from his run and went through his routine. Back in his living room he stretched, did some pushups, setups, and other random exercises. He then showered and dressed and left his home for Amber Duffy's condo. Wheatley followed, making note of her address. When he realized the couple was watching the LMSU game on television he dropped back, went to The Lookout for a sandwich and to gather the other items that he needed. Wheatley wasn't opposed to an occasional line of cocaine -- a "bump" the weekend, recreational users called it – but he didn't partake on a regular basis. He knew where to get what he needed with the safety of no idle talk. With Chap cash he made a $10,000 purchase. He paid a half dozen known small-time movers five eight-balls each to share the price-hike story if anybody asked. The rest he saved for his return to Price's house.

Wheatley listened to the final minutes of the Black Bears' 41-10 victory over Georgia State on the radio as he returned to Amber Duffy's condo. He then watched as the couple left in Price's car. He followed them from a distance on the winding mountain road to The Eagle's Nest, then returned to Price's home.

He had work to do. He was counting on Price returning home alone at some point. Wheatley thought of the morality, mentality, and sensibilities of the middle class people with which he was dealing. The people he normally encountered were not community pillars. They screwed on first dates -- on first meetings, often standing up against the walls or on sinks in filthy bar bathrooms. They got drunk on week nights -- on week days -- were often jobless and not above illegal activity, like sexual favors for drugs. They were petty thieves that would plant evidence, participate in frame stings with Wheatley behind the camera, pretty much anything shy of armed robbery. It was the dabbling of criminal activity by society's seedy underbelly, executed at night, in the shadows, seen only by the moon, with little threat of ever being caught. Wheatley didn't believe Price, a saint by comparison, would be having pre-marital relations with Amber Duffy that evening, and he was correct.

Wheatley parked a couple of streets over from Price's home in front of a stretch of three empty lots young kids used as a makeshift playground and walked in the safety of autumn's early darkness to the alley that led to his back door. He watched closely and saw no sign of neighbors in windows or doors when he - with gloved hands - picked the lock of the back door knob, which took mere seconds. In the house he sat down at the kitchen table and allowed his eyes to acclimate to the darkness. He could see the glow of a street light shining into the front room. Wheatley pulled a green surgical cap out of his jacket pocket and put it over his slightly greasy hair, matching the surgical booties he had pulled over his shoes when he'd stepped into the door. Once he was more accustomed to the darkness, he walked to the front room and stood looking through the sheers covering the window. He saw no activity from those neighbors either so he shut the drapes and went to work.

With a small flashlight in hand he looked for the black notebook he'd seen Price carrying in the past. It was on the dining room table, his file of the case was on top of the pile. Wheatley then searched the rest of the notebook for any other clues or hints that might lead the police to him or Roberts.

There was nothing. He put the file on the washing machine in the utility room by the back door. He sat back down on the couch.

Price owned a coffee table that had a compartment underneath in the middle which held a few magazines and a book. Wheatley stacked them so they took up but half of its two-foot width. He then placed the largest bag of coke that he had, filled a small coke spoon and carefully sat it on top of the coffee table, then sprinkled the remaining powder on three sides of its outline with a two-ounce bag, as though a bag in a stack had broken. He returned the larger bag to his pocket and rubbed it clean. Then he tossed a couple of the tiny bags into the compartment. The larger bag he then stashed in Price's dresser in the bedroom … buried in the sock drawer, knowing it would be found later. And the outlay in the coffee table, he hoped, would be considered a second – and stolen - bag. Wheatley then sat back and waited, with a 45-caliber semi-automatic, complete with silencer – the Evolution-45, in hand.

When Price came through the door he flipped on the light, took his coat off, and hung it in the closest. He didn't immediately see Wheatley, which is what the intruder wanted. When Price was nearly to the kitchen door, Wheatley cleared his throat, startling Price. He turned and faced Wheatley.

"So I was right," Price said.

"Your biggest mistake," Wheatley said, his southern drawl more pronounced.

"It's all about money, huh?"

"Damn right."

Price tried to rush Wheatley – also what Wheatley had hoped – but there was no way to close the 15 feet between them in time. Still sitting comfortably on the couch, Wheatley squeezed off two shots, hitting him just where he wanted to, in his right side of his chest.

Price went to his knees, stunned and wide-eyed from the pain, gasping for breath. He then fell to his side. Death was inevitable. Wheatley waited a long minute, then with his foot rolled Price to his back, his left arm becoming trapped underneath him. The blood from his wounds was filling his lungs and seeping into the tan carpet. Mindful of the crimson liquid, Wheatley kneeled, placing one knee on Price's right forearm. He shoved a couch pillow under Price's head to prop it. With his gloved left hand he covered Price's nose and mouth, cutting off his air. Price began to struggle weakly, though he lacked the strength to free his left arm. With his right hand Wheatley reached and grabbed the tiny spoon. Once in his grasp and in the proper position he uncovered one of Price's nostrils. As Price instinctively tried to fill his remaining lung capacity with oxygen, he snorted the hit of coke. Wheatley then stepped back to watch Price drown in his own blood, without the courtesy of a kill shot. He pulled the pillow out from under his head and tossed it on the couch. As he continued to watch he smiled wryly and laughed under his breath.

Wheatley then unlocked the front door and opened it, leaving the living room light on. He twisted the silencer off his gun as he walked to the back of the house, grabbed the case file and cautiously exited through the back door, the knob of which he relocked with his left hand, mindful of not getting any coke residue on the metal. He took off the surgical booties and hat, stuffed them in a pocket, and walked quickly through the darkness back to his car, a black Corvette. He drove down Price's street, window open. When he was in front of Price's house, he fired two shots in the air. By the time any of the neighbors looked through their windows, he was long gone.

A few men in the community came out to investigate. It was one of them who found Price and called the police.

14

There had been a mostly one-sided connection between Amber Duffy and Ben Wright when he was a freshman at Lookout Mountain State University. Driven as he was, Wright knew he would most likely be redshirted that first year on campus. It is the norm in college football and usually necessary and helpful to give the arriving high school players a year to acclimate to the entire college routine. Wright, though, was not the normal freshman. Having spent his final high school spring in beefed up versions of the training and preparation he'd been doing since he was 13-years-old – lifting weights, running agility and quickness drills, working on his throwing and footwork deficiencies with his father after studying the game film from his senior season – he enrolled at LMSU in June, took a class in each of the three overlapping summer sessions, and worked with his new teammates in all volunteer drills and workouts.

For Coach Rosemont, a dilemma was approaching like a storm that crept over Lookout Mountain. He had a big decision to make. He had a senior quarterback, Paul Anderson, who was above average, probably one of the best three quarterbacks in the Southwest Conference, but not necessarily what Rosemont called a "gamer," one who could carry the team on his back in the final seconds. His arm was respectable throwing short, but he wasn't much of a deep threat. Pragmatically, Rosemont figured the Black Bears would win seven games that year, maybe eight with a little luck. But if Anderson went down with injury, his backup, Steve Green, was a liability.

Opponents would be able to gang up on the run knowing his arm was suspect.

As August two-a-days progressed, it was obvious that Wright was head and shoulders above Green. And if Wright were given Green's reps he could challenge for Anderson's job. But freshmen still made rookie mistakes under fire, and Rosemont knew that it was best to follow the plan, to redshirt Wright, leave Green as the backup, and pray Anderson didn't get hurt. That was the gamble. If Anderson was injured in game eight, would he burn Wright's redshirt year after keeping him off the field all season? Possibly, but that would certainly be a waste. It would depend on many factors: how good the season was going, how severe Anderson's injury was, and if there was a bowl game at the end of the rainbow.

As it stood, Wright began fall classes as the unmistaken, coveted, and popular "quarterback in waiting" and that was quite a title to have as a freshman on a campus of so many. Given his nature to absorb knowledge, and as a journalism major, it was natural for Wright to spend some of his free time in Jim Winkler's Sports Information office. It was the nerve center of LMSU athletics, and the pipeline to the outside world. There was also a young lady named Amber Duffy employed there. While work was accomplished at a rapid rate and many interesting projects such as sports media guides were written, designed, laid out, and taken through the print process, there was also a lighter atmosphere in the S.I.D. office than in some of the more rigid departments on campus. The thought of her kept Wright up at night... Amber Duffy, a 25-year-old *woman*. She was beautiful in the most dignified, eloquent way. Her face was the last image he would see before he fell asleep.

She so possessed his mind he was almost giddy in her presence. He found it difficult to relax and be himself around her. As October rolled into November, he made a few awkward advances for a lunch date. She found him adorably amusing. Amber saw it more as the flirtation of a kid, but she did realize even then that he would mature into quite a man. In truth, she was still hurt from her break up. She made it clear through Susan Potter, a female graduate assistant that, though she was flattered, if she did break the employee-student dating code, it would not be with a freshman.

As football season ended with a less than satisfying 6-5 mark – no bowl game - and the holidays approached, Wright's visits to Jim Winkler's office became less frequent. He had submerged himself in his studies with a goal of finishing the semester with straight A's. A goal he would attain again and again. Spring practice brought on the beginning of his reign as the No. 1 quarterback, and his unending quest to do it as perfectly as possible. As Wright matured he still looked upon Amber with fondness, but he'd become more businesslike in his approach to everything. His trips to the S.I.D. office were usually precipitated by a media request for an interview. Thus, the sizzle that had once dictated his teen-like actions simmered into the maturity of a man who personified focus.

Amber remained in the Office of Sports Information through Wright's all-conference sophomore season, until she felt her work would take on greater meaning if it were evolving higher up the academic ladder. Her move to the associate AD's office was still related to sports by definition, though much more to the business side of it. It was the necessary first step. For the past ten months Amber and Wright had seen much less of each other than they had in the previous two and a half years.

On that Sunday afternoon meeting, with the pain of Price's death still looming, there were no quick resolutions for Amber and Wright, except that she didn't drink coffee. Wright was nearly finished with his first cup while she still daintily bobbed a tea bag in her hot water. Wright was pressing Amber to remember anything different about Price's routine the previous week.

"There were a few things different, now that I really think about it," she said, quickly squeezing the hot excess liquid from her tea bag with her index finger and thumb and placing it on a napkin. "On Monday, he was out of the office the entire morning. If he'd had meetings I would have known about them. So he was doing something else... maybe investigating. He said he was investigating yesterday morning, too."

"Ok. So he was on to something. We'll have to figure out where he was. What else?"

"He visited Jane Haynes in the Business Office," Amber said. "She pays the bills essentially."

"That could be big," Wright said. "You could take care of that one tomorrow. See what he was doing."

"I will."

"Anything else?"

"Well yes, actually. This is not that strange except that, Dwayne was always all business, you know? He wasn't in to gossip around school or anything. But this week he asked me what I knew about Max Milovich. That may not be significant, but I thought it was odd after what, five months on the job? It stood out."

"Yeah, I see what you're saying. Obviously I don't know Dwayne's work habits, but I got that sense about him, too. A Navy man and all...

chiseled," said Wright, his mind still churning on the information. "I knew Max pretty well, saw him at the Ron Bennett visitation but I didn't get to talk to him. Maybe I should pay him a visit tomorrow just to find out what he thinks about the guy who took his job being murdered. He's still in the area right? What company?"

"Ridgecrest," Duffy said, recalling her and Dwayne's discussion with Bruce Fellows. "Bruce explained that to Dwayne that day in the office when he asked about him."

"I'll pay Max a visit."

"That might not be a great idea, Ben. We don't know what is going on here. Obviously it's pretty serious. I would never forgive myself – and the town would hang me by a rope – if something happened to you."

"Oh, nothing's going to happen to me. You talk to Jane, I'll talk to Max. We don't even have practice tomorrow. Coach is letting everybody heal up a day. They're just working with the freshmen. I'll just go over and catch up with Max."

They exchanged cell phone numbers and walked back to the parking lot outside of the police barracks. As they did, the sun briefly emerged from a break in the clouds.

"About half a season," Wright said.

"What are you talking about?"

"The length of your shadow. Look at it."

Amber turned and looked down at both their shadows. The sun warmed her back, which she appreciated.

"So?"

"About a half a season. Your shadow gets longer from the beginning of football season in August, to the end in November… and then even more if there's a bowl game to work towards. Has to do with the tilt of the earth from the sun as fall turns into winter."

"I know about the equinox and all," Amber said. She smiled, amused by the presentation of his rationality.

"It's something I've just always loved about football. That and the dew on the grass in the mornings. In August, on the practice field, your shadow is short, not too much longer than your body, even at the end of the day. But as the season progresses, and hopefully the wins pile up, when you walk off, your shadow is longer. It's a little more pronounced at home than in Tennessee. I can tell that too though. It's something my dad and I always talked about."

"And he was your coach?"

"We won a lot of games together."

"You really love it, don't you?"

"It's the greatest game."

"Would you still say that if you were here for baseball or basketball?"

"Probably. It's the greatest orchestration of men. Timing, precision, strength, battle, art, speed, beauty. It has it all."

She looked up at him admiringly as he spoke. She respected his whole-hearted dedication to his sport. Of course she agreed – her enthusiasm watching the game with Dwayne Saturday popped into her head -- so she said nothing. She let his words linger.

"Ok, call me if you think of anything else," Wright said.

"I will. I'll talk to you tomorrow."

"Oh, and Amber, I am sorry for your loss. I'm glad you're helping me though."

"Thanks, Ben."

Wright watched Amber pull away, then walked to his own vehicle, a ten-year-old red Jeep Cherokee, given to him by his parents. The SUV still looked good despite 170,000 miles. That was another trait he inherited – or a learned behavior – from his parents besides faith and football, they both took care of their vehicles, and they expected their sons to help and follow suit. The remaining time on Saturdays - after the boys' sports events - was used for chores.

He cranked the ignition then put both forearms on the wheel. He thought for a minute about Price. Could he have misjudged him? Price seemed sincere about his relationship with Jesus Christ. Anybody who says it out loud usually does. He was likeable. Wright had never seen evidence of what the police were saying; never seen him talking with the party crowd on campus, or the party players for that matter. Amber hadn't either. She obviously liked Price and she's an intelligent girl.

"Stick to your instincts," he said out loud as he shifted his sport utility vehicle – his truck, as he still liked to call it - into drive. "They haven't failed you yet."

That statement reminded him about the crush he had on Amber as a freshman. Those feelings were still there. She hadn't changed at all, maybe just a more mature beauty. There was something different, he felt, in the way she stood listening, looking into his eyes. He didn't know exactly what it was, but it lifted his soul.

15

Monday was catch-up day for the *Pineknob Herald*. Dwayne Price's murder was discovered on Sunday morning after Saturday evening's deadline. The three local television stations all ran brief stories. Each interviewed Tennessee State Police Investigator Robert Mills. The print story ran on the front page of Monday's paper, below the fold. Despite the extra day to dig, there was no more information than what the TV stations had been spoon fed by the State Police. Lookout Mountain State University president William Everett provided a brief quote, but the overriding drug sentiment released in the police statement caused both the police beat writer, Eric Thaxton, and Dr. Everett to avoid the usual obligatory fluff about losing a key and likeable employee.

The murder of a middle-class white adult male in Pineknob would normally have crippled the town, causing a feeling of uneasiness throughout. While there was a buzz on the street and in the businesses around town, once again the drug implications left the townspeople with an excuse to not care, to look the other way, even to say this newcomer Price received his just reward. Besides, there was Black Bears football to talk about. The polls had come out before midnight Sunday evening. Never before had LMSU been in the Top 10 in the nation, cracking the barrier at No. 9. Though he usually met with reporters on Tuesday, Coach Sam Rosemont's phone rang non-stop Monday morning with interview requests. He loved the attention his program was getting, mainly because he felt it was well-deserved. Both Danny Smith and Ben Wright were being touted as potential All-America selections, and Wright-to-Smith highlights were a constant on both television and the internet.

It was business as usual in the other buildings at LMSU that morning as well. Amber Duffy didn't want to, but feeling the administration would think she had no right to bereave, she pulled herself together and went to work. While she hadn't necessarily bought in to Ben Wright's notion that they could shed new light on Price's case, she planned to seek out and talk with Jane Haynes.

Dr. Everett and Charles Nester met with their Director of Safety and Security, Pete Crawford, and instructed him to have his staff quietly inquire about the possibility of Dwayne Price selling cocaine to students on campus.

"I can't stress the sensitivity of this, Pete," Everett said, with Nester looking on blankly. "If you find anything affirming, we can't let it get out. This could be a recruiting nightmare. It could set back enrollment efforts for years."

"There was certainly no indication of it up to this point," Crawford said. "Of course there never is until you're hit with it. I've come to expect the unexpected in this business."

"Well, date rape and internet orgies are violations we can't control," said Everett, deliberately looking at Nester. "But by God it's a whole other kettle of fish if prospective parents find out we hired a drug dealer and gave him a nice window office on campus."

After Crawford departed with his instructions, Nester took issue with Everett's statement.

"Now wait a minute, Bill," Nester said. "You're not putting the blame of this thing on me are you?"

Secretly he wasn't. But Everett was shrewd enough to know a scapegoat was often needed in these situations.

"Did you do a background check on Price?" Everett asked.

"No. You know we don't do background checks on potential hires. That would cost thousands a year," Nester said.

"But the compliance director! That calls for a little more discretion don't you think? If your watchdog is lawless what have you got?"

"I really don't think that Price would have been low enough to sell to students," Nester said, "even if he was selling drugs off campus."

"Oh, yeah, I see, a drug dealer with a conscious, right?" Everett said, showing no respect for his athletic director. "Let's just hope Crawford doesn't find out Price's entire list of customers was students. Or that it was a student or students that killed him! Hell his murderer might be sitting in Psych 101 right now."

"All right, that seems far-fetched," Nester said.

"Really? I hope so for your sake. Go ahead and get human resources to run ads nationally for Price's job."

"Ok. I'll take care of it immediately."

"Was Price working on anything overly intriguing? Or was it the usual Clearinghouse red tape."

"When we met last week, it was just the normal stuff. Nothing special."

"Then you should be able to handle his role for a bit?"

"Yes. No problem," Nester said, though his insides were tightening from the lack of respect he was feeling.

Nester left Everett's office with his normal professional remorse, though he was not quite bright enough to grasp Everett's high level of

169

disdain for him. Still Everett's indignity ate at Nester. He went on his way feeling a little less secure in his job, and daunted by the prospect of assuming Price's duties. He tried to think of another way to lessen the burden. Maybe he could bring on some grad assistants. Ultimately though, both jobs would suffer, just as they had the year before.

From a perspective of time and mental health, Amber Duffy knew that walking into Jane Haynes' office was like stepping into the blade of a buzz saw, but she had no other recourse if she was to find out what Price had been doing. A good 15 minutes went by as Jane rehashed the sights and sounds – including the shots -- of the time surrounding Price's death. That was followed by a full 20-question inquisition into what Amber knew about the topic.

"I really don't know any more than what has been reported, Jane," Amber said finally in a saddened tone. "I would like to help the police though. See, I don't think he was selling drugs like they're saying, do you?"

"No. Not for a minute," Haynes said. "You can tell certain things about people. He did *not* seem the type to me. He had a tough side, but he was kind."

"Me either … and I agree. Do you remember what he came over here for last week by chance? I think it's important."

"Oh sure I do. He had a list of businesses. He wanted to know how much we'd paid those businesses over the last 10 years. He said Charles Nester wanted to trim the budget. I hit an extra printout last week just in case I was asked what I was doing for two hours… stuck it right here in the drawer. Would you like it?"

"I sure would," Amber said, taking the document from her. "Thank you so much."

Amber knew enough about Pineknob and had heard plenty of conversation through her years around the department of University athletics to realize that the list Jane Haynes gave her must be a list of Chap Roberts-owned businesses. Some, like Roberts Printing, Roberts Fuels, Chappy's Bar and Grill, and PayDirt Uniforms, were no surprise. Some of the remaining establishments, such as Ridgecrest Insurance and Financial Services, Lookout Ford and Chevrolet, Liberty Fuels, R& R Brick & Block, R&R Construction, Pineville ABC Store, Pineknob Heating & Cooling, Pineknob Real Estate and Rentals, Mountain View Steak and Seafood, The Lookout, and The Bear Claw were jaw droppers. She began, as she studied the list, to comprehend the scope of Roberts' empire, and the tens of millions of profit the entire operation must generate annually.

Ridgecrest Insurance and Financial Services jumped off the paper at her, filling her with dread, as she began to suspect a connection between Max Milovich and Price – or at least in the compliance position -- and now Roberts. The paper shook in her hand as she thought of Ben Wright, who, eager to experience a true investigation, had just pulled into Ridgecrest's parking lot perched two thirds of the way up Lookout Mountain.

Even more than at the police station the previous day, Wright was immediately recognized by most of the employees moving about the offices there, many of whom were LMSU graduates. Wright approached an attractive receptionist in her mid-20s sitting at her desk in an open foyer, which fronted the glass-walled structure, and requested a visit with Max Milovich. After a quick phone call, Max appeared.

"Ben Wright, great to see you," Milovich said, shaking Wright's hand grandly. "You've got some season going... Top 10, undefeated. Most people thought it was impossible."

"Steady growth," Wright said, with a modest smile.

"And a couple of All-Americans," Milovich said, referring to Wright and Danny Smith. "I used to be a quarterback in my playing days – before I got to LMSU. I never had a target like Smith though. That's got to be a blast."

"It is. He's a world-class athlete. Have you been making it to the games?"

"Yep, sure have," Milovich said, leading Wright to his office in the back right side of the room. "Season tickets. First time I had to do that. And, I'm able to wander up to the Ridgecrest box sometimes."

"Oh, yeah, this place does have a box, huh?"

"Nothing but the best... right beside Roberts Printing. It's great to have to invite clients up to. You know, the big commercial accounts and all."

"So, how's it going up here? Miss the University and your old job at all?"

"Sit down, please," Milovich said, extending his hand to the two open chairs in front of his desk. "There are aspects of it I miss. I'd say the interaction with the coaches and athletes being the biggest... all the people. That's probably why I'm so glad to see you. But in all, this is a much better job. Lots of growth potential."

"I saw you at Ron Bennett's wake. He was a teammate of yours I assume. I'm sorry."

"Thanks, Ben. He was a good guy... just abused himself. His wife and kids – they're going to miss that man."

"Did you hear about Dwayne Price?"

"Yeah, I did. Another tragedy... a real shame. Is that why you're here?"

"Well, I suppose. I got to know Dwayne a little bit. He was going to be our FCA advisor. I just don't believe his death was over drugs, Max. I don't buy it. So, I wanted to ask you if there was anything about the job, I don't know, that you felt threatened by? Anything that you ran into that could have had those consequences?"

Milovich was a 6-foot-3, still-fit man of 37, with brown eyes, matching hair with more length than a regular business cut, combed straight back and shaped perfectly. He cared about his good looks and took care of himself. He sat back in his chair quietly and looked at the ceiling. A former athlete – he'd walked on LMSU's football team and was a celebrated special teams player -- he was never one to be intimidated easily, when he was growing up, when he was the compliance director, or now. He looked at the handsome superstar sitting across from him, and then over Ben's shoulder into the open room of cubicles behind him. He could feel eyes on him, though none were apparent.

"No. I never felt threatened," Milovich said, with a complete disregard for the truth. He envisioned Jim Wheatley relaying Chap Roberts' vague but suggestive offer to him ... 'You can get on board at Ridgecrest or be removed, your choice,' Wheatley had told him.

"Especially to that extent," he continued. "I guess I was lucky. In the few years I was there, not one violation that I knew of. Everybody was playing by the book, I suppose."

Wright looked at Milovich closely, trying to read him. There was some hole in the story, but he didn't know yet what it was.

"So how did you get on here?"

"They were creating an internal auditor position," Milovich explained. "I graduated with a double major, accounting and business. So it was a perfect setup for me. It's still like being a compliance guy in a way. I just don't report to the NCAA. And I make three times the money. Higher education doesn't pay squat unless you're part of the President's cabinet. It's better for my family."

Wright decided to wrap it up, though he wasn't completely satisfied that Milovich was coming clean. He left his cell phone number with Milovich in case he thought of anything else. As he said his good-byes a couple of employees stopped him for autographs for their children. In the opposite end of the building from Milovich's office, the company's Chief Executive Officer, Jack Perry, picked up the phone and dialed Chap Roberts' cell to discuss Milovich's popular visitor. Roberts wasted no time in calling Jim Wheatley, who planned an afternoon visit to see Milovich.

When Wright returned to his Jeep, he saw that Amber Duffy had called while he was inside. He redialed and found her to be excited with news. "What are you doing for lunch?" she asked. "We need to talk about this in person."

"I'll pick you up in 15 minutes," he said, pulling out of the Ridgecrest parking lot on his way back to campus.

Twenty five minutes later Amber and Wright were facing each other at a booth in a little campus hangout called simply Rick's, an institution which had taken the act of flat grilling and deep frying to a level of artistry.

"I'll have a BBQ, hold the bun, a side of pasta salad, and an unsweetened tea," Amber said, to a round waitress named Eloise, fifty-ish, who had seen so many college students come and go in 30 years, she was unfazed by the celebrity status of Wright. Besides, she knew him well.

"Just a double cheeseburger with everything, fries, and a chocolate milkshake please, Ellie," Wright said with a smile.

"If you keep eating like this after you're finished playing, boy, you're going to end up looking like me," Eloise said.

"I'll scale it back when I retire," he said, as she walked off. "But I'd be skin and bones now if I didn't. Coach runs us too hard."

"Uh-huh," she said, "I've heard that before."

The two watched Eloise walk back to the window to shout their order.

"Who's Grace?" Amber asked, pointing to a worn, leather bracelet Wright was wearing almost under the watch on his left wrist. The bracelet read Living for GRACE.

"It's an acronym: God's Rewards at Christ's Expense," Wright said. "I use it as a daily reminder."

Amber smiled.

"That's nice," she said finally. She was taken by Wright's maturity and dedication to God, his studies, his sport. He was uncommonly anchored and together for a college junior, for any man she'd ever met actually.

"So what's the news, because my meeting with Max was pretty much uneventful. Other than a feeling I had," Wright said.

"Well, I got the exact list Dwayne picked up from Jane Haynes and why," Amber began excitedly, handing the paper to Wright. "And I've made a few calls. Chap Roberts owns every business on this list. And apparently he owns others ... some bars that do a lot of gambling business."

"Wow. Oh, man, there's Ridgecrest. Chap Roberts owns Ridgecrest?" Wright asked rhetorically, digesting the information and the possibilities.

"Yeah, he does," Amber said. "And get this. These businesses charged LMSU over $10 million last year."

"Ok. Well, there's nothing really wrong with that if they're legitimate businesses providing services, right?" Wright asked.

"Sure. But why was Dwayne checking? He must have had something else on Roberts.

"He's entrenched in the football program. He's our biggest contributor *and* Coach Rosemont's best friend somehow. I mean with a backstage pass to everything. But, again, there's nothing wrong with that either."

"There must be something out of sorts," Amber said, looking up and smiling as Eloise dropped off their drinks in large plastic glasses. Nothing handled by students at Rick's was breakable. "Thank you."

"Thanks, Ellie," Wright added, waiting for the woman to depart. "Well, here's the thing. If Chap owns Ridgecrest, and this blows my mind, he must have gone after Max. He talked like his job was almost created for him. Max could have found something – caught them in something."

"And then been bought off," Amber said.

"Right."

"So what was the feeling you were talking about?"

"Just that he was hiding something … Now I'm sure of it. I'm going to have to keep working on him."

"Should we go about it another way?" Amber asked. "Maybe tell Mills this? If Dwayne was killed over it, we could cause Max to be next."

The couple looked at each other without saying what they both were thinking, that *they* could be the next victims.

176

"We should get more before we go to Mills," Wright said. "This doesn't prove anything."

Jim Wheatley pounced like a cat from around his van, propping Max Milovich's hunter green Chevy Trailblazer door open with his left hand.

"Hi Max … long time," said Wheatley.

"Jim Wheatley. What can I do for you?" Milovich was leaving the mountain for lunch, when he was met by the unwelcomed visitor.

"Oh, come on Max. I know you're glad to see me. Heard you had a visitor."

"Who are you talking about?"

"A young gent named Ben Wright."

"Man, word travels fast around here."

"There's no need for any reminders is there?"

"About what?"

"About how important it is that you keep your mouth shut? About your personal health and well-being?"

"He was just in the area and wanted to say hi. Nothing more. That's what good people do."

"Oh really? Good people, huh? That's relative to where you're sitting isn't it?"

"Meaning?"

"Meaning I don't care if it's Ben Wright or Bill Clinton, the wrong side of me is the wrong side of me. Now, if you value your life you'll remember that."

"Look, Wheatley, Ben and I were friends when I was on campus. He has an off week. He stopped by to say hi. What else would he be doing here? Or are you admitting to me you had something to do with the death of the new compliance guy."

"What I'm telling you is to stay on the team," Wheatley said, stepping closer. "If you're not, your options are slim. And your family may suffer as well for your ill-advised choices."

"Don't worry. I bought in," Milovich said. He was steaming under the surface. He felt he could pulverize Wheatley in a fair fight. He also knew Wheatley would never fight fair. "I just want to work this job and get paid to do it."

"That's good to hear," Wheatley said, allowing Milovich to shut his door. "Don't make me come here to see you again."

Monday was one like no other for Sam Rosemont. The national media was already making its way to Pineknob. On Tuesday, ESPN, FOX Sports, ABC, and CBS were all creating stories for that evening and for Saturday's pre-game shows. It was a shame the Black Bears didn't have a great game scheduled, Rosemont thought, because they were definitely the story of the week. National TV would have been a sure bet.

Due to the off week and the overflow on Tuesday, Rosemont offered the local beat writers some time with him on Monday. The Southwestern Conference coaches' conference call was each Monday morning. The call, five to eight minutes with each coach around the league, was access for all writers to get quotes for the stories they would work on that week.

Because Michael Kelly, of Chattanooga's *Daily Register*, just happened to be in his office at 10 a.m. listening on an extra line when Janet

Randolph called relaying Rosemont's message during the other coaches' segments, he was able to scoop his competition on the Danny Smith for Heisman Campaign story. Rick Bayless, who listened to the conference call from home with plans of a league notebook for Tuesday, missed her call, and assumed the week's schedule would be normal.

Sitting in Rosemont's office later that day, Kelly quizzed Rosemont on the depth of Smith's talent.

"That blocking play Saturday got every NFL scout, coach, and GM salivating," Rosemont said. "Did you look at it again later on the highlights?"

"Yeah, I did," Kelly said. "That's some acceleration."

"World-class speed," Rosemont said. "There's no denying it. His 40 time is not off the charts, but Murvin's is damn respectable."

"Like, what, 4.5?"

"4.4. And he blew by him like Murvin was tied up in a block. He's got unbelievable game speed… football speed."

"Some people are saying 'Sure, but he's facing 5-8, 5-9 corners with average talent from a mid-level league,' " Kelly said.

"Yeah, that's true. But mark Coach Sammy's word, it won't matter," Rosemont said. "Danny Smith will do what he's doing now in the NFL … whenever he chooses to go. Eventually they'll have to double-team him there, too. And as far as this Heisman thing goes now, I guarantee you there aren't five players in the nation with as much talent as him whether it's recognized now or not. And here's the kicker, he's just a pup."

"Just getting started, huh?"

"Oh, you don't even know," Rosemont gushed. "He doesn't run crisp routes, his hands will get much better, he'll learn to drag his toes on the sidelines on out routes … there's nothing tougher than trying to beat a corner at full speed then make your legs go dead as your making a catch. It's an art."

"Do you expect him to come back?" Kelly asked.

"I expect him to. His education will do him some good. I expect all my players to graduate."

"Come on, Coach."

"On the record, you got my answer," Rosemont said. "Off the record, no way in hell. It doesn't take Matlock to figure that out. Would you come back? The kid's family doesn't have anything… never has. This time next year Danny Smith will be doing fine financially – better than either one of us - setting the NFL on fire, and there will be no one happier for him than me."

LMSU's assistant coaches were busy all day studying film on Southern Methodist University, the Black Bears' third and final non-conference game of the season. It was a great opportunity against a once respectable program, but still 12 days away, which gave Rosemont that newly acquired "courting feeling" in regards to Jennifer Newton. After all, the freshmen were still going to have their Monday Night Football. He should have his as well, he thought. She, as a phone call proved, was hoping for his company, despite giving her a bit of the cold shoulder at the radio show on Thursday.

"You did the right thing, Coach," she said. "You didn't hurt my feelings or anything. I understand."

Her attitude made her even more enticing. Rosemont watched much of the highly-spirited contest, then moved over to Billy Reed, for consultation and an exit excuse.

"Billy I've got a late meeting. Remind the freshmen, regular schedule tomorrow, the veterans will be back on schedule Wednesday. And the coaches meeting will be at 8 a.m. for the SMU briefing. Ok – sound good?"

"Sure, Coach. We'll be ready down to the final frame. They look pretty tough. Everything ok with you?"

"You betcha.' Don't worry about me."

But that was exactly what Billy Reed was doing. It wasn't like his boss to get distracted during the season. And Linda Rosemont was like a second mother to him, he couldn't believe Rosemont was treating his marriage with such disregard.

As Rosemont drove to Jennifer Newton's apartment, he called Chap Roberts, who had used Monday to catch up with his many general managers around town. Roberts was now at the Lookout, checking up on his bookie's evening action, but he also had placed a call to Betsy Parrish's cell phone hoping for a conquest.

"I'm heading over there," Rosemont said. "I figure I might as well keep it going while I can."

"You mean keep it up?"

"Well, yeah, something like that. I'm sure she'll get tired of me eventually, find some young stud."

"Not with your personality coach, you dirty dog. I love it: a cheater created in my own image."

"Easy now. You'll have me turning around. I'm not in your league. Are you in town tomorrow? Let me buy you lunch. I've got to tap dance for the national media at 1 o'clock. You can help me rehearse my lines."

"I'll pick you up at 11:30."

At 8 a.m. on Tuesday, Ben Wright was inside Ivory Facilities Building, heading towards the quarterback meeting room to watch some film on SMU. He ran into Rosemont in the hallway.

"Coach, could I talk with you a few minutes before my 11 o'clock class?"

"Sure Ben," Rosemont said. "We're meeting now, how about 9:30?"

"That'll do. Thanks."

At 9:30, after learning four ways he could exploit SMU's defense, Wright sat promptly waiting in Rosemont's office when the coach came back from his meeting.

"What's on your mind, Ben?" Rosemont said. "Are you enjoying your break -- as the leader of a Top 10 team?"

Wright laughed. "That feels really good, Coach, believe me. But actually, this Dwayne Price murder has me troubled."

"Troubled how?"

"Well, I got to know him a little bit. He was going to be our FCA advisor -- though it wasn't official yet. But we talked about our faith some... you know, had some good conversation. I just don't believe he could have been selling drugs."

"Son, people fool you sometimes. They're not always what they seem," Rosemont said. "It happens every day to people a lot smarter than you or me."

"I know. But there's more to it. I hesitate because this is about your friend, Chap. I've been looking into this a little bit because Dwayne had started seeing Amber Duffy. And, well, she doesn't believe it either. Dwayne had gotten an accounts payable list that had all these businesses that Chap owns. I mean, he bills the University over $10 million a year. But what

183

struck me as odd was that Ridgecrest was one of them, and that's where Max Milovich went to work. More like his job was created for him."

"I see where you're going, Ben," Rosemont said, in truth, taken aback by the $10 million figure himself. "But son, you've got to understand and see the big picture. There aren't too many of them in these parts, but Chap Roberts is a unique business man. I mean, he's so diversified his picture ought to be in Webster's with the word. He's like Tennessee and Georgia's Donald Trump. I poke fun at him all the time, but the truth is, his business is more than I can comprehend."

"I understand that, Coach. I do. But I think Dwayne was on to something," Wright said. "I don't know what yet. But I don't believe he was dealing drugs. She and I are going to figure it out."

"Don't you think you might be running a naked bootleg here?" Rosemont asked. "No protection... I like Amber but she's no blocker. I don't want you getting in over your head."

"I've got my classes licked, Coach," he said. "And you know I'm not going to neglect football."

"Listen, I don't want you messing around in this. Someone has been killed. I'll do a little checking myself, ok?"

"That sounds good, Coach, thanks," Wright said, with no real intention of backing off.

Michael Kelly's story in Tuesday morning's *Chattanooga Daily Register* made for great copy. The headline read "LMSU's Heisman Push Gives Smith Well-Deserved Opportunity." Having the time on Monday evening, and presumably the scoop, the *Register* blew it out ... dominant art (four columns by 10 inches) of Smith hauling in a Wright pass. It was essentially a fluff piece, but a timely feature on Smith's development and potential, and it made the sports editors at the *Chattanooga Times* hopping mad at Rick Bayless. He'd whiffed on another breaking news story. He seemed out of touch with the beat. If they'd known how bad it really was, they would have stuck him at the desk for the rest of his career, taking calls from Little League coaches and churning out line scores.

"Well you know, Mondays are the closest thing to a day off I get during football season," Bayless said to his editor, in the weakest defense since season one of the Tampa Bay Buccaneers' existence. "Janet Randolph could have called me at home, too."

The result for Bayless was probation. One more slipup in a three-month period and he was history, at least from the beat.

The worn-down reporter left home early for Rosemont's press conference, hoping to get some one-on-one face time. He arrived at the coach's office just after 10 a.m., and as he began to speak, nerves frazzled, he broke down crying.

"There's just so much pressure to get stories first," Bayless said. "They told me the beat would be the hardest thing I ever did in my professional life, but I didn't realize. Nobody here seems to like me ... or confide in me. I'm going to get fired."

Rosemont looked at Bayless in disbelief, thinking "Well the world needs more grave diggers, too." But the coach went against his own grain for an instant.

"Didn't I give you a nickname? Come on, you can't get more 'in' than that Righteous Rick," Rosemont said, but with southbound patience. His harsh tone took on greater edge. "Now, do you want some constructive criticism? Cause I'm not going to sit here and blow sunshine up your ass.

185

Except for August, I only see you on Tuesday's and Saturdays. That's not enough. The other guys are here for more practices... talking to assistants. Talking to players. Even if it's about stuff they're not going to write about. I heard from Jim Winkler about that stunt you pulled, stopping all the black guys and asking them if they were Jerome Jones. Do you think those guys are idiots? They know you don't have a clue who they are without nametags."

"That's one of the few times I wasn't prepared for an interview. My media guide is usually in my car but I had left it in my apartment," Bayless said weakly.

"I don't care where you left it," Rosemont blasted. "You ought to have the damn thing memorized. I let you guys on the sidelines for practice. You should know faces without numbers. You think they're going to respect you or trust you after that? That's why they ignore you. And you could have avoided it if you'd just asked Jim for help. That's like trying to force a pass into triple coverage... usually something bad happens. Jeez, you're a nice guy but you've got to learn to think on your feet. Now you're going to have to excuse me -- or pull it together and ask some questions."

"Janet could have called me at home," Bayless said. "We're not bound to a typewriter like the old days."

"Are you kidding me? Leave her your number," said Rosemont, giving the thumb over the shoulder motion. "We'll see if we can't write the story for you next time, too. I don't want to have another conversation like this again... ever. Now get out of here, please."

As Rosemont was giving Bayless the boot, LMSU Director of Safety and Security Pete Crawford shared with Charles Nester and Dr. Everett that his men had found one student willing to confirm he'd purchased cocaine from Dwayne Price. In truth, he'd lied for the grand sum of $500 courtesy of Jim Wheatley.

"Well, that's just fantastic," Everett said. "Any other great news? A ring of prostitution? Or maybe the international students are having drunken orgies again? Well, I'll not be attending Dwayne Price's wake this afternoon. Let's pray the media doesn't find out about this. Do you have to share it with the police?"

"Well, we normally work in complete cooperation with all law enforcement agencies," Crawford said. "That's a relationship we've developed for our own purposes. It wouldn't be right to withhold information."

"But they've got all they need," Nester said. "It's not like this thing is going to go to trial. From what I hear they think the shooter was some out-of-state transporter who got greedy."

"That's right," said Everett. "We could have come up empty here."

"Yes, but, and I don't think it's the case because he said he went home for the weekend, this student could be a suspect," Crawford said. "Students get into some heavy activity. You see it. Some like to dress and act like gangsters even when they're not. But some actually are."

"Let's hold on to it for now," Everett said, "and see what the police come up with on their own. Let them tell us something for once."

"Yes sir," Crawford said, exiting the President's office. The President shot a seething glance of annoyance at Nester. Nester held his tongue, turned, and followed Crawford out the heavy oak door.

17

Chap Roberts picked Coach Rosemont up just as he said he would, at 11:30 a.m. sharp, for a meal with his old buddy at the University Inn. At least, Chap assumed that was where they were going since the coach said he was going to buy. But Rosemont, once again filled with doubt about Roberts, had other ideas.

"Let's drive through this Bojangles' and have us a quick picnic," Rosemont said, pointing up the street. "It's as beautiful day … little chilly. Are you in for half a bird? Come on … high times."

"Ok, Coach," Roberts said. "You have heard of cholesterol though right?"

"Honey, give me an eight-piece box, with two sides of mashed potatoes and gravy, beans and dirty rice, biscuits, and two large sweet teas. You want tea?"

"Yeah, sure."

"How about some corn on the cob with that too, Coach," said the voice on the other end of the box. Rosemont scratched his cheek, looking at Roberts.

"I guess I've been here once or twice. Yeah, honey, corn sounds good too. Now make sure we get a couple of big breasts in that order, doll… I don't want a bunch of skimpy thighs."

"You know you're double-starching," Roberts said matter-of-factly, as though it were the only issue with the mammoth order. The coach gave his college mate a suspicious glance out of one eye.

As Rosemont concluded his drive-through flirting, leaning into his friend to do it, Roberts watched the customer activity across the street at a Speedway gas station. "I need one of those," he said to himself. "Look at the traffic." It was then he noticed Max Milovich getting out of his Trail Blazer and walking to a pay phone. As he pulled his hand out of his pocket with the change necessary to make a call, Roberts could see in plain view Milovich's cell phone in its holder on his belt. Coal was chucked on Roberts' blood pressure. Perhaps due to paranoia, but also with knowledge of Wheatley's visit, Roberts surmised that Milovich could only be calling the cops. Unless he was cheating on his wife, too.

Ten minutes later, the two friends were about to sit down to a picnic table at the base of Lookout Mountain. "I'm going to make a quick call," Roberts said, walking away for some buffer space. Rosemont enthusiastically pulled the fried skin off a plump chicken breast and folded it before sticking it in his mouth.

"Mmm, you go ahead," Rosemont said, eyeing his next bite of white meat. "But you better hurry. Get it while it's hot."

Wheatley was number one on Roberts' speed dial.

"I just saw our buddy Milovich at a pay phone at the Speedway on 16th Avenue. Are you out and about? You better check your sources at the police station."

"I'm close, maybe I'll catch him."

"It was about 10 minutes ago."

"I'll hit the redials," said Wheatley, who was just leaving his apartment to start his day. The murderer didn't sleep much, but he usually worked until three or four in the morning, smoked his last cigarette by five.

189

Roberts joined Coach Rosemont at the picnic table for a heavy meal and light conversation. Rosemont vented about Rick Bayless breaking down in his office over missing the Smith for Heisman story.

"Can you believe that wimp?"

"You're talking about tears... wet, salty tears?"

"Streaming down the man's face. Like a child!"

"Wow. Well, Bob Knight said it best: 'We all learn to write in second grade. Most of us go on to greater things.' "

"A man after my own heart," Rosemont said. He snatched up a drumstick and bit with his normal vigor.

Once lunch was concluded, Rosemont quickly took on a new demeanor. Roberts was still thinking about what Milovich might have been up to when Rosemont abruptly changed his tone.

"Chap, I'm having second thoughts about this Price murder. I've heard some things that make me believe he was on to you."

Roberts looked Rosemont in the eyes as his facial expression quickly changed from inquisitive disbelief to pure anger.

"He was on to *us,* buddy. He knew we were paying the props. You know that. He followed Wheatley around with them. I was trying to protect you and your program. I can give money away if I want to."

"Well, yeah, but it goes a little deeper than that," Rosemont said. "You're billing LMSU over $10 million a year. How has Everett been letting you get away with that?"

"Everett, that damned lowlife ... he's got his hand *deep* in my pocket - squeezing my balls," Roberts said with disgust. "I've more than doubled that prick's salary for the past 10 years. He's set."

"So he's getting a kickback on your over-billing? Jesus, Chap, that's extortion. When did you lose control of your life?"

"Damn it, Sam, grow up. Ok, yeah, I wanted more," Roberts said, with a dismissive, annoyed look.

"You're making more money then you could ever spend. Why fleece the school?"

"It's not the school, it's the state and all its taxation. It just did my heart good to stick it to them. But you're no different. We all have it … those who ascend to high places. There's something driving you."

"To be a great coach… I haven't killed anybody."

"Who's to say? You're no saint. You break the rules. What about when someone like Ron Bennett dies… only one of *your* players? You pushed him to be stronger. Did you supply him? Did you allow the supplier to hang around? Aren't you responsible?
Besides, you break God's rules," Roberts said, getting up and walking to his Mercedes. "Let me show you something."

In his trunk, Roberts grabbed a stack of grainy, black and white, 8x10 glossy photos of Jennifer Newton riding Rosemont like he was an entry on Derby Day at Churchill Downs. Roberts took his wallet out of his back pocket and dropped it in the trunk, palmed a loaded snubbed nose .38 caliber pistol and slid it into his pocket, then walked back and threw the stack of photos on to the table so they'd slide apart in front of Rosemont like a deck of cards.

The demands Max Milovich received from Jim Wheatley on Monday kept him awake that night, like hot cinders burning his brain, causing him to toss and turn. He was tired of threats, especially when it came to his family.

He rationalized that if Wheatley and Roberts got caught, Ridgecrest, and thus his job, would go on. He didn't want to see Wright get hurt, he wanted this Black Bears season to continue as it had, and ultimately, he knew a shit storm was coming and he wanted to remain out in front of it. Detective Robert Mills was quoted in the paper, so it was Mills he requested when he called anonymously on Tuesday.

"You're on the wrong track on the Dwayne Price murder. He found out something. Chap Roberts is paying the football non-qualifiers -- the Proposition 48s – for alleged work. That's how they can afford to come here and stay their first year. That's where it started with Price. Check out Jim Wheatley, Roberts' hatchet-man. Or should I say henchman. He probably planted the drugs. Keep it to yourself. They have spies everywhere … big payroll."

"Who is this?" Mills asked. "Why don't we meet?"

"I've got to go now, but I'll call back. The money is real … serious money… Chap cash they call it."

Wheatley just missed Milovich at the Speedway, but he hit redial on both pay phones and sure enough, the second one answered, "Tennessee State Police. How may I direct your call?" Furious, he drove straight up to Ridgecrest and pulled next to Milovich's SUV. A quick glance around the parking lot revealed no witnesses. Wheatley stepped out and dropped to the ground, rolled on his back and shimmied his head and shoulders behind the passenger side front tire, knowing wheel fronts are the few places rubber hoses are used in the brake line system. He found the brake fluid line of the Trailblazer and gave it just a nick -- a tiny slit -- with his pocket knife. After all it wasn't even 1 p.m. That would be plenty of time for the brake pressure to drop. He was up, in his car, and out of parking lot in less than two minutes.

"I might go down but you're going to bleed, asshole," Wheatley said to himself.

Shortly after 5 p.m., Milovich left the office with his co-workers, searching the parking lot for Wheatley as he walked. Once inside his Trail Blazer with the engine running, he felt relief. He turned on to the winding descent hoping he could put his fears behind him. It wasn't until the sixth curve that he realized he had trouble, as he stomped the floor with his brake pedal.

Immediately he began looking for the best place to crash, but the winding switchbacks offered only rocky walls or mountainous cliffs filled with pine trees. At the next curve to the left he saw what he thought was an opening into a bit of flat ground. He went for it, but an unseen low boulder caused the SUV to flip on to the driver's side. It slid 30 feet, then rolled over and over down a steep embankment. The vehicle's inertia was stopped by another huge boulder, crushing the roof of the car when it did. His airbag deployed after hitting the initial rock which kept Milovich from death and a massive amount of facial trauma. But his left leg, left arm, and six ribs were broken. The ligaments in his left knee were ripped apart when his leg wedged oddly in the steering column. His spleen was lacerated as well.

Despite enormous pain he was pleasantly taken aback to see a single file line of six deer moving towards him curiously investigating the commotion, and not recognizing a human form. Two fawns, still with their spots, hopping playfully on unsure legs, led the way followed by two doe, and two young, spiked males, the second of which stopped and grazed in front of his truck before moving on. It was as close as he'd ever been to a spike. He could see the fuzz on his four-inch antlers, just beginning to show the splits of adulthood at their ends. He could hear in the distance the snort of a buck, probably the dad. It made him think of his own children. He smiled weakly before he passed out from the pain.

18

Dwayne Price's memorial service was scheduled for 1 p.m. on Tuesday, at Jenkins Funeral Home. Price had no immediate family that could be found, nor a will, so in a case such as his the state of Tennessee freezes the victim's assets to make sure all outstanding debts are paid. Price did have a small amount of life insurance, but it still listed his parents as the beneficiaries. He had no real money to speak of outside of that $250,000 insurance policy, and had no equity in his home, which he'd purchased just months before. His Honda was nearly paid for. At any rate the price of a decent burial was covered.

Wright had told Rosemont that morning that he was going to Price's memorial service, and that since the veterans had the day off he would deal with any media that needed him when he got back. He'd made arrangements with Amber Duffy to pick her up outside of her building at 12:20 p.m.

She wore a modest, mid-length black dress that seemed to him to make her appear delicate, which he assumed – though obviously physically fit -- that she was. The neckline was low, but she wore a black scarf as well, to go along with her black shoes and black sun glasses.

Wright jumped out of his Jeep and jogged around to open the door for her, and though she smiled at the sweet and mannerly gesture, she found it unnecessary. His stereo was playing the compact disc of a West Virginia band, Good Country Folk. The lyrics, which played while they began their short trip in silence, were:

I've been thinking hard every night,

worrying about the way things might be.

Getting high with the fire flies, blending with the stars.

Trying to see in to the future, wondering how I got so old.

And knowing that this little town can't hold me...

But there's some things you just can't dwell on.

Sometimes you stumble and fall.

Some people must live and learn, and forget about the past.

But sometimes the lesson's never learned.

"That's nice," Amber said, relaxing into her seat. "Has anybody here learned any lessons?"

"I don't know," Wright replied. "I talked to Coach Rosemont this morning about everything. I told him what we found out about Chap Roberts."

"What did he say?"

"Well, nothing about that," Wright said. "But he did seem surprised. He told me we should stay away from it, and that he'd look into it."

"That's good, I suppose," she said. "Of course, Chap is Coach's best friend, right? How far is he going to go?"

Inside, a white guest book sat nearly unsigned in a foyer of blue carpet and ivory walls. Obviously Felix Jenkins, the proprietor, was a Black Bears fan, too. The foyer led to two open doors, and a moderate viewing room, full of 40 empty chairs except for a few employees; Bruce Fellows, Jane Haynes, Mary Shell, Charles Nester, and an open casket containing the youthful but rigid Dwayne Price. Amber walked ahead to pay her respects. As Wright followed, the cell phone in the pocket of the navy blue sports jacket he wore along with a blue and red tie and gray slacks, began to ring.

"Oh, shoot. I meant to turn that off," he said, as he walked to the back of the room. He didn't recognize the number.

"This is Ben."

"Ben, this is Robert Mills. Do you remember me?"

"Oh, yes sir. Of course. What can I do for you?"

"Listen, I don't want you to be alarmed. But I got an anonymous tip from someone saying this Price murder all started because he found out that Chap Roberts was paying the team's props for work they don't actually do. Would you know anything about that?"

"No sir," Wright said, he turned to see Amber looking at Price in his casket. "But it makes sense. I've wondered sometimes how some of the guys do it... you know, afford to stay. But Amber and I found out that Chap's businesses are charging the University the mint ... over $10 million a year. It's got to tie in somehow."

"You're right. Well, listen, this caller mentioned Jim Wheatley. Now, we know him too. He's a thug ... does all Chap's dirty work. Do you know who he is?"

"No, sir. I don't think so."

"He's a small, wiry guy. Tough though. We're trying to track him down right now. You keep your eyes open," Mills said. "And be careful. He may have heard you two were at the station Sunday. If you see or hear anything, give me a call, ok? Don't try to do anything on your own. This is my cell too."

"Yes, sir, I will. Thank you, Detective."

The pain and injustice associated with her friend's death was still an open wound to Amber. Tears streamed down her face as Wright, Jane, Mary, and Bruce Fellows all stayed close to comfort her. Charles Nester, wearing a charcoal suit, sat quietly by himself two rows back. He looked to be in a solemn mood over Price's death but in truth was thinking first about the additional work on his plate, then the events that brought him to where he was sitting, including the tongue-lashing he'd taken from Rosemont the previous Thursday.

Pastor Mark Culpepper from First Baptist Church of Pineknob delivered a short eulogy. He seemed to be a gentle man, tall and thin with graying hair and reading glasses perched at the end of his nose. His voice was not deep or loud, but he didn't have to strain to be heard with so few in attendance. After reading Price's obituary word-for-word, he launched into some scripture.

"I have been crucified with Christ," Culpepper read, "and I no longer live, but Christ lives in me. The life I live in the flesh, I live by faith in the Son of God, who loved me and gave Himself for me. Galatians 2:19-20.

"When you encounter people you find difficult to love, God expresses His unconditional love through you. I pray this sentiment wasn't lost on the soul that slew Dwayne Price. But I somehow doubt it. Find comfort in the fact that our brother is in a better place, in the Kingdom of God, no matter how tragic his earthly exit. Please bow your heads with me in prayer."

As they pulled away from Jenkins Funeral Home Amber untied the scarf from her neck and placed it on her seat.

"Take me anywhere but work. I can't go back there today, Ben," she said. "It's just too depressing."

"Do you want to hit the mountain?" Wright asked, loosening his tie and unbuttoning his collar. He'd already shed his sports coat, laying it neatly in the back before getting into the driver's seat.

"Sure. It's a beautiful day."

The couple didn't know that behind them, a few cars back in his black Corvette, was Jim Wheatley. Realizing that Detective Mills likely had the drop on him and Roberts, Wheatley was ready to leave town. When he left Ridgecrest, he went straight to his Roberts-owned apartment, where his own stash of cash – around $45,000 -- was hidden. He had nothing else of value other than a couple of weapons and some clothes. He stuffed it all in one duffel bag – other than a second gun, along with his .45, and one knife, which he pocketed in his jacket. He threw the bag in his trunk. He could have just left, headed for Texas via Georgia, Alabama, Mississippi, Louisiana, then into Mexico, but the thought of Wright somehow influencing Max Milovich to come clean with the cops, thus casting the blame for Price's death on him and Roberts, enraged him, outweighing his sense of safety or freedom for himself. "I'm going to make that snot-nosed superstar pay," Wheatley thought, knowing he'd find him at Price's funeral service.

Coach Rosemont looked up from the pictures Chap Roberts had just tossed his way. At first he was surprised. He felt the bite of betrayal on his neck. He thought of the conversations they'd had through the years urging Rosemont into infidelity. And he remembered the most recent talks – trusted talks -- they'd had about his relationship with Jennifer Newton.

"Go ahead, keep them" Roberts said. "There's plenty more where they came from."

"You son of a bitch," Rosemont said.

"Well that's hurtful," Roberts said. "I knew you'd turn on me when the heat got turned up. I was right again."

"I'll just go to the cops ... and to Linda. You can't hurt me with this," Rosemont said, holding up a photo.

"Oh that's just the tip of the iceberg, Coach. Let's see. Can you prove that you haven't been betting on football games? My bookie says you have. You call my cell phone all the time. I placed the bets. You'll be stripped of your record. That's just for starters."

"Nobody would buy that," Rosemont said. "Nobody who knows me."

"Now listen, Sam, you ass. We can still get out of this ok. There's no real proof about Price. I'll get the best lawyers in the country."

"No, it's over," Rosemont said, standing and stepping out of the picnic table. Roberts did the same. "This can't go any further. You've lost it. Your cash can't buy your way out of this. What were you going to do, blackmail me with these?"

"No. Just persuade."

"Well it won't work. I know right from wrong."

"I can't believe it's come to this," Roberts said, suddenly and awkwardly reaching for his back pocket. Instinctively, Rosemont turned the corner of the table and charged, plowing Roberts – his right hand still in his back pocket -- into the dirt with his shoulder. Straddling him, he began pounding Roberts' face with his right fist, a championship ring slicing his skin. Roberts was bleeding profusely when a glancing blow enabled him to squirm enough to pull the gun from his pocket. Roberts fired, hitting Rosemont high in the chest. The bullet's impact sent the coach backward and to the ground, unconscious from the pain... or dead.

Roberts kicked Rosemont's legs off of him, stood up, and left his oldest and closest friend in the dirt to die -- if he wasn't dead already. Looking around and seeing nobody, he took the pictures he would have

touched in his delivery to the table, left the ones in the middle of the stack –
thinking it would make the crime appear executed by a common
blackmailer. He put the fingerprinted pictures and the lunch trash in the
trunk of his Mercedes and drove away, not caring even to look back or
worry about his own blood all over the crime scene.

Turned towards Wright in her seat, it was Amber Duffy who first
noticed the black Corvette tailing the quarterback's red Jeep Cherokee as the
couple was driving to the outskirts of town and on to one of the many
mountain routes.

"Do you know who it is?" she asked.

"No, but Detective Mills called when we got to the funeral home. I
meant to tell you sooner," Wright said, continuing to look ahead. "He's with
us now."

"That's good news. What brought him around?"

"He got a tip. It must have been from Max … said that Chap Roberts
has been paying our props. That must have been what Dwayne found out,"
Wright said, looking into his rearview mirror. "This guy might just want by
so he can open it up."

Wright saw a "scenic overlook" ahead and hit his blinker. He turned
right into the gravel pull off. The Corvette pulled in as well. As the driver
opened his door and stood up, Wright looked closer in his side view mirror.

"I know that guy!" he said, putting his SUV into drive and hitting the
gas. "That must be Wheatley. Mills mentioned him. I see him in our offices
sometimes."

Wright whipped his Jeep back on to the highway, spitting gravel as his tires reached the asphalt. Amber looked behind them. "Here, call Mills," Wright said. "It's my last received call."

"What should I tell him?"

"Tell him we found Wheatley! Oh man, he's on us already. We can't outrun him."

"Officer Mills? This is Amber Duffy. I'm with Ben and this Wheatley guy is following us. We're on Mountain Route 6, heading up. Ok. ... He said he's on his way with some troopers. He said bring him back to town if you can."

"What? Do you see a turning circle? This guy's a nut," Wright said, pulling the knot in his tie until the free end released and it came off into his hand. He threw it over his shoulder in the back. "We can't outrun him in this thing. I'll bet we can beat him on foot though. There's a trail up here in a mile or so. You want to try it?"

"I suppose. Wait. He'll have a gun. Won't we be easy pickings on a trail?"

"Maybe... we could ambush him. Knock him out and tie him up or something till Mills gets here. You in?"

Mills was trying to pull up beside them but couldn't because Wright was hogging the center line. "Yeah... ok," she said. "You're right. We can't outrun him."

"I'll try to get him to wreck into the back of me. Maybe we'll get lucky and he won't have his seatbelt on or something. There's a good straight stretch coming up."

As Wright pushed on the accelerator, another Good Country Folk song, this one with a fast-paced rhythm distinguished by the hammering of guitar strings, began on the stereo:

Submerged in the passion of the eyes that look upon you

with a love that lasts forever and forsaken by no other

till you go away and figure out that

men will kiss the ground you walk on

I have done the same but they are happy, strong, and rich and famous

"What *is* this?" Amber said. Her short laugh breaking the tension.

"It's good stuff," Wright replied, looking over with a youthful grin. "I saw these guys at a fair in West Virginia.

"Well, it fits today," she said, turning up the volume.

Now you want to be alone and search the world for something better

I will gladly let you go 'cause misery kept is bound to fester

But I wish you'd known me when

I was young and couldn't bend

Love was free and easy then but time moves on

and now I feel I'm

Long past being pretty

I'm long past being what I was

Time can change the way you stand but it cannot break the willful man

so be the girl you want to be, see the things you long to see

travel roads and burn the bridges

fan the flames that whisper set me free...

"Ok, are you ready?" Wright shouted, again looking into his rearview. "He'll ram us I think. Be ready to hit that trail."

Wright slammed on the breaks, and instantly the unsuspecting Wheatley drove underneath the Jeep's rear bumper. The impact of the Corvette's low bumper caused Wright's rear wheels to blow. Both drivers lost control, swerved, and crashed. The Jeep took out a pine tree, Wheatley's 'Vet went nose-first into the side of the rocky embankment.

"Are you ok Amber?"

"Yeah, I think so," she said, kicking off her shoes. "Let's go. Do you see him?"

"No. Let's move."

The couple ran to the trail as Wheatley shook the cobwebs from his head. His dirty hair was down in his face. As he pushed it back, he saw Duffy and Wright moving to the trail through his rearview. He began to unfold his battered body out of his totaled sports car. He touched his chest to make sure his .45 was still in his jacket, pulled it, and began running after them.

Wright, with the confidence of a young athlete, wouldn't go too far. He picked up a broken limb along the trail -- about three feet long and four inches in diameter. He swung it once, like a baseball bat. He found a thick pine tree close to the trail, and sidestepped his way into its branches.

"Amber, you go over there and wait," Wright whispered, pointing to some rocks. "Stay behind."

Wheatley slowed to a jog, then to a walk. Not hearing their steps, he sensed the ambush.

"I got your buddy Price and I'm going to get you both as well," Wheatley said, laughing as he walked. "The big guy paid me but I would have done him for free. It's a shame it had to end this way. Some people just don't know when to quit. You never should have gotten involved."

Wright timed his swing perfectly, but there was quite a bit of give in the piece of pine he'd chosen. Hitting Wheatley on the bridge of his nose, the impact stunned him, but didn't knock him out. His gun fell to the ground behind him as Wright's stroke knocked him backwards a couple of steps.

He shook his head to regain his senses, some small bits of bark falling off his face. He laughed when he saw the much larger Wright coming at him again with the branch. Wheatley was a government-trained, Vietnam-polished, expert at hand-to-hand combat, and he instinctively knew that taking down the youthful Wright would be easy work.

He caught the branch on Wright's next swing with his left hand, then with his right punched the young man hard on his left cheekbone and followed with an uppercut into the quarterback's gut, striking his solar plexus and stealing his wind. With his left he let go of the branch but instantly found the pressure point in Wright's right wrist and twisted it out – te nagi -- forcing him to his knees. He punched Wright twice more with his right hand as he continued to hold Wright's wrist with his left hand. One of the blows cut Wright. Warm blood ran down his cheek. Wheatley drew back low with his right for a palm strike, his intention to send the cartilage of quarterback's nose into his brain. Dazed from the punches, Wright's bleeding head bobbed about. Wheatley dropped Wright's wrist and grabbed him by the hair on the top of his head.

"See ya, boy," Wheatley grunted low, under his breath.

Amber Duffy fired the gun. The huge blast echoed across the mountain range. The bullet hit Wheatley in the side of his forehead. Eyes wide with a stunned look, Wheatley's knees buckled as he slowly twisted from the bullet's impact and fell backwards, crumpling to the dirt in slow motion. He lay on his back, feet folded under, looking up to the sky as the crimson blood poured out of his head, through his greasy hair, around his ear and on to the ground.

Wright would always remember how Amber looked when his head turned to her. She was beautiful. Her bare feet were shoulder length apart, her knees slightly bent and locked for her aim and to brace for the gun's impact. She held the handle with both hands, arms extended and locked. Her form was as perfect as the shot that put Wheatley down. Part of her hair had fallen into her face from the run. The smell of gunpowder filled the air, and a bit of smoke swirled upward. As she dropped the gun, Wright stood up and hugged her as tightly as he could.

"You saved my life," he said.

She could only smile, letting out in broken waves the frightened breath she'd been holding since she took aim and pulled the trigger. Her hands and body began to tremble.

"You do owe me," she said, with nervous laughter, reaching up and touching his bruising, bloody cheek. Wright looked deeply into Amber's brown eyes and they kissed for the first time. "But I'll let you pay me back."

Again they kissed, this time a long, passionate embrace. As they broke, she looked up into his eyes and gave another short laugh. She said softly, "You Ben Wright?"

"For the first time in my life."

19

Sam Rosemont would not die from his wounds that afternoon. Pinned underneath his former friend, Roberts' shot angled up in his chest cavity and shattered his collar bone. The bullet exited the back of Rosemont's shoulder. He regained consciousness and dialed 911 on his cell phone while still lying on the blood-soaked ground.

"Chap Roberts just shot me," Rosemont told the 911 dispatcher, after identifying himself. "I'm at the park at the base of the mountain. Chap is driving a silver Mercedes XL-3."

Using a picnic table as a brace, Rosemont struggled to his feet. He picked up the remaining pictures of Jennifer Newton making love to him and sat back down on the table's seat. He thought the grainy black and whites captured the girl's uninhibited beauty. "Riding high in the saddle," he thought to himself. "She's a good girl." Then he inhaled a broken breath as his eyes watered with guilt. What had he done? How would Linda react? She'd be crushed to see this. He was barely recognizable except for his distinctive profile, though the angle of the shot was from more of a bird's eye view as far as capturing him. His strength waning, he put the remaining pictures in a nearby trash can, making sure they were buried beneath other papers. He sat back down, weak from his blood loss. He could hear the ambulance approaching.

Though the broken bone made the pain excruciating, Rosemont was pressing on the entry wound as best he could with a navy blue Black Bear golf shirt he'd gingerly taken off, when help arrived. He was sitting on the table's bench in a blood-soaked V-neck T-shirt about to pass out when the doors opened. A police cruiser pulled up as well.

"What happened here, Coach Rosemont?" asked a young patrolman, as the two Emergency Medical Technicians made a quick diagnosis of Rosemont's wound.

"My best friend just tried to kill me," Rosemont said in a weakening voice. "Shot me like a dog in the dirt."

"And who is that?"

"Chap Roberts."

"Let's get him up," said one of the EMTs. "We've got to get an I.V. in him quick. He needs blood. Coach, can you walk a few steps with us or do we need a stretcher?"

"Why did he shoot you, Coach?" said the patrolman, whose brass nametag read Derek.

"He's dirty. I didn't know how dirty," said Rosemont rising to his feet with the aid of the EMTs. "I'll tell you everything. Just get me to the hospital. Keep me among the living."

The EMTs continued getting a SAMPLE history in the ambulance from Rosemont. Patrolman B.A. Derek remained to preserve and observe the crime scene as more help arrived. It took only minutes to find the pictures.

Chap Roberts drove straight to Chattanooga Metropolitan Airport. He kept his passport in his briefcase at all times, and it was always in his car, for just such emergencies. Or what he considered emergency visits to international girlfriends -- when time allowed. Thus, he was not a stranger to the airport employees. He was looking anything but inconspicuous with three gashes on his face, the blood from which he had been mopping up with a hand towel taken from the golf bag in the trunk of his car. The blood had finally coagulated, but he certainly didn't look like the typical first-class patron. He sometimes rented a private jet, and that isolated departure area – parking and boarding – could be completely discrete... one on one. He wished he'd had that foresight today.

He tried to book himself on a flight via New York to Paris. Roberts had large sums of money stashed in Swiss accounts, among others. But the news of the shooting went over the police radio quickly, and he was ultimately surrounded by cops at an airport ticket counter. He surrendered without incident, having tossed what he thought to be a murder weapon in the Tennessee River during the drive.

With his money, connections, and pedigree he knew he could ultimately beat the rap, of course. When he learned of Jim Wheatley's fate, he was in a holding cell back at the state police barracks. The wheels in his head really started churning. He'd cut Wheatley loose. He could pin the whole Price fiasco on him, as some seedy, night life sidebar. "I didn't know anything about the drugs," he'd say. If President Everett kept quiet, the extortion and kickbacks may not be revealed. For the Proposition 48 deal, he'd probably just get a fine from the Internal Revenue Service. He didn't care what kind of penalties the NCAA would impose on LMSU, hell he was just doing it to make money and get laid. He had no real loyalty. If Sam had just played ball... if he hadn't had to shoot Sam, he could have steered clear of the whole damn mess.

If he had to, Roberts would hire a team of lawyers that would make the O.J. Simpson trial look like a bunch of kids running a lemonade stand. With his initial phone call he touched base with his local corporate lawyer, Winston North, with the instructions to do just that... start assembling a team.

Blood loss became a serious issue as Rosemont was taken into emergency surgery upon his arrival to Pineknob Memorial Hospital. The tissue damage, especially the exit wound, was extensive due to the close range of the shot. His collarbone exploded, fragmenting into many dangerous shards. His left arm was in a sling, and he was wearing an unfashionable black-dotted, gray hospital gown when Linda came into the room.

"Do you know there's a policeman out there in the hallway, Sam?" she said, as she walked to his side and kissed his cheek.

"Yeah, he just needs a statement. I think I should call a lawyer though."

"Sam, what is going on? Why would Chap shoot you?"

"We need to talk, honey," Rosemont said, taking his wife's hand in his good right hand. "I'm afraid I've screwed things up royally. There are some issues with the team and with Chap. That'll come out later. But with us too... I'm afraid, well... I've had an affair."

"What? You mean recently?" Thoughts swirled in her head. She broke her grip with his hand and instinctively held out her to catch herself. Her eyes closed. She was dizzy, nauseous. She reopened them and sat down in the bedside chair looking up at her husband of 41 years. The blood drained from her face.

"What do you mean recently?" the coach asked.

"Well, I'm not stupid Sam. Or at least I didn't think so. I hoped and prayed back when we were young that you wouldn't cheat on me on all those road trips. But when you're having babies and raising them, you're so tired at the end of the day you can't hold your eyes open, but you know that

210

cry is going to come in the middle of the night. You watch your own body sag and grow weak, you start having doubts."

"I never did back then," Rosemont lied. "But, I wasn't there for you. I was always worried about climbing the ladder."

"So why now? Who is she?"

"That doesn't matter, does it?" Rosemont asked. "I guess I got a little power trip going -- at Chap's urging. I was running too close with that bastard. But I still shouldn't have done it. I lost sight of what's important."

Tears streamed from Linda Rosemont's eyes as she sat quietly. She seemed to draw in and look even frailer, and that hurt Rosemont more than 100 bullets ever could.

"Honey, I'm so sorry. I could give you more details but that doesn't change anything. It was a couple of times and it's over. I know you can't forgive me now, but I want to make it right. I love you. You are the love of my life. When we were together again the other night, that was home to me."

Linda looked up at Sam, the man she'd stood beside for so many years, through highs and lows, multiple homes in ten cities, wins and losses, hits and misses on the recruiting trail, good and bad stories in the media, raising their four children. Ultimately she loved him, and she'd stay by his side until the end.

"So why did he shoot you? Was it over a girl?"

The coach put his head down, slightly relieved. "No. I wish. It goes a little bit deeper than that."

It had been a busy day for law enforcement in Pineknob. Two shootings and a single-vehicle wreck, all on the mountain, all within an hour of each other, all related. Detective Robert Mills now believed he had most of the pieces of the puzzle in front of him. He just needed to make them fit. He thanked God for Amber Duffy, Ben Wright, and the fact that he'd kept a semi-open mind. He didn't want to miss anything, and he felt that Chap Roberts now saw himself as a larger than life figure… above the law. He wanted him to pay for every crime he could make stick.

Mills thought back to earlier that day. He was the first to make it to the mountain -- with one cruiser in tow -- for the aftermath of Amber Duffy shooting Jim Wheatley. The scent of gun powder from the bullet's busted cap still lingered and Amber and Wright still embraced when he arrived on the scene.

"Are you two all right?" Mills asked, surveying Wheatley's resting place. Then looking up at Wright and making a mock punch in the air he added, "Look's like you took a couple of shots, Ben."

"Yes, sir. He definitely knew how to handle himself in a fight," Wright said, rubbing his cheekbone. "If it weren't for Amber, I don't think I would have made it."

"You both probably should have stayed in the car."

"Well, we knew we couldn't outrun him in the Jeep. And, where were we going to go?"

"We couldn't see how we could turn him back to town," Amber added.

"So, I thought we could beat him on the trail. Then I got the bright idea to try and knock him out with a branch… didn't work."

"But you made him drop his gun," Amber said.

"Did you think about trying to just hold him once you got it?" Mills asked.

"Well, I didn't think. I just reacted. He was about to try and kill Ben doing that thing," Amber said, shoving the heel of her palm forward and backward.

"Just one shot? It was certainly dead on," Mills said, "if you'll pardon the pun. You know how to shoot?"

"My grandfather and my father taught us," Amber said, "on the family farm."

"He admitted it, Detective," Wright said, getting back on subject. "When he was following us on the trail, he told us he killed Dwayne."

"Yes, that's true," Amber agreed. "He was quite proud of it. He said, 'The big guy paid me but I would have done him for free.' Is that right, Ben?"

"Exactly," Ben said.

"Really. Meaning Chap Roberts, I assume."

"Who else?" said Wright.

"This will test the hearsay exceptions," Mills said, thinking ahead. "That wraps everything up neatly on this end for you two. Oh, for the report, he started following you when?"

"He must have been waiting after Dwayne's service," Amber said.

"I wonder what he'd have done if we'd been in two cars?" Wright asked.

"I don't even want to think about it," she said, though graphically brutal visions flashed in her mind.

"As deranged as he was, he probably would have retaliated on both of you, one at a time. Thank goodness you were together. Well, this should do it. I'll call you if I need more. Ok?"

"Sure," Wright said.

213

"Looks like you won't be driving that Jeep back down the hill. The officers there can give you a ride back to town, wherever you need to go," Mills said, looking up the hill. "We'll have your vehicle towed as well. Do you think you need to go to the hospital? Might need a few stitches."

"No. I've had worse…. It's embarrassing, really."

More police cruisers and an ambulance arrived during the trio's talks. Now, at the top of the trail there was the commotion of the news media trying to move down to get shots of the scene and Wheatley's corpse. Word had gone over the scanner that included the name Ben Wright, so a frenzy had begun. Mills was in charge of the investigation. He looked at his watch. It was 3:13 p.m.

"Officer Gilbert, tell the media I'll have a statement for them at 5 p.m. down at headquarters," Mills said, having grabbed the nearest available patrolman. "And, will you and your partner take these two back to town please? You can tell the media that they are not under arrest, but were acting in cooperation with law enforcement."

"Thanks, Detective Mills," Amber said. "For everything."

"Yes, sir, we appreciate it," Wright said, extending his hand.

"No, thank you," Mills said, shaking Wright's hand. "I have to admit, if you two had dropped this the truth might not have come out. Oh, one other thing. The anonymous tip… any ideas?"

"It was probably Max Milovich," Wright said. "He had the compliance job before Dwayne. Went to work for… well, he works at Ridgecrest Insurance and Finance."

"I'll check that out after the press conference. You both should be there when I make the statement really. The media is definitely going to want to speak to you."

"No. I deal with it all the time," Wright said. "Amber, do you want to?"

"Not me," she said with a smile. "That's not my game."

20

Pain and increasing soreness were not utmost in Chap Roberts' mind as the walls of his holding cell began to close in around him... although both were extreme. Getting out, and staying out, was. With barely room to turn around, feeling caged like an animal, his mind raced. He could not go to prison. He'd run first. He'd never considered himself claustrophobic but as he looked around this dark, cold 8'x 9' box, he could barely breathe. And he was quite positive he couldn't get laid. He could live on the cash he had stashed overseas. Leaving his wife, Gina, was barely a concern... non-existent. Would she get what he left behind? He did at least hope for her that was true.

Winston North was able to procure the first installment of Chap's defense team, a hotshot criminal defense attorney from Chattanooga named Steve Jackson. Not yet 35, Jackson made a name for himself representing criminals in the most newsworthy trials.

There weren't a great deal of high profile crimes in Chattanooga, so he traveled some at times, remaining within the borders of the state. He had his own firm, was harshly direct in his speech, and wasted no time. He was thin and good-looking at just under 6-foot, light brown hair with a well-groomed business cut, a distinctive prominent nose and a sleek jaw line, no signs of aging. He had an Ivy League look to him, but he was pure Tennessee when he spoke. He'd grown up in Chattanooga, was a UT-Chattanooga Moc, and resented like Hell having to go to Knoxville for Law School because of his love for his hometown.

He relied on only one employee, Margaret Davenport, who was accomplished at everything from accounting, to organization and research. When North called, Jackson was not in the courtroom which was fortuitous. He'd heard of Chap Roberts, and, seeing dollar signs, news clips and newspaper ink, he was willing to drop most everything to represent him. Roberts was going in front of a judge that afternoon to set bail. The charge: attempted murder.

North brought the two together in a dingy holding room smaller than the walk-in closet in Roberts' 8,500-square-foot home.

"Mr. North briefed me as best he could, sir, on the drive down," Jackson said. "What kind of case will they be building, Mr. Roberts? In other words, what else is associated with the case?"

"First, cut the formalities, please," Roberts said. "We'll be spending too much time together for that. He's Winston. I'm Chap. All I'm worried about today is getting bail set, ok? Then we'll work on the case."

"I see. Well, attempted murder is a tough burden for the state to prove."

"Yeah, and look at me," Roberts said, turning his bruised and cut face from side to side. "If I didn't have the gun, I could be dead."

"Self defense? Well, let me play devil's advocate for a bit. Why did you bring a gun to this… ahem, picnic lunch we'll call it?"

"Look, Sam and I have lunch twice a week. It was his idea to get away from the madness for a few minutes. I thought we were going to The University Inn."

"Reasonable. And the gun?"

"It was in my trunk. I have a permit for it. Luckily, I had the foresight to grab it."

217

"Did you have it on you at the beginning of lunch?"

"No. I went after it mid-meeting."

"So, the conversation turned bad or what? I mean, what was the purpose of this lunch, Chap? Post-50-year-old buddies don't usually get into down-in-the-dirt fist fights during lunch, especially millionaires. You just don't hear about that every day."

Chap raised his hands shoulder height, palms forward as if to say stop.

"Ok – and I appreciate the understated humor in that – but look, this is going to be your dream case. It may go pretty deep. But we've got to let the dust settle on it a little bit. I don't know all the particulars right now."

"Meaning they'll come up with more?"

"Meaning we will seek clarification on some matters… see where things stand on some issues."

"And you'll one day tell me what these *things* are?"

"Well, their case has to be disclosed, right? Just get bail set. I'll pay whatever."

"You'll probably have to come with 10 percent of a million, maybe two… 100 grand, Chap… cash," Jackson said.

"Don't say that," Roberts said, thinking of all the times Rosemont used the phrase Chap cash for a joke.

"What, 100 grand?

"No, Chap cash… oh, just forget it. So, do you foresee any problem? I've never been arrested before."

"You wouldn't flee would you?"

"Hell no! We're winning this battle."

"They picked you up at Metro, right?"

"Yeah, but that was just a knee-jerk reaction," Roberts said, looking over at the ever quiet North. "We plead not-guilty, and you tell the judge I've got a half billion in business interests I'm trying to protect. Oh... and a wife."

"What's her name?"

"Gina."

"Of how many years?"

"Let me think. She's my college sweetheart you can say... nearly 38 years.

"That might be enough," Jackson said. "Two issues on my mind: I despise not knowing all aspects of this case going in, but due to time restraints I'll let it slide if you assure me you will come clean with everything. Secondly, I'm all the defense team you'll need on this so save your money. Now let me some take pictures of your face for the file."

The judge sitting in for arraignments that day was near the end of a long, distinguished career. His name was Oliver Henry Buffington – Judge O. Henry Buffington – a name his mother chose due to her love of the writings of William Sydney Porter – pin name O Henry -- and a kinship she felt with him due to his being born in Greensboro, North Carolina. She was born Clara Fulks in Winston, North Carolina, in 1896, and as an avid reader, sought Porter's stories – mostly in magazines -- as much as possible. Her love of books led her to become a librarian – she studied at all-women's Salem College. By then the dash had officially been added to Winston-Salem. After a couple of years there she migrated east to Wake Forrest, procuring a position at the University at the original campus, north of Raleigh. She fell in love and married a professor of English Literature, Dr. Robert A. Buffington, who spent much of his free hours in her library there.

Once expecting their first child in 1920, the couple decided if they were blessed with a boy to use Oliver, a family name of Clara's, and Henry, not only for a literary reference and show of respect for literature, but to inspire the boy into his own love of reading and writing. It did. Henry's hungry mind craved books. But in his youth, as the biography of Porter became more widespread, Henry Buffington was fascinated that Porter had allegedly embezzled from a bank in Austin, Texas, and was imprisoned in Ohio. He vigorously read literature involving crime and imprisonment, and studied the relevant laws while growing up. He was also athletic. He grew long and ran quickly and spent the time he wasn't reading on a baseball diamond, where his reflexes and strong throwing arm helped him excel as a third baseman.

He attended Wake Forest for next to nothing due to his parents' employment there and earned degrees in both Political Science and English – literature option of course – in just three years. He also walked on and made the Demon Deacons baseball team, cracking the lineup as a junior and hitting a respectable .286. Once accepted, he chose to leave his parents and the region's cigarette industry to study law at Vanderbilt University in Nashville, Tennessee, although his three years there were separated by what he called "888 days of service" in the Europe theatre with the United States Army fighting War World II, which wasn't exactly accurate but he liked the roundness of the number. He came home to visit his parents and their nurturing needs, and then was back in Tennessee before V-J Day.

He returned to his studies a reluctantly wiser man, having experienced the gruesome and horrific face of war. It was then he met his wife-to-be, Mattie Henderson, a jewel of an undergraduate at Vanderbilt. The couple married but never had children. It was the poor health of her parents that led him first to practice law then to garner a judge's robe in Chattanooga. Since there was a state police depot in Pineknob – essentially to cover a district that included Southwestern Chattanooga and Pineknob, a rotation of judges was continually scheduled for the courtroom there.

Buffington had remained handsome in his senior years and had kept his hair, which was now a soft silver and a little unruly when not freshly combed. The lines around his eyes, forehead, and mouth had grown deep, and the skin on his thin body loose. All his movements were deliberate, but he felt fortunate to be able to move at all.

He was a widower of eight years when Chap Roberts' case landed on his bench. He'd planned to retire sooner but when Mattie died of complications from cancer he no longer saw the need. He still enjoyed reading and did so in all his free time. He took his meals with books and they followed him to bed. He'd finally decided to quit working and he was going to do so at the end of the year. He looked forward to spending the winter's more harsh months in Florida, where a few of his friends had migrated.

He was known as a fair judge, quiet and patient, and preferred no interruptions when hearing a case. Lawyers learned quickly he did not care for the limits of interrogation to be pushed when questioning a witness simply due to his aggravation with having to speak following an objection. When he did speak his voice's volume was so low that every attendee strained to hear him. Knowing that, the court members would be utterly silent, the shuffling of feet, all bodily movement would cease so that his words and meaning could be absorbed.

When Steve Jackson stood and answered "not guilty" to the charge of attempted murder, Assistant District Attorney Luke Rinehart, a small, squirrelly, dark-headed white man in his early 40s, felt the need to address the court.

"Your honor, before you make a decision on bail I want to point out that these photographs of Coach Sam Rosemont and an as-yet unidentified female were found at the scene of the crime, and similar photos were found in the trunk of Mr. Roberts' car. This leads us to believe, your honor, one, that Mr. Roberts was either blackmailing Coach Rosemont or using the photos as influence, and, two, that this is only the tip of the iceberg in his criminal activity. Also, a known employee of Roberts' was shot earlier…"

Judge Buffington raised his hand for Rinehart's silence," This is not the time to plead your case as you know, Mr. Rinehart. Attempted murder is alone enough to render a conclusion on this occasion. Mr. Roberts, you are a man of means therefore if I grant bail I must do so in a way that you will hopefully feel. I want you to think hard too while un-incarcerated. The world is a much smaller place than it once was and being a hunted man is in itself a prison. While you are worldly and intelligent, don't sell short the abilities of law enforcement, bounty hunters, and international manhunts. This trial will begin at 9 a.m., here, one week from today. Bail is set at $5 million."

21

As passengers Amber Duffy and Ben Wright ascended Lookout Mountain. A sense of safety, and finality washed over them for the first time in days. They sat in the backseat of a police cruiser with just a few inches of space between them as the car negotiated curves, one passenger's body would slide and their shoulders would touch and rest against the others'. After this happened a few times they both smiled and looked deeply into each other's eyes. Amber slid her petite hand into his battered one, and that solitary gesture spoke volumes, adding validity to the kiss they'd shared in the euphoria of victory over Wheatley. Wright looked at her hand in his and thought about awkwardly trying to make conversation with Amber when he was a naïve freshman. He leaned his head back and smiled.

It was with a new found appreciation of the precious present and the events of the past few days crescendoing into that afternoon's life threatening adventure that Amber let her intentions be known when she closed the front door of her condo behind them. She'd played it quite innocently in the Pineknob police cruiser. "Ben, why don't you get out here with me and I'll run you back to the dorms in a bit... I'll put something on that cut on your face." she'd said.

Once inside her door, she turned to Wright, reached to his broad, athletic shoulders and they again kissed. Wright felt the heat of her lips, her mouth, and tongue on his. He could even feel temperature in her palms rubbing from his collar bones to his pectorals and on to his ribs and abdominals.

"I want you to hold me," Amber said. "Please... will you do that? Make love to me?"

"Since you said please," he answered quietly with a smile. "Do you know how many times I imagined this when I first came here? I thought about you all the time. You were on my mind constantly."

"Oh, yeah? Did you ever see us in the shower?"

"Uh... no."

"Neither did I. But that's where we're heading first."

"Well, that's good anyway because I'm about to bust."

Amber laughed. "You can use that bathroom there," she said pointing down a hallway at the far end of the living room, "give me a few minutes, then meet me upstairs."

Though she had never utilized it with a lover, the condo she purchased was part of a village for the younger sect. The master bath had both an oversized tub with the hardware situated in the middle so both users could lean back comfortably while facing each other, and a large, glass-walled, walk-in shower.

When Wright knocked on her open bedroom door, Amber wore only a white, terry cloth bathrobe.

"Come in, and take your shoes off," Amber said, turning and facing Ben's knock. Amber let him slide his socks and black, slip-on dress shoes under the end of her bed before she stepped to him.

"Cozy," Ben said, touching her robe at her shoulder.

"I thought you'd like it," she said, smiling and gazing into his eyes.

"I like that too," Wright said, pointing to a majestic, aerial panoramic of Ludlow Stadium, the sky over Lookout Mountain to the West orange, just

224

minutes before darkness. The stadium was filled, mostly with fans wearing blue. It was the only object related to sports he'd noticed in her home.

"My grandfather gave me that when I graduated," she said, looking over at the photo, which hung on a wall by itself, between the doors to her bathroom and closet. "He knew how much I love LMSU football."

"Knew?"

"Yes. We lost him last winter. He lived on that family farm I mentioned to Mills."

"I'm sorry, Amber."

"It was tough," she said, tears forming in the corners of her brown eyes. "He knew you were going to be a great one. That's what he said. He'd come down to some games with my dad and brothers."

Wright held her in his arms.

"So, is this real?" he asked after a moment, leaning back, which he had to do to look into her eyes when they were so close.

"It is for me," she said. "I know what you're asking. What's the difference between now and when you were a freshman?"

"Well, yeah... although, I..."

"I think you are on the threshold of greatness as a *man*," she interjected. "I'm not talking about football. You're so generous and charitable already – you're such a good person. I watch sports on the news. I see when you're at hospitals or camps. There will be doors thrust open for you because of who you are. I'd like to be there. You can help so many people. I can't even give blood sometimes because of my weight."

"Too heavy?"

They both laughed as Wright shifted the tone of the conversation.

"Well, you know I wouldn't be here if I didn't think we had something," Wright said, taking off his watch and placing it on her bedside table. The thin leather bracelet remained, a worn symbol of his Christianity.

"I do know that," Amber said. "And you know what you said earlier? Well, you've been in my mind as well these last few days… constantly. I guess it took Dwayne to bring us together. I always liked you, Ben. It was just different three years ago. It had to be."

"I know. I was just a kid, but my feelings were real. What about now?"

Amber stepped closer and began unbuttoning Wright's shirt. "Now? Now I'd leave my job if I had to… to be with you. If that's what you want."

"I want you… whatever it takes, though I hope you wouldn't lose your job. And, I'd throw God in there with Dwayne, too, as far as getting us together."

"It's funny… like familiar," she said. She loosened the terry cloth restraint on her robe and turned her attention to his pants. "I don't feel the least bit awkward about this."

Wright stood confidently, her tugging and pulling at the fabric of his pants was making him grow. "First impressions," he thought.

"I don't either," he said.

She slid his pants over his hips and down his legs, helping him to step out. "I like the boxers," she said.

"I box in dress clothes… extended briefs for jeans and shorts," he proclaimed proudly, snapping the waistline of his blue-paisley-on-white shorts with his thumbs.

Amber led him into the bathroom and turned the hot water on in the shower. She slid her robe off her shoulders, hung it on a hook on the wall, and stood fully nude in front of Wright. She did her best to stay fit, was proud of her body, and was not a woman who spent her life wishing for larger breasts. Hers were perfectly rounded and firm, beautiful ivory skin curving upward from below.

Wright's hands seemed even larger than they actually were when he put them on her arms. He lightly slid his fingertips across her chest at her collarbones, stopping briefly at her suprasternal notch, up her neck, then down her jaw line. She closed her eyes. His hands went to her breasts, his fingers cupping them from below. He'd never expected to be granted the freedom to roam Amber Duffy's body but now he had it, and he knew it would last forever. He saw steam rising toward the ceiling so he slid off his boxers, re-opened the shower door and led her in.

He tested the water with his hand, added a bit of cold, and stepped into the strong stream, her hand still in his. Amber followed and turned her back to the water at first, then she faced the spray and let it hit her forehead. She ran her fingers through her hair, as the water ran down her curved back. She made room for him to do the same. He had to lean over to get his head wet.

"You can adjust that if you need to," she said.

"That's all right. It's fine."

They began to kiss again. As they did, Amber reached for a bottle of scented, liquid soap, and, breaking the embrace, squirted a generous amount in her hand. She sat the bottle down and nodded her head at Wright.

"Have some… for me."

He lifted his hand. She put hers on top of his and turned it on its side slowly, allowing the thick liquid to run into his hand. She then rubbed her palms together, sharing her supply equally, and put them on his chest and began to rub, first to his neck and shoulders, then to his abdominals and hips, and between.

He followed her lead. She submitted, her hands venturing to the back of her head to pull her shoulder-length hair into a wet ponytail. He found when he arrived at her tiny waist that with his thumbs at her belly button, his middle fingers nearly met on the small of her back. He ran his soapy hands all over, but he did not penetrate her. He caressed her gently. She threw her head back, slapped a hand to the wall for balance, and exhaled with euphoria. Ben picked her up easily and held her at his waist, her legs wrapped around him. She began to gyrate slightly, her back naturally arched with desire.

"I don't want the first time to be in here," she whispered, her elbows on his shoulders, her fingers running through his wet hair. "Get the soap off of us."

He turned his back to the stream and let it run over his shoulders, hitting Amber in the face and chest. They were so tightly locked that a pocket of water began to form at Ben's waist. They began to kiss wildly with all the out-of-control passion two lovers could feel without actually being in the throws of lovemaking. Strands of her wet hair fell into her face. It was all he could stand. She was so beautiful. He loosened the tight seal he'd created with her body against his and the water fell to his feet. Holding her in his left hand, her wet, strong legs clinging to his waist, he turned off the water, opened the glass shower door, and stepped out. Her weight of 103 pounds was nothing for him to handle. She grabbed a towel off the hook beside her robe as Ben walked her back to her queen sized bed and laid her down. As they began to kiss again, she reached and put him into her. She'd not made love in many months, almost a year. Despite anticipating the feeling, her eyes grew wide as he slowly slid himself in, then retreated slightly, before he moved forward until his entire length was inside her.

Ben knew if he took it slow early he could last a long time. He wanted to impress her as a lover. Amber was in no hurry either. They were caught up in the rapture of experiencing each other. He was turned on by her taste, her softness, and her attitude and her beauty. He'd craved this moment for years now. She was attracted to the scent of his skin, and his large, strong, athletic body as well as his humble nature and his innocence. He was more than twice her weight. At one point, she rolled on top of him. He would never forget that vision. She turned her head to the side, eyes closed with pleasure, as her leverage gave her all of him. Her movements and her pleasure intensified. As she climaxed, she leaned back and reached for Ben's thighs.

"I want you. I want it all... in me," she said, falling forward, her face just below his jaw. She lifted her head and looked in his eyes in an instant of humor. "Give it to me, please."

"Yes, Ma'am."

He rolled her back over and after a few minutes finished with all the athleticism he could muster. His face was flushed, his youthful eyes vulnerable when he achieved his orgasm. Holding on to his shoulders tightly, Amber came a second time. They looked deeply into each other's eyes, smiling in that moment after, when nothing could be more right. After he caught his breath, he slowly pulled away and rolled to his back.

"That's the greatest thing that's ever happened to me," he said, looking over at her and reaching for her hand.

"You weren't too bad yourself," Amber responded, exhaling with laughter, and searching for the towel she'd brought with her from the shower. She grabbed a pillow.

"Here, sit up a bit," she said, placing the pillow behind him. She slid herself under his arm and laid her head on his chest. "Truly, that was fantastic. I could get used to it."

"You will."

"I want to."

"I do too," he said.

Amber rubbed his pectoral with her finger tips as the conversation waned. Neither felt a need to speak as their euphoria slowly subsided. The action of the day was taking its toll, the silence comfortable. Ben's eyes closed. He was close to nodding off.

"Oh, look, it's almost six. We should watch the news," Amber said. "Think they got Mills on?"

"Yeah, I guarantee it, if he really made it back by five o'clock."

Amber picked the remote up off the night stand.

"I don't usually watch TV in bed, unless I need to know a Black Bears score," she said. "I just have it on when I'm getting ready in the mornings or cleaning."

"From now on, if it's a game I'm in, I'll call you with the score."

"From now on, if it's a game you're in, I'll be there."

22

There were certain aspects of the investigation that Robert Mills could not share with the media, although word had spread of Coach Rosemont's shooting and Chap Roberts' arrest. The media contingency that day was 25 strong and abuzz, and beginning to connect some of the dots. Mills stepped up to the podium, set up inside the police barracks for such occasions, a drab gray wall with no backdrop behind him, with a prepared statement.

"I want to thank you all for coming. There are elements of this case that cannot be discussed because there is an ongoing investigation. Therefore, I will not be taking questions afterwards. There were actions taken today that still need to be clarified. What I can tell you is this: A local man, Jim Wheatley, was shot and killed today. An All-Points- Bulletin had been put out on Wheatley – he was wanted for the murder of Dwayne Price, the Lookout Mountain State University employee who was murdered in his home early Sunday morning. It turns out this was not a drug-related crime. Price was set up. Wheatley framed him. Any and all discussion of Price in drug activity was false. The city, county, and state police would like to apologize for that. Jim Wheatley was shot in self-defense by a Miss Amber Duffy, a local woman and a LMSU employee, who was protecting her own life and the life of LMSU student Ben Wright. Law enforcement owes a debt of gratitude to Ms. Duffy and Mr. Wright for their efforts in shedding new light on this case. In addition, Coach Sam Rosemont was shot today in an altercation. I'm told he is in stable condition and resting comfortably. That's all I have for you."

Mills stepped away from the podium as a flurry of questions sailed his way. The level of noise jumped as cameramen began breaking down their equipment hoping to speed back to their stations to edit before their 6 p.m. newscasts: "Why was Chap Roberts arrested?" "Did Roberts shoot Rosemont?" "Did Wheatley work for Chap Roberts?" "How did Wright get involved?" "How is this all related to the football program?" "When is Roberts' arraignment?" Mills didn't look back, he just kept walking quickly out of the room.

When Ben Wright heard the news about Rosemont, he sat up in bed quickly. Amber, laying against him, did so as well out of necessity. "Oh my gosh! Coach got shot? I need to call him."

The newscast that Amber and Ben watched also had clips of them being led away from the mountain trail on which Wheatley was shot. It then cut to Mills' verbal thanks from the podium. Immediately, their phones – Wright's cell, Amber's cell and home line - starting ringing.

"Should we?" Amber asked.

"I don't want to. But people could be worried."

"I guarantee somebody will call your parents. You should definitely call them."

"You're right. This is going to get crazy though," Ben said, grabbing her hand. "You know what? It'll be all right if we go through it together."

"We are," she said.

With that Amber reached for her cell phone on the night stand, and Ben rolled out of bed naked to retrieve his cell phone from his pants, neatly folded over a chair. A new chapter of their lives had begun.

Sam Rosemont also saw the news, Linda by his side, from his hospital bed. His paternal instincts for Ben Wright caused a siren to go off in his head. He reached for his cell phone and called.

Wright, who was speaking to his mother at the time of his call, felt he'd done all he could to explain the situation and ease her mind, so he used the beep of a new call as an exit excuse. "Mom, Coach is calling me, so I'd better go now."

"Wait, now Benjamin, you're sure you are ok?"

"Mom, I'm better than ok. I'll call you back tonight. I love you, bye-bye. ... Coach? How are you doing? I just heard."

"As did I, young man. I told you to stay away from that situation, didn't I?"

"Well, yes. But Wheatley followed us. We didn't have a choice. He told us, Coach. He admitted he killed Price and that Chap put him up to it."

"Did he say anything else?"

"No, not really. But he didn't think we'd be repeating it.

"I see. You're both lucky, that's for sure. Are you ok?"

"Yeah, just a cut and a couple of bruises on my face. What about you? I heard you took a bullet."

"Shattered my collar bone. I'll be alright eventually. I was lucky too, they tell me."

"That's good."

"I'm afraid I've made a mess of things though, son. That's hurting me a lot more right now. I've got to come clean. It's going to cause some damage, but your future is secure. That's the main thing. You stay on the high road and you'll be fine. I've never coached a more talented, dedicated player than you Ben."

"I appreciate that, Coach. But what can I do to help with this? Detective Mills told me about the guys getting paid."

"Nothing. Don't start any crusades for me. I'll land on my feet. You didn't know anything about the props so just say that if the NCAA asks you. That's all that matters. Where are you?"

"Uh, I'm at Amber's place right now."

"Oh, yeah... you two sparking?"

"We're past that," Wright said. He laughed nervously.

"Well, that's good. She's a great girl. Think of the story you'll have to tell your children. Look, Ben. I've got to go. I don't know if practice will be mine to hold anymore."

"What?"

"I'll be addressing the team I'm sure, later this week. But like I said, just stick to what you're doing. You'll be fine. I love you, son. It's been an honor coaching you."

"I love you too, Coach. Thank you for everything. I'll be seeing you soon though. Bye now."

Wright clicked the end button on his phone. He sat on the edge of the bed, staring off into nowhere.

Amber had finished her conversation before him, and sat quietly listening. She reached and put her hand on his shoulder. "Are you ok?"

"I hadn't thought about it before. Nothing is ever going to be the same from now on."

He looked over at Amber. He could see the caring in her eyes. She was propped up against her pillows, sitting, still naked, under the bed sheet. He turned toward her and took her hands in his.

"If I left here early, declared for the draft, would you marry me?"

Tears filled her eyes. She tried to fight them back but one spilled and ran quickly down her check. She smiled. All she could say was "Yes."

23

"Lack of Institutional Control" sounded like an innocuous term, unless you were the manager of that institution, i.e., the CEO of the University. For that soul, there was no greater insult. A college president deems his or her mind superior to most. If the complex masthead of employee function is a mirror of the president's mind, a representation of their master plan, then its failure or breakdown can be considered nothing less than a weakness of that leader's thinking. And that cuts against the grain of the president like the physical devastation of a child.

In Dr. William Everett's mind, the gray blemish in athletics was a calculated gamble, and worth the risk since he was lining his own pockets for a brighter future. Thus he suffered from no self-doubt. Smiling inwardly at his Latin skills, he remained the *Valde mens vel rector*, the great mind or leader. Still, he needed one piece of information. He didn't think that Coach Rosemont had any knowledge of his arrangement with Roberts, but he wasn't sure. Everett only wished that somehow Roberts had perished with Wheatley on that fateful day. He planned an afternoon hospital visit to chat with, and possibly dismiss, the most popular man in the county. Everett hoped he could gain the information he needed without going to Roberts. He also needed to confer with Charles Nester, though he knew his athletic director wouldn't make a move without him. It was really Nester's place to speak with Rosemont, but given their relationship and Nester's weak backbone, Everett knew Nester wouldn't object to his visiting the coach. He could offer for them to do it together, but Everett most certainly did not want

Nester to know he'd taken Roberts' payoffs through the years if Rosemont did have that nugget of knowledge. "I'll tell him he can make the announcement that Sam's fired... that'll be enough for him," Everett thought.

Since there was a mushroom cloud of despair hovering over Pineknob from what became tagged Black Tuesday by LMSU football fans – and because the Black Bears program was already making national headlines for its current 7-0 undefeated season – the NCAA came in hard and swift. Rather than the normal advance investigative team, college athletics' governing body froze all current business and sent the full whack, interviewers, investigators, judge, jury and executioner. Its president, Dr. Nicholas Peabody, even planned to fly in to announce the findings, something he rarely did unless he was assured a great deal of national exposure. His underlings booked a dozen rooms at The University Inn, and ironically, took their dinner each night at Sam Rosemont's Restaurant.

Displaying uncommon efficiency, the group flew down from Indianapolis on Wednesday morning. They were checked in and had interview schedules by the afternoon. While every LMSU staffer who would remain after the fact hoped the process wouldn't bleed into the next week, Lisa Vickers, the NCAA investigations coordinator, assured it most likely would.

Vickers, still single at 33, also doubled as Dr. Peabody's booking agent and travel scheduler. His position made him a sought-after public speaker, and while he could have raked in large sums of cash to do it, he accepted no payment other than an honorarium of first class travel and hotel accommodations. Vickers' inside track to the boss gave her an additional aura of purpose that made her rude and difficult. In her mind, she didn't

237

arrive at a destination to smooth feathers but to ruffle them. It was in an agitated state rather than the opposite that the truth typically emerged, one where friends and co-workers spilled the beans on other friends and co-workers. With the institution under investigation and already in a collective panic, Vickers' attitude often helped the house of cards to fall.

She was a tall, stoutly built brunette, a former University of Massachusetts soccer player. She wasted no time in her dealings and abhorred nonsense. In fact, colleagues who wished to have any fun on the road usually had to slip away from her to do it or display blatant disregard for her authority. Vickers' attitude was, the entire day was the NCAA's if the team was on the road working.

Sam Rosemont was an early riser. The aches and pains of his athletic career usually got him out of the bed much earlier than he cared to be. But in the hospital, despite a strange bed, the painkillers meant to offset the shock of a bullet's invasion of his body was helping him sleep well past breakfast and nearly till 10 a.m.

Linda was the first to his room on Wednesday morning, she brought coffee that they shared. When Everett arrived, Rosemont politely asked his wife to scare him up "something to nibble on before lunch."

Dr. Everett was dressed in his normal college president business attire, today a pin-striped navy blue suit, white shirt, and solid red tie. He tried to be stoic in his demeanor, but as with most people, when they got around Rosemont a little adoration came into play. Especially when the coach, even in his weakened state, greeted Everett with, "William the Conqueror, man, I must be dreaming."

"Good morning, Coach Rosemont," Everett said. "How are we feeling today?"

"Oh, I've been better. I'm ready to get back to work though."

"Looks to me like a few days off would do you good."

"I'm not going to let my butt get used to *this* bed."

Then, as though the pleasantries were for Linda's benefit as she exited, both tones became sharper. Everett sat down in one of two guest chairs at Rosemont's bed side and threw his left leg over his right knee, his hands together in his lap.

"Well, you've really got us in a bind down there Sam… you and Chap. I've got the NCAA getting off a plane. They've got their axes sharpened. I'm sure there's going to be a hail storm. What else are they going to find out?"

"Nothing. I let Chap help the props out, to give those boys a chance at a better life when no one else would. Is that so terrible?"

"Well, you know the rules better than I do Sam, but doesn't that mean you've been using illegal players? Ineligible players… in every game you've coached?"

"Not the first year."

"They'll strip us of every win, won't they? Not to mention what they'll do with us in the future."

"They'll take a few scholarships… we'll be all right."

"I'm afraid the future can't include you, Sam. The infraction was just too blatant… total disregard of the rules. You should work for the Atlanta Falcons, the way money was being tossed around. This is collegiate athletics. I'll buy out your contract, but I can't have you running the program anymore."

239

"Let me see if I can come up with another scenario," Rosemont said. He wanted to keep his cards close to the vest. "You could take the old 'first mistake' stance. Suspend me for a month, four games, the rest of the regular season, with no pay… or I'll donate it to charity. Then, if we do make it to a bowl game, I'll be back in the saddle. For that, I'll keep any information I have outside the realm of football to myself."

Everett laughed.

"What information?"

"I think we both know. I'm not as dumb as you think there, Will. I've picked up a big gem on you… so spare me any more self-righteous speeches."

"I beg your pardon?"

"Please, I'll admit it. I didn't know until yesterday. I really thought you were better than that."

"I'm afraid you are misinformed. I've - "

"You presidents have it made – house, car, food, utilities, everything fixed by maintenance, every bush and blade of grass manicured by grounds," Rosemont interrupted, grimacing as he tried with one arm to boost himself higher in his bed. "Your entertainment budget is more than my lowest assistant's salary, for Christ's sake. I'm sure you were socking away 100, 150 grand a year from your *regular* salary."

"The perks, Sam, are why one ascends to this level. Higher Ed is a labor of love and service. With this," he said, tapping the side of his head twice with his index finger, "I could be the CEO of a Fortune 500 company, pulling in millions a year."

"Wait, wait, service to who? I'll admit, you're not a bad president. But you spend a lot more time with donors than you do students."

"That's service 'to whom,' by the way," Everett said. "Fundraising is a constant. Bricks and mortar cost money."

"I'm sure some of your Board friends have your money working for you, too. But that's good… well done. I always wondered though, why wasn't Chap Roberts on your Board?"

"His business practices cut against the grain of many."

Rosemont laughed, shaking his head. "Hello, black kettle, I'm the pot. You just didn't want those worlds colliding, did you. Best to keep him at bay…"

"This is getting us nowhere, Sam. The semantics of my job is not the issue. We need to talk to Chap," Everett said, leaning in and lowering his voice. "I may get fired if I don't fire you – I think I can talk my way around that - but I most certainly will if the Chap deal comes out. Then you'll get fired by my replacement. If Chap just told you yesterday, I doubt anyone else knows. Wheatley's dead, who else would he have told?"

"You're right. I can't think of anybody. So you're willing to keep me if Chap and I keep quiet about you?" Rosemont asked, studying Everett's face hard for a betraying clue. "Looks like I've got to go make up with my best friend."

"Well, he made bail yesterday. So he's out."

"Tried to kill me on Tuesday, and he's out roaming the streets," Rosemont said, again shaking his head. "Unbelievable… You know, Dr. Everett, I'm thinking, somebody really *has* to get fired. Don't you think? Let's talk about Nester."

"All right," Everett answered thoughtfully, leaning back in his chair.

"How can you stand having that putz work for you?"

"He serves his purpose."

241

"Now would be the time to get rid of that nimrod. Nobody respects him. Do you think other athletic directors do? He's a weak link - vegetable lasagna. You're only as strong as your weakest link."

"It would give the perception that he was partially guilty," Everett said.

"Partially? *He* lost control. He had no idea what was going on in athletics. He's too worried about his next speech… or making sure he's not discovered as a fraud."

"I can see the rational. Although, he could make a lot of noise if he's fired."

"Just transfer him then. Let him keep his salary," Rosemont said. Then in his best Everett imitation, stately and dignified, " 'Charles, I don't want to lose you, son. How does special assistant to the Provost sound?' Or, stick him in the alumni house. Let him be your star fundraiser."

"I like it. If he doesn't like the transfer, he can leave."

"It'll go a long way with the NCAA too," Rosemont said.

Outside Rosemont's door, Max Milovich, had hoped to say hello to his colorful former colleague, since they were sharing a hospital. As a former player, he and Rosemont had gotten along well until Roberts and Wheatley interceded. Milovich quietly turned his wheelchair, and did his best to get back down the hall to his own room without being detected.

24

The NCAA's blanket investigation of LMSU began Thursday morning. Coach Rosemont had called Janet Randolph and the assistant coaches that knew props were being paid and instructed them to serve him up as the guilty party -- that the Black Bears were going to "fess up and take their medicine." Discharged later that day, he even made his own appearance.

Amazingly, the only assistants that had any knowledge of the pay arrangement were Billy Reed as Rosemont's program confidant, Nick Blanch, who doubled as recruiting coordinator, and Stacks Osborne, the strength coach, even though props would come from all the assistant coaches' recruiting areas. The reason the majority of coaches were unaware was because a player's efforts to become academically eligible if they weren't already would normally take them into the summer before they were to first report. By that time, Rosemont, Reed, or Blanch would have taken over the recruiting process, determine whether or not the player was worth the risk -- and could be discreet. Talent-wise, they were always players touted nationally as top recruits, tremendously gifted athletes that big-time programs wanted but ultimately would not wait on if the athlete was struggling academically. LMSU's community college served as an on-campus prep school, and that gave Rosemont an upper hand when a recruit's options dried up before his eyes. The staff would keep the player on the line, then either Blanch, Reed, or Rosemont would ultimately negotiate the secret deal with the player and parents.

"That's how it worked," Rosemont said, looking across his desk at Lisa Vickers, who studied the coach's body language for signs as he spoke. Mostly she saw pain, though he attempted to cover it with insincere humility.

"Once they were on campus here, we'd gather them and one of Chap Roberts' guys would pick them up, take them to a business, drop them off, pick them up a half hour later. They got paid on Mondays."

"Very neat, Coach Rosemont," Vickers said. "And I understand from Janet Randolph the now-departed Jim Wheatley would deliver Chap Roberts' cash payments. How did you come up with the per hour amount?"

"Does it really matter? Lot of water under the bridge since that conversation, honey. The equation was set up so these young men could survive... eat and pay their rent and utilities. And it was a lot less than the scholarship value of room and board."

"Is that something you're qualified to determine... while blatantly disregarding the rules?"

"I was just trying to give these kids a chance. You know, college isn't easy. From my experience the players that don't make the grades usually end up on the street. And I don't mean the streets of Amherst."

"You flatter me, Coach."

"We all have reputations, darling... the good, the bad, and the ugly."

Vickers' face turned a slight shade of red. Her features then went flat as she weighed Rosemont's comment. She cursed herself for letting down her guard. Reading the bios of top NCAA personnel was just a few clicks away on the internet. Having weathered the slap of the insult, she cleared her throat.

"So setting up the illegal payments was about the players' welfare and not your program getting blue-chippers that wouldn't have given LMSU any consideration early on?"

"That's right, though I wouldn't say no consideration. This program has come a long way and it's not been because of the props... though they have done their part as well, once eligible."

"Everybody has been forthright about this issue, Coach, and I appreciate that. But is there anything else that needs to be reported? This is your one opportunity to come completely clean. If I find anything else later – academic fraud for example – I... the NCAA, won't be so understanding."

"Well, you're about as subtle as a sledge hammer," Rosemont said. He fumed internally, pissed he had to deal with "this Vickers" in the first place. "But I like that. No, we don't take tests for our kids, we don't strong-arm professors, we don't pay prostitutes to take care of recruits. If someone's getting laid, they had it coming, if you'll pardon the pun."

"I *will not* pardon that, sir, though the statement is true enough about this program," Vickers said, standing quickly and jamming her notebook, pen, and – after turning it to the "off" position -- a tiny tape recorder into a soft leather briefcase. "Good luck to you, though that won't help much now."

Vickers stormed out of Rosemont's office, slamming the door behind her. Seconds later Janet Randolph entered to find Rosemont, reading glasses on his nose, examining the pill bottles on his desk.

"Are you all right Sam?"

"Oh, yeah," he said, putting one bottle in his left hand, still in its sling, and twisting off the top with his right."

"She was steaming. Aren't you worried about what she'll do?"

"She was going to do the same thing either way," he said, popping two pills into his mouth. "I might as well let her know how I feel about it."

The NCAA's investigative team was all over Lookout Mountain State University -- all over Pineknob - for those two days. They were, if anything, thorough, talking with not only staff, professors, tutors, players, trainers, landlords from which props rented homes. Through the information provided by Amber Duffy, Ben Wright, Jane Haynes, Janet Randolph, Bruce Fellows, Max Milovich, the visitors were able to put together the steps of Dwayne Price's investigation. Vickers even spent time with Detective Mills, comparing notes.

Milovich was interviewed by Vickers, whom he'd met once before at a NCAA Compliance Seminar, and a male underling named Steve Kapp in the hospital, in the lobby of the third floor, just down from his room. Vickers wanted Kapp there to observe because she was hell bent, despite his weakened condition, to ostracize Milovich for abandoning his oath to the NCAA and taking the job at Ridgecrest Insurance.

"You understand that there were threats to my family, Lisa?" Milovich asked. "It may have been wrong – I may have acted incorrectly -- but at the time I was under extraordinary pressure and feeling all alone."

"But later on..."

"Maybe I should have contacted your office after I was out, sure. Once I started my job I never saw Jim Wheatley again and that was a relief. Ten months later Ben walks into my office and it started all over again."

"The threats?"

"Well, yeah."

"But you were on their team."

"Wheatley – which always meant Roberts -- didn't want any information passed along."

"About their criminal activities?"

"About the past, mainly. I obviously inferred that Price's murder wasn't drug related."

"But you kept quiet. You've heard of withholding evidence?"

"No, I called Mills… anonymously. But that can be proved."

"Let's back up. How did you find out props were being paid when you were the compliance director?"

"I had had my suspicions… this is a small town, you see things, purchases, high-dollar meals, expensive jackets. Then last season, three props moved into a house that rented for about $1,400 a month at the time. I knew the players' backgrounds. There was no way they could afford the place, not and pay utilities and eat. So I started sniffing around."

"How did you confirm?"

"I called their landlord. He said he stopped by for the September rent and the boys paid in cash. So at the end of the month I started watching them as best I could, hanging out near the facilities building more than normal. I watched two of them walk out of Janet's office, turn the corner, and start counting out the cash."

"And then?"

"It was just then that I bumped into Coach Reed. He saw what I was seeing," Milovich said, looking out the window at a beautiful fall day on the mountain. "You know, those three, they just came to party for a semester. They didn't even try to study. It really is a great thing when a prop gets eligible and plays."

"I'm sure it is," said Vickers.

"Anyway, it was the next day that Wheatley came around for the first time."

"Chap didn't offer you the job immediately?"

"Wheatley was meant to intimidate first, that made the job seem like a great compromise."

"Did you get yourself a signing bonus for a payoff?"

"I resent that," Milovich said, though he had been given the shiny new Chevrolet Trail Blazer. As the interview progressed, he pondered whether or not to mention the conversation he'd overheard the previous day between Sam Rosemont and William
Everett. Vickers' attitude helped him make up his mind… he'd save it for a later date. "I'm tired now. That's all I have for you. Thanks for stopping by."

"That's fine. I think we've got the picture," Vickers said.

Ben Wright was at home again Thursday, back on the practice field. Though he normally wouldn't, he allowed himself a bit of gregarious behavior with his friends. Between it being an off week, the unexpected surprise of Coach Rosemont sitting on the sideline on a bar stool, and the fact that he was in love, he couldn't help himself. Though one side of his face was bruised around the healing cut, his arm was fresh and from his inverted-release, the ball was snapping off his fingertips. He'd blistered the first team defense for five touchdown passes in a short scrimmage. All the players were excited. Banter flowed as wildly as the Tennessee River.

"Come on 12, give me a chance to score," running back Steve Lake said.

Safety Buster Cantley screamed "Enough, enough, give us a break coach… we ain't gonna have no confidence next week."

"Ben's burnin' them. Burning Ben…" Little Murvin Rivers added, "No, give me one more route, Coach, I'm having a blast."

Even Danny Smith, prone only to talking smack to defenders, got into it, using the name pun. "He's Ben Wright, Ben Wright on *every* throw… *every* throw."

Wright asked Reed, the special teams coach for field goals, if he could kick one. Reed looked over at Rosemont, who shook his head affirmatively. Wright, who was also the backup holder in case a fake was ever needed or for some reason second-string QB Lyle Loftus – the holder - ever went down -- lined up his kick. Loftus called for the snap, put it down, and Wright, who had never kicked, not only shanked it, he kicked so high on the ball he caused a low trajectory missile - directly into a lineman's butt.

The team roared with laughter. Wright, again uncharacteristically, turned and limped away from the spot as though he had a physical disorder.

"Ok, ok, that's enough for today. Gather around here men," Rosemont shouted, as the team circled him, removed their helmets, and took a knee. "I know you all have heard a lot of stuff over the last few days and I'm here to tell you that some of it is true. I screwed up. I'd rather you heard it from me… We don't know exactly what is going to happen as far as the NCAA is concerned, but it could be bad. We should know by this time tomorrow. I want you to know something though. The rule that I broke has no bearing on your success on the football field. You're undefeated – and I guarantee one of the top five teams in this country. What you have achieved as a team has been through hard work and dedication. Whatever happens to me or this program, I want you to please remember that. You can achieve the same success in life by applying the principles that you have here. I'm proud of all of you. Ok, shorts and hats tomorrow and Saturday, but get your lifting in. All right... groups. Give me one... 1-2-3 BLACK BEARS!"

Many players approached Rosemont, touched his back, shook his hand, offered encouragement, before jogging off to meet with their respective position coaches. Then Rosemont found himself alone at the 35-yard line. He turned and walked towards the facilities building thinking, "I've got to find Chap."

25

The autopsy performed on Jim Wheatley's body provided little more information than was already known. Shot in the head by his own registered gun, his lung tissue dark brown from cigarette smoke, near-cirrhosis of the liver from drinking a steady diet of whiskey. Prints were taken from his corpse to have on file, though no other prints were found in Dwayne Price's home. The thought being, some old crimes might be solved with the prints in the system. Wheatley's body was then sent to Jenkins Funeral Home for cremation. The state of Tennessee used the seized money from Wheatley's wrecked Corvette for payment, the rest went into the policemen's widow's fund.

It was at the funeral home that Rosemont found Chap Roberts. Rosemont had intended to drive to Chap's three bars as his first effort to find him. He didn't want to break phone silence for a meeting, especially since there would be a record of the call. He wanted to surprise Chap too, to see how he reacted. He was on his way to The Lookout when he spotted Chap's car outside Jenkins'. Rosemont backed his car into the spot beside Roberts' Mercedes, which was parked perpendicularly against the drive through awning of the majestic, white-painted brick building, driver-side to driver-side, and waited.

He was hesitant to turn up the radio as he waited. He didn't want to hear bad news about his program, but he flipped his station to Sports Radio 790 "The Zone" out of Atlanta. Rosemont was relieved. He heard only what he considered mindless chatter about Saturday's games. Top of the order was the home squad Georgia Tech, which was hosting North Carolina State. "Everybody thinks they're a football coach," he said out loud, leaning back against his seat's head rest after adjusting his sling a bit. "I'd play Georgia Tech in this parking lot for fifty bucks."

Rosemont was dozing ten minutes later, still physically exhausted from his body's ongoing recovery. Roberts' footsteps awoke him. Roberts, dressed business casual in charcoal slacks and a gray tweed jacket, the bruises on his face just reaching their full potential, was carrying a plain, silver urn in his left arm as he came round his car digging for his keys with his right hand. He was oblivious to Rosemont's car.

"What the hell are you going to do with that?" Rosemont said in a low-shout, startling Roberts so much he nearly fumbled the urn.

"Damn it, Sam!" Roberts said, truly mad but unable to withhold a bit of laughter as well, adrenaline suddenly searing through his veins, his heart pounding in his chest. "You scared the shit out of me."

"Is that Wheatley?"

"No, it's my pet dog Rudolph."

"It's a good thing that's nickel plated, or he wouldn't have made it out of the parking lot. What are you going to do, flush him down the toilet?"

"What do you want?" Roberts said. His eyes scanned the area for anything or anybody unusual. "We can't talk."

"Why not? Cause you tried to blow me away? Seems like my choice... and you *obviously* don't obey the law. Why don't you stick that thing in your trunk and get in. I've got something I want to tell you."

Roberts hesitated at first, perused the area once more, then did just as Rosemont asked. As Rosemont pulled out of the parking lot haphazardly with one hand on the wheel, Roberts quickly buckled his seatbelt.

"You wouldn't try to shoot me out the windshield would you?"

Rosemont just looked ahead and continued to drive, ignoring the comment. "So what're your plans... prison?"

"I'm not seeing it."

"Really? You must be smoking something."

"I don't think anybody can pin the Price thing on me," Roberts said. "You know how volatile Jim was... in fact, you could help me there. You could help me with attempted murder as well."

"Well, I might... if you're willing to play ball. Let's cut the sugarcoatin' shit. Here's the deal. Everett is willing to let me stay on if we can keep him from getting fired."

"You mean if I don't tell anybody that that jerk's hands are so far down in my pockets he's scratching my knees? Why should I do that for either of you?"

"Well, let's think about it a little bit. You're going to do some time... maybe not much. If I'm still the coach, a few years from now we'll be right back where we were, except for paying the props. You'll be up there eatin' biscuits and bangin' chicks while I'm getting my team ready... still the toast of the town, still doing 100-dollar handshakes with my stars. People have short memories. It'll all blend together like the seasons."

Roberts' scowl melted away, the downturned corners of his mouth rose.

"Here's a bonus. Nester's out as AD."

"Hmm. Early Christmas for you," Roberts said. "You guys *are* starting to use your heads."

"Look, I don't know why you had to have those pictures taken. You and I are on the same side, man. Then when you tried to use them on me, I went a little crazy. But we go way too far back to let this end our friendship."

"Well, I certainly would have regretted it if I'd gotten off a good shot and you'd died... my profits would have turned to shit if it got out that I'd killed Sam Rosemont."

Rosemont looked at Roberts, weighing his comment, sincerity versus humor. Roberts was staring straight ahead, still nervous over Rosemont's one-handed driving. He looked over and smiled. Both men laughed.

"So how's the shoulder anyway, any permanent damage?"

"You ass... there shouldn't be."

"What about with Linda? Did you come clean?"

"That woman is a saint. It's the hardest thing I've ever done. We're going to be ok though, thank goodness."

"All right, final question, then get me back to my car. I've got important business elsewhere. What about the NCAA?"

"They've got this tightly, tightly-wound woman named Lisa Vickers leading their team. I think we're gonna burn. She played soccer at UMass... I pissed her off pretty good."

"Is she gay?"

"No, I don't think so. Indifferent, most likely. She's a Peabody warrior."

When 5 o'clock came, Amber Duffy was relieved. She tried focusing on her work most of the day, only to find herself drifting back to the events of the past couple of days. Ben Wright had stayed over Tuesday evening. A Chinese restaurant was about all that would deliver in Pineknob other than pizza joints, so they had some egg rolls, fried rice, and hunan chicken with mixed vegetables sent over. They ate downstairs, wrapped in blankets, made love for a second time, and fell asleep in each other's arms.

Amber dropped him off at his dorm the next morning as she went to work, with plans for him to make it over again that night.

"I may need you mid-day if I can get a rent-a-car. It depends on what I can find out from the insurance agency. Or I could just get a buddy to run me," he said, pushing opening his passenger-side door.

"Now, you know I'd be glad to," Amber said. "Just call my cell. We can have lunch if you want."

"I can do that today," Wright said. "Normally I take my lunch and watch film. That'll be great. It'll have to be a quickie though."

"Are you talking dirty to me?"

"Now, there's an idea worth pursuing… what's your stance on library loving? Little fantasy of mine…" he said, pulling his door back to a closed position. "With you."

"We'll have to think about that one. It would be my last day at work if we got caught."

"Ah, that place is a four-floor maze. Once you got lost in there you'd have all the time you needed. Just wear a skirt."

"You're giving me twinges just talking about it."

"Should we go back home?"

"You stay focused," Amber said. A seductive smile followed. "We've got our whole lives in front of us."

"I can't help it. I don't want to be away from you," he said, finally stepping out of her vehicle. "I'll call you."

Later, after his efforts to get a rent-a-car had fallen through, the couple had lunch in the St. Elmo's district of Chattanooga at Blacksmith's Bistro and Bar. They sat outside on sunny afternoon – far removed from campus -- and watched the Incline Railroad go up and down the mountain. Amber nibbled on a salad while Wright devoured a Blacksmith Burger, homemade fries, and a bowl of gumbo.

"I don't guess I really need a car, if you'll give me a lift now and then," he said.

"Why don't you bring a few things over tonight… some lounging clothes, some clothes for class, a toothbrush, whatever else you need, just to have *in case* you stay over."

"Oh, if you say I can, I'm staying over," he said, with a boyish grin.

That evening, he studied at her dining room table while she left to work out and pick up some groceries, for a light, late dinner. She walked in and their eyes met. She walked to him, carrying four plastic bags of groceries. She bent slightly, and kissed him passionately. Both their hearts soared. She walked towards her kitchen and stopped. "Are you getting hungry?"

"You know I'm always hungry."

"Eventually, you're going to have to start eating more sensibly."

The enthusiasm of that kiss spoke volumes, she thought, and it warmed her as she walked from her office on that cold, late October, early Thursday evening. The sun was just beginning to set though it was only fifteen minutes after five. Thinking of Ben that morning, she'd parked in an area by the football stadium, closer to the dorms, and she'd given him the spare key to her car just in case he needed to run somewhere or wanted to put some more "overnight items" inside.

As she approached the facilities building she could see Ben, walking up the ramp that led to the parking area with a reporter – ever accommodating she thought. The most convenient locker room access was at field level. As football players often do, he carried his shoulder pads -- with his practice jersey still properly affixed -- by the face mask of his helmet, which was stuck through the head opening in the pads. The T-shirt he wore underneath was now exposed and drenched with sweat, though it wasn't yet cold enough for steam to rise off the wet garment or his body. With his other hand he gestured. The two were obviously in deep conversation about defensive schemes or something related to passing choices. The reporter still had a tape recorder on, and had it stuck out ahead of the QB as they walked. Ben extended his hand into the horizon as though reading the safety when Amber entered his sight line.

"Hey," he said loudly, and smiled. Michael Kelly looked up and noticed Amber for the first time. The trio reached the summit of the ramp simultaneously. "How are you doing?" Ben said, reaching and rubbing Amber's arm with the palm of his hand.

"Oh, I'm good," She smiled at the stranger.

"Amber this is Michael Kelly, of the *Register*.

"Hi, Amber, nice to meet you."

"Likewise," she said. "Ben, you must be freezing."

"Starting to be, I was hot when we finished," he said.

"Oh, Amber Duffy, I just made the connection, I'm sorry," Kelly said. "You're the hero of the week... yes?"

"I don't know about that. We had some excitement."

"Yeah, that must have been something. Are you two... dating?"

"Engaged," Ben said, glancing at Amber. She returned the look with a what-are-you-thinking glare. "Though not for publication."

"Pre-engaged," Amber added.

257

"Oh, wow, congratulations," Kelly said, sincerely. "I'd love to do a feature on you two, I'm sure that readers would eat it up. I mean, once this NCAA thing is over..."

"And the trial too, I'd say," Amber said. "We might be old news by then."

"I doubt it," Kelly said.

"Well, maybe. We'll have to talk about it."

"Mike's the best on this beat," Wright said, looking at Amber. "I trust him like family."

"Oh, yeah? You've got an endorsement there," Amber said. "We'll see about the story then."

"Ok, well think about it," Kelly said. "It's great to meet you, Amber. Ben, I'll talk with you next week. Oh, actually, if I could get a reaction from you tomorrow evening if it comes down that would be great."

"That's fine. Just call my cell."

"Ok, thanks."

As Kelly walked away, Amber and Wright shared a quick kiss. "Are you coming with me?" she asked.

"Yes. If it's ok. Did I put you off there?"

"Well, that's just the first time it's been thrust out there... and to a sportswriter. That could be about as public as it gets. We should talk about it."

"I agree. Can you give me 10 minutes? Come inside and wait upstairs here. Everyone's pretty much gone except the coaches."

In the hallway of the facilities building, a place she'd been many times before in official capacity from the Sports Information Office, she walked slowly, half daydreaming, looking at the team photos from

258

yesteryear. She noticed Max Milovich in one, his hair down to his shoulders, and remembered that she'd learned of his fate that day, and that she should tell Ben. Next in line on the walls were the framed jerseys of players that had gone on to the NFL. Other than the décor, the place felt like a morgue, cold, with a lot of open air, brick, and glass. All the coaches were back in their offices working. She thought about Ben, and their future. His enthusiasm with Michael Kelly was understandable, and she did want to marry him. But they hadn't even told their parents or friends, hadn't gone on a real date. Right now the story could be construed as an older woman seducing a college student... a LMSU employee. She laughed.... older woman. She wasn't 29 yet. She could still pass for 22, 24 for sure. It was just the perception of their love – their affair - that she worried about. It was certainly too soon to go public. If he didn't go pro and came back for his senior year, she should definitely find another job. That wouldn't be a problem.

Wright re-emerged from the downstairs locker room showered and dressed. They kissed again, and walked out of the building, arm-in-arm, into the Tennessee night.

"I meant to tell you what I heard about Max," Amber said. "Apparently Wheatley cut his break line and he had a bad wreck coming off the mountain."

"Oh, wow. He's ok though?"

"Pretty beat up, I heard."

"We should go see him."

About the time the couple reached Amber's condo, a Chap Roberts-paid executive, Aldric Prideaux, walked into the bar at the University Inn, dressed to the nines in grayish-blue Louis Vuitton. He was a native of France, brought on board at Ridgecrest to develop international commercial insurance business. A former professional tennis player that flirted with World Tennis Federation's top 25 status, he was 35 with dark hair and eyes, tan, chiseled features, with a cleft chin that was enhanced by his perpetual 5 o'clock shadow. At 6-foot-5 he had a serve that perplexed his opponents but his backhand became his Achilles heel as he attempted to rise through the ranks. He still had the cutting physic of a man who trained fifty hours a week for his sport.

Roberts had met him through Aldric's mother at the French Open, a tournament for which the player had always set his sights but never finished better than the round of 16. Roberts had a fling with Aldric's mother in Paris. After a few awkward seconds, the two men recognized immediately that they had at least one common trait: a need for women. Not perpetual, everlasting love, but the next conquest. In that regard, Aldric was still at the top of his game. Roberts thought it would be interesting – just for laughs -- to send his newest vice president down to the University Inn with an agenda that included Lisa Vickers and sunrise in Paris.

Prideaux sat at the curved end of the bar at the University Inn, which was adjacent to the hotel's restaurant. He was turned partially towards the tables in the bar, only two of which were filled. The first table sat a middle-aged couple having dinner, the second a group obviously working, traveling, and now celebrating – if you could call it that -- together. Their interviews completed, summarized, and shared among their team, Vickers broke down and called for a round of drinks. Her encounter with Rosemont had her feeling vilified, the impending verdict, which was maximum severity, vindicated. She was in the mood for a drink. Their waitress was apparently

260

off delivering food in the restaurant, so Vickers approached the bar to order a second round.

"It seems you and your friends are celebrating, yes?" Prideaux said, lifting his glass. "Cheers."

"Oh, thank you," she said. "But I have nothing to drink."

"Well, our friend here can fix that. Not to be rude to your colleagues, but would you care to have one with me? My treat."

"Oh, I don't know."

"Please, I'm having just one or two more while I wait for my taxi."

"Send those to the table, please," Vickers said, taking her neat Martini from the bartender's tray. "I'll have one with you."

Sliding from his bar stool he helped her on to hers, the gesture an actual ploy to get inside her personal space and to show his height, which was deceiving while he sat. Because of his height, one of his pickup techniques through time was to identify the tallest girl in a bar and ask her to dance or to share a drink. He knew that 6-foot women don't often get hit on by insecure, 5-foot-10 males.

Vickers willingly craned her neck to take in his stature.

"I am honored," he said, picking up his glass and tapping hers. "Please, what are you called?"

"My name is Lisa. And yours?"

"I'm Aldric. Aldric Prideaux."

"Oh. Are you… French?"

"I am. But please, let's talk about you. Your friends and you, what are you celebrating?"

"We're not too popular. We're from the NCAA," she said. "Like getting a visit from the grim reaper."

261

"I'm familiar with the organization but not the reason for your visit," Aldric said.

"You're from out-of-town?"

"Heading home now, actually."

"Where?"

"I plan to be in downtown Paris for breakfast."

"Wow. That sounds wonderful," she said. She took two enthusiastic sips of her drink.

"May I?" he asked, motioning to the bartender.

"I suppose," she said, though she was beginning to feel the first one and a half. "Thanks."

"Have you been to Paris?"

"Not yet."

"Do not wait too long. And take that special someone..."

"That may cause the wait."

"A woman as strikingly beautiful as you? I don't believe it."

"It's true," Vickers said, looking into her drink, and then at him, flattered by his remark. "Are you married?"

"I don't believe in it."

"I'm not sure I do either."

"So why no man... your work? What are you doing here?"

"Dissecting a local football program for rules violations."

"And you travel around doing this all the time?"

"Pretty much."

"I will say no more about it."

"Why not?"

"Aghh. No. I don't want to offend."

"Please."

"This," he said, motioning, palm up, with one hand at her, down her body, then over to her colleagues, "is a tragedy. "I guess you to be near trente ans... 30 years old. You should be joyous... partying and taking lovers, seeing the sun rise with new people. Not be this rules watchdog. Did I tell you my business?"

"No."

"That's because it's *only* my business. I do not let it rule my life or what I want to do. I do enjoy the travel it allows, but even then, I work very little and experience much. I was up on the mountain top earlier and was told I saw into seven U.S. states. What beauty!"

They both took sips of their drinks. Aldric drained his, glanced at his watch, and motioned for another. He knew the flight schedules even if he didn't actually have a ticket. Vickers was in deep thought. "Have you been to the mountain top my dear? Any mountain top... lately?"

She looked at him sadly, just barely shaking her head no. "I haven't."

"You need to go there," he said, seductively stressing the word need.

"I do have unmet needs," she said, looking up at him again.

She was vulnerable. She would take him to her room right now. He could make love to her, but that would spoil the agenda Chap Roberts prescribed: "Get her out of town, or drive her crazy." He was becoming aroused as well - he could feel her opening up - but he had other friends around town he could make love to later. He leaned closer to her. He thought she would accept a kiss if he offered, but he didn't want to spoil the moment... or her yearning. He didn't want her guard to go back up with her colleagues twenty feet away, though they were happy to be rid of her.

"What will you do about it?"

"You're leaving now? You can't stay awhile?"

"I could push my departure a bit and tighten it at the airport, but you would only regret that encounter."

"No, I don't think I would," she said, touching his pant leg just above the knee, taking notice of the contrast from his cap to his massive quadriceps underneath. "You're flying to Paris tonight?"

"I call it my historic figure flight: Kennedy to de Gaulle. Would you like to come along? The plane is never full."

She laughed. She was much more attractive when she smiled, though she didn't do it much. "I would love to come along... "

"I could show you Paris, be your tour guide. I don't have to leave again until next Wednesday."

"I am so tempted, but it is impossible," she said. "I have important business here tomorrow. I don't even have a passport."

"Oh, there are ways around that. You don't look so threatening."

"It is out of the question," Vickers said, with true regret. "I wish we'd met yesterday."

"It is unfortunate," Aldric said. "Do you have a business card? I'll email you next time I am in America. You will then have mine in case you come to Paris. Perhaps our paths will cross again."

Vickers gave him her card, he took it, and put cash on the bar for their drinks.

"It has been a pleasure, Miss Lisa, he said, leaning in and kissing her cheek."

"Good-bye," she said, and she watched him walk away. He extended the handle of an empty travel suitcase in the hall, and walked away. Vickers signed for the first two rounds of drinks and walked out of the bar without acknowledging her team.

Back in her room, feeling a little drunk, she showered and dried herself partially, then stood before the room's mirror, naked. She still had an athlete's body, though her tone had begun to soften. She turned down her bed and lay on the clean, white sheets. She felt so alone and empty. Looking at the ceiling, the fingertips of her right hand softly glided over her lower abdomen and then to her thigh. Aldric's handsome face was on her mind. She considered masturbating. Instead, she began to cry, wondering when a man would come into her life, yet knowing her lifestyle hardly allowed it. She was devoted to Peabody, but he was hopelessly married. She refused to date a colleague but those were the only men with which she interacted, other than men from her cases. She pulled up the cover and rolled on to her side. It was 8:15 p.m.

At 9 o'clock a "courier" dressed in brown but with no UPS markings delivered a small box addressed to Rosemont to the main office in the facilities building. Billy Reed intercepted the young man in hallway and signed for the package, recognizing him as a Chap Roberts employee. Reed brought the box into Rosemont, who put a sharp letter-opener to the tape. It was a pre-paid cell phone. Within seconds it rang. The ringtone was "The Victors."

"You know I hate Michigan," Rosemont said, as he answered the phone. Across, the desk, Reed was laughing.

"Thought it was a good idea for you to have this in case we need to talk," Roberts said. "This is a throwaway for me as well. Anyway, I've got one thing to share right now."

"What's that?"

"I sent my stud Aldric down to the hotel to try and entice Miss Vickers to fly off to Paris with him."

"What? Why?"

"Just for the hell of it... fly in the ointment... and to see if he's as good as me," Roberts said. "I couldn't do it with my face looking like it does. Plus, Betsy was working. Anyway, I thought if she went, at least it would cause a snag or two for those bastards."

"You're sick. What happened?"

"I'd call it a success. She didn't go with him, but she asked him to stay. He had her squirming in her skirt when he left to catch his 'pseudo' plane."

"How's that going to help us?"

"It's not. But, you know, men get shot down in hotel bars all the time – I do - and have to go back to the room with nothing but a woody for company. If a woman wants it, she gets it. I hope this girl is up all night."

"That's just mean, Chap."

"You think she's going to be nice tomorrow?"

"You're right. Good work."

26

Chap Roberts case had both sides of the judicial system – Assistant District Attorney Luke Rinehart and Defense Attorney Steve Jackson – scurrying for information. Rinehart had been hard at work for days learning all he could about Roberts' sometimes sadistic methods of doing business.

The black and white glossies made one fact certain: Chap Roberts was perfectly willing to bend a law or two in the name of business expansion. The pictures at the Rosemont crime scene hadn't vacated Rinehart's desk or his imagination, so he put out feelers to a dozen or so former business owners Roberts had bought out. Sure enough, three times out of twelve, Roberts had used a gentle persuader, photos taken while the target was having relations in an unplanned, non-spousal encounter, to nudge that person to sell. Roberts paid fair money for the businesses. It was only after the deal was closed that the naïve seller realized the sex had been set up by Roberts. By then the recipient was living the good life, too humiliated to seek retribution. And of course they'd still been unfaithful to their respective spouses, no matter the circumstances of the encounter. Blackmail, though not officially practiced by Roberts, was always a phone call away.

That wasn't the only chink in Roberts' armor. Rinehart had found Milovich as well, and Max was willing to clear the air. He assured Rinehart that Jim Wheatley was not acting independently of Roberts in the case of Dwayne Price. In his personal history with Wheatley, he never did.

"Do you have any proof?" Rinehart asked.

"You mean like a taped conversation? No," Milovich said, bandaged and bruised in his hospital bed. "But I'll give you an example from Wheatley's return to my life. When Ben Wright came to visit me the other day, Wheatley showed up an hour later to intimidate me. The only way he got that call was from Chap."

There was nothing iron-clad, but Milovich's first-hand experience, combined with what Ben Wright and Amber Duffy said they were told by Wheatley, a case was certainly building, Rinehart thought.

"I'll give you another lead," Milovich continued. "Wheeled down to say hi to Sam Rosemont, who do I hear chatting it up but Sam and William Everett. The implication I heard was that Chap was paying Everett off for his fleecing. Also, wait and see if Charles Nester doesn't go down as the fall guy in all of this."

Rinehart also got a complete picture from Detective Mills on what went down, and the amount of cash in Wheatley's car when he was shot. Wheatley certainly lacked the conscience to refrain from wrongdoing, but much of what he did took financial backing. It was clear that Roberts was the bank. It was also revealed that Roberts' bars constituted at least three-fifths of the illegal gambling in the area. Sticking Roberts with tax evasion and racketeering seemed weak, but hey, Rinehart thought, "It was good enough for Al Capone."

Steve Jackson had a come-to-Jesus meeting with Roberts that morning concerning the case, and the defense attorney was preparing for the old courtroom sidestep. Roberts gave Jackson a greatest hits list of what to expect in his moral assassination, from paying the Props right on down the line.

"Listen, give me the weekend to think about this," Jackson told Roberts. "We have a pre-trial meeting and disclosure update with Judge Buffington Monday. I may have to come see you again on Sunday."

"Do what you have to. But remember, please, I'm not built for serving time. Life's too short. So if you need more help, by all means get it. Or let me get it for you. This is not the time to skimp. Besides, Sam's on our side now."

"It really doesn't matter, Chap. Your malicious wounding was within an inch or two of a willful homicide. And by having the gun on you, they could have argued it was premeditated. You're just lucky you missed his heart."

The NCAA's mid-Friday-afternoon press conference and release of its findings on the Lookout Mountain State University football program left its fans so thoroughly disappointed they walked out of their businesses, discussing the violations with each other in the streets. Live coverage by the local affiliates of the major television stations showed fans in the streets discussing their remorse and showing their solidarity.

For some closer to the program, there was outrage. Coach Sam Rosemont boiled over when he heard the NCAA sentence, which came from Dr. Nicholas Peabody himself in an oracle befitting a 16th century Lutheran minister. He was even dressed in black.

"All former partial qualifiers still in the Black Bears program must repay immediately the funds allocated by booster Chap Roberts to retain eligibility," Peabody said.

He continued with the major violations, the dreaded "lack of institutional control" and the rest, like they were bullets of a power point presentation on eternal damnation rather than the critical maiming of a football program.

- Every LMSU game in which a former partial qualifier participated must be vacated… now considered a forfeit.
- Eight full scholarships per year will be forfeited for four years from the LMSU football program.
- LMSU will not be eligible to compete for Southwest Conference championships for four years.
- LMSU will not be eligible to compete in bowl games for four years.
- LMSU will remain on probation for three years after it returns to regular status.
- No monies of any kind may be accepted by this athletics program from booster Chap Roberts for three years. He in turn is banned from attending LMSU athletic and booster events for the same period. The institution is to do no business with a Chap Roberts-owned entity.

"Don't punish the kids," Rosemont shouted, as soon as he, Peabody, Everett, Nester, and Vickers were behind the closed doors of his office. "There's no way they can afford to pay that money back now. At least let them try and earn it over the summer… please."

"Paying back the money, Coach Rosemont, is the only way they can reverse the unfair advantage you afforded them," Peabody said, stoically. "If it were not the middle of a season, I could grant them some time. The only alternative would be to sit the underclassmen out of your remaining games, then they could have the extra time. I'll allow that. Your seniors would have but the one option. I'm sorry it-"

"You're not sorry about anything," Rosemont said, "so don't say it. There's so much illegal shit going on out there constantly. Are you that blind? And taking eight scholarships is way out of line. We might as well drop back to I-AA. It'll be like starting over."

"I guess we'll get to see how good a coach you really are," Vickers said, interrupting. "Frankly, I don't know how you've retained employment. But it's interesting to hear you say please now."

"I didn't say it to *you*," Rosemont said. "But I heard you said it last night."

The card deck of her thought process shuffled quickly, as all eyes centered on her, especially Peabody's. Her temperature began to rise. Her neck and face became red hot, her hands fidgeted at her coat pocket. When she comprehended his meaning, a hurt look came over her face. Rosemont's sexual implication was greater than the actual encounter with Aldric Prideaux. It was only Rosemont that interpreted her willingness to take the man to her room equating to a "please." For the others, not knowing what was happening was far more sinister, far more elicit. But mainly, despite taking the major hits, he just wanted to piss her off one more time.

"What was the point of that?" Vickers said. She stormed out of the room.

"I'm inclined to agree with her about employment, Dr. Everett," Peabody said, when the door shut.

"It was all one big mistake, wasn't it ... one misjudgment? That's our stance. And it's Sam's first one," Everett said. Then, glancing at Nester, "We've already informed you of our employment changes."

271

"Spin it how you want. But you know he knew exactly what he was doing the entire time... nine years. It's more a crime than a violation," said Peabody. "I will admit it seems Coach Rosemont wants the players to get their degrees. But he should be made an example of for the blatant disregard of the rules. Had you fired him, we may have been able to go a little lighter on the program."

"We'll roll with the punches," Everett said. "Thank you for your time, Dr. Peabody."

Rosemont was impressed by Everett's blunt treatment of Peabody. When he left the room, Everett turned his attention to Nester, who was sitting quietly in the corner. Everett had been holding off on the upcoming conversation but was primed for it now.

"So, Charles, how do you feel about fund raising?"

Nester looked up at the two men with surprise, as though he were invisible, and never planned to be in a conversation the entire day. "I do feel a change needs to be made," Everett continued, "in the management of athletics."

"This had nothing to do with me or my job. This was all Sam."

"Well, yes and no," Everett said. "You had no idea what was happening. You lost control of the situation in your department."

"William, uh, this is preposterous," Nester tried to stammer out, as Rosemont took a turn quietly enjoying the moment. "You're shifting the blame."

"No, I'm shifting the perception," he said. "It had to happen. Don't fret about it. You'll keep your salary if you accept the transfer quietly. No media for now. Sam and I will handle it for this situation."

"Are there any other options?"

"If not fundraising, you're going over to work for the Provost... hash out academic policy. Or, you can leave LMSU. I'll accept your resignation. Don't look at it as a demotion, Charles. We're going to need a great recruiter of donors now that Chap is out of the picture."

"I suppose... ," Nester said. He stood facing the wall, his back to Everett and Rosemont, suppressing a maddening need to explode with anger, "I'll give it a try."

"I thought you would. It's the right choice, Charles. It's an exciting game," Everett said. He stood looking into a round mirror on Rosemont's wall, smugly adjusting his tie. He shifted his weight to glance at the back of Nester's head through the mirror. "We'll have some special building projects coming up for which money must be raised. Plus, this situation may compromise the generosity of some. There's nothing like closing a naming rights deal... you'll love it. Now Sam, should we go out and address the media?"

"Yes sir. No hard feelings, huh, Charles?" Rosemont said, sticking out his hand with all the sincerity of a schoolboy who'd shot spit wads at lunch then framed an unsuspecting classmate with the principal by sticking the straw in his hand. Nester thought about all the insults over the past few years, how Rosemont had never given him his due respect.

"We'll see," Nester replied, lightly gripping Rosemont's hand for an instant with his dainty, four-finger handshake, then releasing.

Rosemont went from the media – same spin, no chance for questions – to his team, which had gathered downstairs in the Black Bears spacious locker room. Most of the team was collectively angry. Their voices could be heard outside the building - drifting off past the ears of fans to Lookout Mountain. They were unlike the players' pregame chants, which would be

273

swallowed up and lost by the noise of the anticipating crowds. When Rosemont eventually asked for quiet, his admission of guilt provided a revelation that struck deeper, a realization that some teammates wouldn't be continuing, that a season with such high expectations – expectations that were finally realized - was lost. The players grew somber. Some of the former props cried, knowing there was no way to come up with the money to return, that this college experience that they'd come to love, was over.

Rosemont gave the team the weekend off, "Come back on Monday with your game faces on," he said. The players began to walk out of the tunnel to the field. They needed to see the end zone, the goal posts, before walking the ramp. They found a few thousand fans on the field – approved by Rosemont through security - fans and students just as hurt, gathered in solidarity, offering encouragement, hoping for some of their own. The LMSU marching band had finished practice a couple of blocks away, and hearing the news, most wandered into the stadium as well, dressed in street clothes, instruments in hand. They began playing the alma mater, which brought another round of tears and cheers. Players hugged fans. Many LMSU employees, just off the clock, walked over and joined in as well. Amber Duffy looked for Ben Wright. When she found him they embraced, and then they kissed. They kissed with no hesitation or reservations of being discovered. Then they turned hand in hand and made their way towards the ramp. Fans patted Ben on his shoulder as they walked, and shouted encouragement. At the ramp they began to exit the stadium. When they reached ground level they turned and looked. The moment was so surreal. What they saw, this outpouring of affection and devotion, was being captured by news crews and broadcast live.

Rosemont looked from his office window, wondering where he would stand in the hearts of these dedicated followers. After all, he was the bad guy. He broke the rules and got caught. He brought all this punishment and sadness down on these people, on this program... his program. He decided to test it, almost wishing for some verbal abuse. After all, he was like a captain taking a lifeboat instead of going down with his ship. He quickly walked downstairs and out the tunnel door.

The first person to see him was a bearded man in his 40s, dressed in work clothes, perhaps a furniture maker. "Coach Rosemont. We're with you," he shouted. "It's us against them!" And like dominoes that multiplied with each row - the measured clap of the fall getting louder as the rows tumbled - the crowd first noticed, then displayed its approval, of Rosemont's presence. They still embraced him despite everything he'd done. If there were some in the crowd that found his actions unconscionable, they were the silent minority. They didn't dare speak out then.

Amber and Ben, still watching from above, turned their backs on the scene. "Nobody down there even remembers Dwayne," Amber said.

"They never knew him," Ben said. "The bad thing is they don't remember why he died. Coach is the hero. If Chap Roberts was down there, they'd probably be slapping him on the back too. I mean, this is going to kill our program. There's no, *'We play for titles,'* now."

"We need to do something," she said.

"We will. The question is what? Is doing that story enough?" glancing back at the field and the ongoing scene.

"Let's go home and think about it."

"We're 0-7 now," Ben said, looking at the ground. He took Amber's arm gently and started walking to the parking lot.

275

"It hurts… but everybody knows the truth," she said. "You stay focused and win the last four. That'll make this season an asterisk worth remembering."

Ben turned and looked tenderly at Amber, who was looking up at him with eyes that showed strength and "don't-forget-who-you-are" pride for him.

"I love you," Ben said.

"I know," she answered, reaching up and touching his injured cheek.

"I love you, too."

27

Chap Roberts had known his banishment from Lookout Mountain State University's football program was inevitable, and he thought he was prepared. But when the call came from Coach Sam Rosemont on his pre-paid cell phone, he suddenly felt alone. He knew it was just the beginning of his isolation.

"It's just LMSU functions, right? We can get together privately if we so choose?"

"Well... sure," Rosemont said. "I wouldn't honor it if that was the case anyhow. They can stick it as far as I'm concerned."

"Let's get a drink then. Gina and I just got in a big fight. I rented a suite at the Inn."

Normally Rosemont would enter the University Inn through the front of the lobby, or through his restaurant's outside entrance, to garner as much attention as he could. That was in the play book. He was typically there to bring attention to the program. Tonight though, he walked into the Inn through the doors at the back of the lobby, and he walked straight to the elevators. Outside the back lobby door, Charles Nester waited for Rosemont to step onto the elevator, then he entered the lobby as well. When he saw that Rosemont had gone to the top floor, he walked back outside into the parking lot. There were only two suites in the University Inn. They were positioned at either end of the fifth floor, the hotel's top floor. Nester, as Athletic Director, had booked the rooms enough for visiting dignitaries to know this.

Nester had to walk across the road to the proper angle to see into the fifth floor balconies. He could make out the coach talking with Chap Roberts in the suite on the east end.

Nester had followed Rosemont from Ivory Facilities Building. He'd watched from a distance on the field as the fans embraced the coach. Nester was stewing internally about the transfer he was going to have to endure. It hadn't even been made public yet, but when it was, this whole mess would be perceived as his screw up. Each time a female fan hugged Rosemont, each time a man slapped him on the back, Nester became embittered. By the time Rosemont had worked the entire field, Nester was enraged. Something in the athletic director's mind snapped.

Dressed in a charcoal gray suit, blue tie, and black wool overcoat, Nester re-entered the building and kept moving until he found a seat at the bar. He was never much of a drinker. He preferred to keep his head at University functions. When he did drink, it was always a whiskey and Coke. That way, with just a Coke in his hand, the boosters he was trying to solicit funds from would think he was having a drink with them. He enjoyed that deception, mockingly clinking glasses with them, the booster's inebriation usually leading to a deeper dip into the checkbook.

Tonight, he ordered his Maker's Mark and Coke, and drank it quickly without turning at all towards the room behind him. As he drank his second, all he could see in his glass was Sam Rosemont. He thought about the insults and disparaging remarks. He thought about the coach's smug behind-the-scenes attitude, and the way he went against the grain in every situation Nester brought up. He thought about what he considered Rosemont's lack of respect for his own university. Rosemont brought this mess on everybody, and he'd been out there on the field an hour ago kissing babies like he was running for the office of governor of the great state of Tennessee. Now he was upstairs consorting with the one man in the river valley with which it was newly forbidden for him to do.

When Rosemont entered Roberts' suite, he found his pal had summoned some old friends. The first was no surprise. On the room's coffee table sat a half gallon bottle of Crown Royal, a 12-pack of 7UP cans, and a brown, simulated wood, hotel room mini ice barrel. Rosemont had suspected that Chap would be getting plastered. His ego was too great to not take the banishment hard. Also on the table were four glasses. As Rosemont stood and studied the situation, the reason for the extra glasses came around the corner of the short hallway that led to the suite's two bedrooms – Betsy Parrish and Jennifer Newton. The girls both wore jeans and sweaters… Jennifer's brown tweed garment was particularly enticing: it cut low in a V, and matched the boots she wore. The revelation of their presence put Rosemont on the defensive, having made his confession to Linda only two days before.

"Hello, Coach," Jennifer said, walking to him and kissing his cheek, then placing both her hands gently and in motherly fashion on his forearm resting inside its sling. "How are you?"

"Hi Jennifer," he said. "Oh, I'm going to be alright. Hello Betsy."

"Hi, Coach," she said. Glad to be summoned by Chap, she bounced over to Rosemont and stood beside Jennifer.

"When I was checking in I found out the girls had a night off – no football this weekend and all," Roberts said. "I *had* to see what they were up to."

279

"Well, it's great to see you girls, truly, but all things considered, it might not be the best idea right now," Rosemont said. There was polite caution in his tone and his trademark smile was a flat horizon.

"I just wanted to say hello, Coach," Jennifer said. "Chap said you'd probably be down."

"Well, I am that," he said, then shifting his attention to the still-bruised Roberts. "You should be too, Sport."

"Oh, I'm mortified, can't you tell? Those sons-a-bitches," Roberts said. "Look, you're here, Sam. Just sit down and have a drink. That's no sin, is it?"

"Are you kidding? Ok, Bartender Bob. But just one."

"Now you're talking."

The drinks flowed again, but the conversation stayed superficial, mostly inane talk about how Betsy spent her days, and how Chap could occasionally "use" her in the mid-morning if she were available. Rosemont had respectfully asked Jennifer how things were at the bank. Finally, on his third drink, Sam couldn't take it anymore. He started into a tirade about the NCAA and the whole situation.

"They should get paid anyway," Rosemont said, of college football players. "All of them. With what we ask of them, the time they spend, the money that's made… especially now that there are 20 games a week on national TV."

"They get a free education, don't they?" Betsy asked.

"But that's not enough," Rosemont said. "A lot of these young men, they don't get anything from their families. They can't *take* anything from their families. Some of them don't have pocket change. They can't buy a box of crackers to have in their room. Then you've got the big schools out there loaning cars and taking care of their star player's family. They don't get caught. They don't get a sniff."

"And all we did was pay the props," Roberts said, getting up to answer a knock on the door. "They weren't even on the team, really."

"Who would that be?" Rosemont asked, his voice starting to slur. "You should check."

But Roberts had already turned the door's flat, silver handle. Charles Nester burst through the door hard and fast, shoulder first, gun in hand, prepared to fire. The weight and impact of the door struck Roberts in the face, knocking him first into the wall, then to the floor.

Nester didn't know that the two women were in the room when the floodgates of his emotions finally swung completely open. When he realized his first shot hit Jennifer in the chest he hesitated briefly, then he realized there was no turning back. He put two bullets in Rosemont, sitting shoulder to shoulder with her, then he shot Betsy in the side of the head from three feet away, the blood spraying back at him and on to his hands, face, and overcoat. The impact knocked her head and shoulders over the arm of her free standing Suffolk chair.

Roberts, finally catching up, tackled Nester from behind. Nester fell, but didn't drop his weapon. Roberts stood and tried to rush him again. Nester, on his knees, fired. The shot spun Roberts, and he twisted to the floor on his stomach. Suddenly there was only silence in the room, and a loud ringing in Nester's ears from the gun, the distinct smell of gunpowder in the air.

He stood, breathing heavily, and looked at what he'd done. He bellowed loudly and grabbed at the sides of his head, his right hand still holding the gun. Tears overflowed, rolling past his glasses and down his cheeks. He put his pistol in his mouth. As he did, Nester caught a glimpse of himself in a reflection from the room's sliding glass doors, which caused him to do a double-take. He had no rational thought, just a feeling of hopelessness and guilt. He realized then that there was no satisfaction in what he'd done. He shrieked again. Saliva rolled from his mouth. He turned his back on his own image and pulled the trigger, blowing out the back of his head. His lifeless body fell with a thud on navy blue shag carpet.

28

The Saturday headline read "FOUR DEAD IN BLOODBATH" with a summary line of, *Among the victims, Coach Sam Rosemont slain in hotel shootings.* It was not a glorious public epitaph for a coach who had become an iconic figure in the area, shot down by his soon-to-be ex-athletic director, in the company of two young women, both innocent victims. The girls' names were not immediately released, pending notification of their families.

Chap Roberts had survived Nester's murderous tirade. The bullet meant for him nearly missed, hitting him less than two inches from his armpit, essentially in the fleshy area between his shoulder and his chest. His lung was spared. The fact that Nester hadn't checked Roberts to see if he – if any of his victims – were actually dead, lent to the theory that he was on a gun-firing rampage, blinded by pent-up emotions that were released when Everett told him he would be transferred. Rosemont rubbed salt in his wound with his coy attitude, then agitated Nester further re-bonding on the field with Black Bears fans. It was a classic case of going postal, just another in a long line of American tragedies.

In the aftermath President Everett first told the police and later the press that Nester was indeed about to be transferred due to the NCAA fiasco, and that cemented in the minds of LMSU fans that he somehow had played some part in the mismanagement of the athletic program.

Linda Rosemont learned of the tragedy from the Pineknob police department's B. A. Derek. Nothing in her life could have prepared her for that visit, that ring of the doorbell on a Friday night. It's the sound parents dread when their teenage children hit the streets, not when the husband is in his late-50s.

"Mrs. Rosemont, I regret to inform you, Ma'am, that your husband is dead. He was shot and killed at the University Inn by Charles Nester. And Ma'am, there are extenuating circumstances…" said Derek. "There were two young women in the room with him and Mr. Roberts. They are deceased as well."

"Is Chap dead too?" she asked.

"No. Stable from what I understand. Spared accidently. "

First her neighbors who saw the police car, then as the news spread, Bill and Victoria Randolph, came to Linda's side to comfort her as she made the calls to their four children, waking them with the news. When that duty was completed, she could no longer be strong. She sat in her navy blue robe on her hand-carved, Louis XV high-backed walnut sofa, a gift from Sam, and had an uncontrollable cry. Victoria Randolph held her, taking note of how frail she felt.

Gina Roberts received a phone call that her husband, Chap, was being rushed by ambulance to Pineknob Memorial Hospital with a gunshot wound, although he was stable. She went to his side, almost reluctantly. She was permanently jilted by what Roberts had become. Before she knew the real story she assumed he'd been shot by the husband of a lover. Following the bullet's extraction, he was placed in a private room.

"I'm leaving you, Chap," Gina said. She no longer knew the man she stared at. She picked up her purse and began to walk out without a good-bye. "I don't think there's any coming back from this."

Staring at the ceiling he opened his mouth to speak, but said nothing. He let her leave.

Roberts' mood on Saturday reflected that of the entire Lookout Mountain State University community: numb, dumbfounded, perplexed, saddened, shocked. Rarely had a town been through such an emotional rollercoaster from the euphoria of a 7-0, Top 10 season, to Dwayne Price's death, the vindication by Ben Wright and Amber Duffy, the NCAA violations and penalties, now these senseless murders, including their beloved coach.

For Roberts it went deeper because he was the only person in town that mourned for Jim Wheatley. Also, despite nearly killing Rosemont earlier in the week himself, he felt responsible for his death now, and for the deaths of the girls. Rosemont was his best friend and he felt he hadn't done enough to stop Nester. He replayed the shootings in his mind. What could he have done differently? The fact was, from knock to annihilation, Nester was only in the room about twenty seconds. The heavy hotel door, Nester's force and full body weight behind it had broken Roberts' nose. A searing pain penetrated his head as he fell to the floor, and it was in that key instant that Nester got the drop on him, moving quickly through the hallway, down two steps and half way across the room to his victims, all shot from near point blank range except for Jennifer, essentially killed by a stray bullet meant for Rosemont. When Nester shot Roberts, he made a quick decision to stay down and act dead, hoping possibly some of the others were doing the same. Through the slit of one eye he watched Nester's last act, a gruesome sight by anyone's standards, though he couldn't have been happier that Nester took his own life.

Lying in the hospital bed that morning his eyes were blackened from the broken nose, which blended with his earlier bruises from Rosemont. He was tender and sore from the gunshot wound. He was beaten and defeated.

285

He thought about calling Steve Jackson and having him change his plea to guilty. He'd just do his time, no more dickering over these petty infractions, no more posturing as an innocent. Then he had a better idea.

Ben Wright and Amber Duffy awoke Saturday morning together, in her bed, to the story of the shootings on local news breaks during the "Today" show. Amber gasped at the news. Sitting up in the bed, Ben went numb. He leaned back on his pillow, and stared at Amber's picture of Ludlow. He just tried to let it sink in. Coach Rosemont was dead. Charles Nester shot him, then killed himself. These two leaders of his college experience, two men he really respected, though Nester to a much lesser degree... gone.

Tears rolled down Amber's cheeks again, as she thought about Coach Rosemont.

"Poor Linda, and oh my gosh, their children -- and grandchildren," Amber said. "They must be in so much pain. I just can't cry anymore. All I've done all week is cry."

She put her head on Ben's chest and wrapped her arms around him.

"Amber, have I told you that I have a little bit of money saved, not much, but more than eight thousand dollars, from working camps and such?"

"That's good, Ben," she said, tilting her head to look at his face, puzzled by his complete change of topics, though he'd yet to utter a word about the massacre.

"I've never wanted for anything," he said. "I've never had to spend money my grandparents gave me growing up. I've led a great life."

"You're lucky. But you've worked hard too. You know what? Your life is just going to get better."

"Let's elope," he said, turning towards her.

"What?"

"You heard me. I want to marry you... today."

"You're crazy."

"No, listen. It will be our secret. We love each other. We have these two days off. We'll still have a ceremony when you want to have it. Spiritually it will be better. God will grant us a 72-hour reprieve on lovemaking, especially with all we've been through."

She sat up on her knees and faced him. She was wearing a blue cotton tank top and panties, her hair was slipping out of a pony tail. He had on a pair of gym shorts.

"It's that important to you?" she asked.

"I just know you're the one for me. I've known it since I met you, even though you wouldn't have anything to do with me."

Amber looked away briefly, though smiling as she thought about it.

"I will want to have a ceremony one day... it's a girl's dream you know. I've got a big family that expects it."

"I understand. Think of the wedding we can have once I'm drawing NFL pay."

"Ok then. How do you want to do it?"

"Oh, I don't know. Let's just drive somewhere... not too, too far. Uh, how about Atlanta or Savannah? No, even better. Let's go to Asheville. We'll stay at The Biltmore. That's just about four hours away."

"All right."

"I just need to check in with the coaches, make sure nothing has changed... see if they know when Coach's funeral will be. It wouldn't be before Monday, would it?

"I don't think so. Probably not… people will be coming in from everywhere."

"He was happy about us, you know," Wright said.

"He was?"

"He called you a great girl."

"That hurts my heart it's so sweet."

"So you'll do it? You'll marry me this weekend?"

"I believe I will."

29

The French Broad River winds lazily through the 8,000 acres on which the Biltmore stands, a summer whim of George Washington Vanderbilt, a grandson of real railroad money. Located just South of Asheville, North Carolina, when the six years of construction was completed in 1895, the 135,000-square foot home was considered the third largest estate in America. The impeccable grounds and gardens leading to the picturesque riverside, fall foliage in part still clinging to the trees, was a perfect setting in Amber Duffy's mind for her secret nuptials to Ben Wright.

The Biltmore is known for its wine and its weddings for the affluent, so after a little friendly persuasion of a young female of the lobby staff, finding a judge was no more difficult than choosing a name. The name they picked was Rev. Luke Means, and he proved by phone to be an amiable enough fellow to suit Amber. The staffer, Cindy Wickline, even agreed to stand in as a witness on her dinner break.

They had decided concretely on three ideas before they left Amber's condo. One, they would dress casually for the ceremony. Knowing the elevation of Asheville and correctly thinking it would be colder there than in Pineknob, Amber chose a beautifully embroidered scarlet V-neck sweater, a black woolen skirt that hit her at her calves, and black leather boots. She wore her hair down. Somewhat limited in his wardrobe choices, Ben grabbed a thin, tan sweater to wear under the only other sports coat he had at school, a brown tweed number. With that he wore faded jeans, and brown loafers.

289

Two, they would exchange rings already in their possession. Amber picked a beautiful emerald ring surrounded by tiny diamonds given to her by her parents. Ben brought along the only piece of jewelry he owned, a conference championship ring he had received in the spring for the Black Bears' hard work and winning ways the previous fall.

The final decision – to make the ceremony more memorable and special - was to allow each other 30 seconds to ad lib their feelings, some message, to each other. "No thinking ahead of time," they decided, which they stuck to, because they shared so much conversation and laughter on the drive over, there was literally no time to concentrate on such thoughts. Amber felt herself at a disadvantage because she wasn't prone to break out into soliloquies, where Ben was already comfortable standing and speaking with nothing prepared before the largest of influential crowds.

They were lucky to book a room at the estate, but a cancellation provided an unfilled opening which they jumped on. There is a hotel on the grounds as well that had openings, but they wanted the full experience of the grand estate if at all possible.

When they left their room and met Rev. Means and Ms. Wickline, they became familiar with each other in conversation as they walked off the South Terrace and on to the extensive grounds, filled with Washington Hawthorns, Japanese Maples, Red Maples, Sourwoods, Black Gums, and Scarlet Oaks. Rev. Means was just old enough, probably just over 50, where he could have been a father to either participant. And yet he had a kind ease about him that made both Amber and Ben comfortable as they all strolled together.

"I'm praying the weather will be nice enough tomorrow to spend time in the Azalea Garden," Amber said, glancing at the sky.

"You know the gardens – all the grounds -- were commissioned by a second architect -- Fredrick Law Olmstead. He created Central Park," Miss Wickline said enthusiastically, not trying to mask that she dreamed of one day being a tour guide. "Richard Morris Hunt, the first architect, modeled the 250 room mansion – 34 bedrooms originally – from three 16th-century French chateaux."

Closer to the French Broad, which was a long walk, they saw an American Beech tree that just seemed to speak to them. The sun was beginning to descend behind the mountains so the couple stepped up close to its roots and faced each other. Amber looked to her right.

"Our shadows. Look, Ben," she said, taking his hands in hers. The intertwined forms stretched twice Ben's length. "That was the day I started loving you."

There was nothing he could add to the thought, so he smiled humbly before he kissed her.

"Is everyone ready?" Rev. Means asked.

The ceremony took all of eight minutes, but both Amber and Ben were dripping with emotions - for each other, for the events of the past week, for the future - so much so that with each word they spoke they fought back tears.

"We are gathered here together at this majestic site, before these glorious mountains and river created by God, to bring together these two fine young people in holy matrimony…"

Amber and Ben stood gazing into each other's eyes, holding each other's hands, and the words seemed to disappear from their consciousness. Even when they each said "I do" it seemed surreal. When the preacher set up their testimonials, Amber came back to her nervous reality, though she remained calm.

"I know in my heart that you are a man who will always love, honor, and take care of me. I want you to know that I will be there by your side, maturing as a loyal wife, and taking care of you and your needs, helping you grow in both mind and spirit. I want to help with charities that I know you'll be involved with. Mostly, I want to grow old with you in the wake of a life filled with children and grandchildren. Know that I love *you* - not your throwing arm, not the touchdowns, or what the public yearns for – but for you: your goodness, your kindness, your dedication, your spirit, your faith. I thank God for what we share."

"And Ben, would you like to profess your love to Amber?" asked Rev. Means.

"I don't know if God had a plan but I know He sees our love as something great. My love for you starts with your eyes, because through your eyes I can see your beauty both inward and outward. I love your sense of humor, and I love to hear you laugh. I love when you walk, and I love when you stand still. You affect me so deeply that it would scare me to be so vulnerable, except I know that our love will always be served. You are now at the top of my dedication list, and whatever I achieve, I will do it for you and for our family and for God. Keep holding my hand and together we will conquer life."

"If there are no objections to these two being wed," said Rev. Means, looking upward from his Bible towards Ms. Wickline, who had a tear in her eye, "by the authority vested in me by the great state of North Carolina, I now pronounce you man and wife. You may kiss the bride."

Ben took one hand and softly reached for Amber's neck, never having broken his gaze. He touched it and slid his fingers behind her head and through her hair as tenderly as he could before he bent slightly to kiss her. Forgetting where they were, so in love and so enraptured in the moment, they held their kiss for a little longer than appropriate, but Rev. Means and Cindy Wickline both just watched and smiled, for meeting the couple seemed to be an exercise in goodness. Remembering then that she was to take a post-ceremony picture, Ms. Wickline turned on a small digital camera Amber had the foresight to bring, and shot the couple in their embrace.

The flash went off in the growing darkness, breaking the kiss. Ben turned to their new friends with a triumphant smile.

"Thanks to both of you for your help," he said. "Could you join us for dinner?" Both respectfully declined. The couple posed for one shot with Rev. Means, and then for three quick shots of just themselves. Rev. Means took the camera and snapped one of the couple with Ms. Wickline as well, "So you'll remember her young face."

Ben slipped the Reverend a 100-dollar bill in a white envelope, shook his hand and thanked him again for his time as the four began to walk back towards the Biltmore. This last action took him from Amber's side, so he corrected that by moving around the group to his right, he put his left arm around her shoulder and held her close as the quartet turned its collective back to the French Broad River.

30

Spurred on by the emails of a half dozen leaders, and in direct protest of the NCAA's severity, the football coaches of America had already decided to vote Lookout Mountain State University in their poll on Sunday night for one last time. When the news of Sam Rosemont's death hit the air waves, it was a slam dunk. The Associated Press Poll, the sportswriters, exercised no such sentiment.

Many of those same coaches arrived by plane Sunday night and Monday morning for Rosemont's memorial service scheduled for Monday afternoon. Jenkins Funeral Home was in charge of the arrangements and embalming the body, but Linda Rosemont accepted Dr. Everett's gesture of using the LMSU's facilities and personnel for everything related to the service, including catered food afterwards for all attendees.

Linda, her children, and the LMSU event staff waited on the weather that morning to make their final plans. If foul weather prevailed, the University's auditorium would be utilized. But Mother Nature cooperated, granting a beautiful early November day, so the facilities staff set up to have the service in Ludlow Stadium on the football field. They placed 300 chairs for family, friends, and VIPs, set up a podium, and created signage stating the stadium seats would be available for viewing by the general public. The LMSU football team, and any former players who wanted to join them – 175 did -- stood and made a three-quarter circle around the chairs that reached all the way to the small stage. That was a site in and of itself – so many large, strong, men dressed in jackets and ties, many of whom could not hold back tears when the speeches began. They joined hands for the opening prayer.

LMSU play-by-play man Bill Randolph mc'd the service. Dr. Everett, Coach Will Reed, Billy Reed, Coach Ennis Ivory and Ben Wright all spoke. The team Chaplin, Rev. Ronald Raines, gave both prayers. Rosemont had always called him "Ronny the Rev" or when he was less playful simply "Reverend Ron." Chap Roberts, released from the hospital that morning, had himself driven to Ludlow's entrance. He watched and listened from ground level, which was halfway up the stadium's stands. He didn't want to be noticed, and he wasn't, despite 3,000 or so fans showing up for the service.

"My first experience with Coach, and something that I observed so many times later, was that he instinctively knew the right strings to pull with players to get what he wanted," Ben Wright said. "When he recruited me, it was the underdog deal. 'Those schools that overlooked you, that didn't even invite you for a visit, you're going to make them all pay,' he told me. 'I can see it in you.'

"Well that was the right angle to take with me. He was like a psychologist when it came to recruiting. I'm sure each and every player standing here could tell you a similar story. Coach made me want to work harder than I ever dreamed was possible. If I'm lucky enough to keep playing this game after my years here at LMSU, I'll think of Coach Sam Rosemont every day I strap on the pads, every time I stick in a game tape and hit play. He motivated me to strive for perfection. Thank you, Coach."

"You get into the day-to-day thing and you stop thinking about mortality," Ennis Ivory said. "For some reason though I once thought about Sam's... and I thought he's so happy-go-lucky, he'll probably live forever.

Despite the fact that his favorite food was 'more, please!' But I was wrong. I'm still struggling to understand this, as I'm sure many of you are. I just hope – selfish reasons not withstanding – there's a football field in heaven and Sam Rosemont is pacing its sidelines, roaring at an official. He was the most competitive player I ever coached, and, as a coach, he was the same way when the whistle blew on Saturday. He made the nation take notice of Black Bears football."

Billy Reed in closing said, "I'm lucky enough to have my father here and yet I feel like I've lost a father. Sam Rosemont took me under his wing and nurtured me as a football coach. He had this amazing ability to assess a situation instantly and combine years of knowledge and experience into a quick answer. He knew the game that well. He could have eventually coached at one or more of what outsiders feel are the top programs in the country -- except that he loved this place so much. He couldn't get past it. You can bet that all those 'football schools' now know Lookout Mountain State University."

With that the crowd couldn't help itself and cheered. Reed walked away from the podium and Rev. Raines gave the final benediction. . For that, joined by Ben Wright and the coaches who spoke, the former and current players spread out and formed a complete circle around the event and again joined hands.

Linda Rosemont looked frail but remained strong, surrounded by her children and grandchildren, as they looked at Rosemont, who was laid to rest in his Navy blue jacket and a Black Bears tie, for the final time. She bent and kissed his cheek, and placed one of his track and field medallions on his hands. It had been in his track uniform that she first took notice of him so many years ago. She wasn't even a football fan when they'd started dating. But he made the same impact on her that he did football games.

When Linda and her family moved from his casket, each and every person in the stadium also filed by to pay their last respects, except for Chap. After the benediction, he returned to his hired ride and continued working on his plan.

The names of Charles Nester, Jennifer Newton, and Betsy Parrish were not mentioned publically that afternoon. Nester's wife, Sally, shocked and confused by the entire episode, had his body cremated, and she took his ashes back to Kentucky to spread. Jennifer's parents lived in-state about an hour, in Sewanee. They took her body home to be buried. Betsy had only a mother, with no real means. Chap contacted her from the hospital and arranged to pay for Betsy's burial and her headstone. On that Monday he also had the difficult face-to-face task of trying to explain to her why she died, why she was in that hotel room. He said he had really liked and respected Betsy and enjoyed the time he'd spent with her, and that she always had this wonderful disposition at work that made other people like her. But her mother, Margaret, was younger than Chap, she'd been around the bars in her younger life, and she sensed what kind of man Chap was.

"I appreciate what you've done, sir, but admit it, my daughter was just a piece of ass to you," she said, holding back tears following her graveside service.

"It's not true, Margaret," he said. "If it were, I wouldn't have seen her more than once. We really had a good time together. I don't know where it would have gone but we were friends… we connected somehow. I can't explain to you how hurt I am by her death. But I am sorry for your loss… for everyone's loss."

While Rosemont's reception went on in the school's commons area, highlighted by a sea of assorted finger foods that could feed 1,000, the chairs were cleared away at Ludlow by University staff. The football team then had the difficult task of putting on the pads and walking back out on that field.

Bud Steel, the fiery defensive coordinator, had been named interim head coach of the Black Bears by Dr. Everett. The first seven wins were now all considered forfeits… from 7-0 to 0-7 in one afternoon. Circumstances could hardly be more depressing. With a potential NFL career in front of him, linebacker Jerome Jones found himself an agent and borrowed the money to retain his eligibility. Most of the other props, with no such immediate - albeit rule-breaking - prospects, cleared out their lockers.

"We have to put the same effort in these last four games that we did in the first seven… and that also means practice, film, and weights," Steel said. "Demand it of yourselves. I know you want to be down, the coaching staff wants to be down. Be mad instead. Let's do what it takes these last four weeks to win. Let's take it out on our opponents. It won't say it in the record books, but we will know for all time what we have accomplished. Who is with me?"

The roar that the Black Bears let out echoed in the stands, rose to the heavens, and could be heard a mile away.

31

Judge O. Henry Buffington sat at his desk Thursday morning in chambers staring at an envelope address to him, delivered to him by Winston North, Chap Roberts' corporate attorney. His defense attorney, Steve Jackson, was present, as was Assistant District Attorney Luke Rinehart.

Buffington's hands showed their age. They were thin, wrinkled, shook slightly, and had age spots. He thought he knew what he had in his hands. His mouth was dry, so after trying to fix the problem by licking his lips, he labored to pour himself a glass of water from a pitcher on his desk. He took a long drink, then exhaled when he finished. He turned the envelope over twice before putting a letter opener to it. He pulled out the contents and re-affixed to the end of his nose the reading glasses that dangled in front of his chest by a string.

He perused the three-page letter to himself at first, then he looked up at North. "Gentlemen, I guess there's no reason to keep anybody outside waiting any longer," Buffington said. "I'll address the court in five minutes, and I will read the parts of the letter that are relevant."

North, Jackson, and Rinehart left chambers and returned to the courtroom, where 35 jury candidates, and four dozen interested parties, including media, Amber Duffy, Ben Wright, William Everett, and local businessmen, some of whom were LMSU Board of Trustee members – capacity - also sat waiting. The bailiff signified Buffington's entrance with, "All rise for Judge O. Henry Buffington."

Buffington moved as quickly as he could for a man of his age, adjusted his robe so it would not bind him, and he sat down, motioning the court to do the same as he did. "Please be seated. Our time is valuable, I don't want you to be here too long if it's not necessary. In fact, jury candidates are excused. You may leave if you please. I'm sure you will be contacted again soon," Buffington said, looking at the three rows filled in the back to his left. Only four of the 35, three men who looked to be labor workers, and one seemingly stressed out mother, gathered themselves and their personal items and exited.

"We were called here because Chap Roberts was – is - accused of the crime of attempted murder, a felony, and I admit sometimes a slippery slope for prosecutors, attorneys and judges because *mens rea* or the mindset of the accused, his intent, his motive, the potential for bodily harm, is never the same in any case.

"Jurisprudence forces us to take a fresh look each and every time this comes up in our courtroom, and to weigh the entire spectrum of the case as we understand it. The pre-trial sharing of information, reports from the NCAA, and from local law enforcement I have received this week shows a scope of activity that reaches much further than this matter of attempted murder. But, for example, Roberts and Sam Rosemont, the victim who, consequently, did not press charges, were obviously good friends. They were dining together when the crime occurred, and they nearly died together Friday night, after the crime, obviously having resolved their differences. Were it not for photos that gave additional criminal intent to Roberts, it could seem that he was defending his own life at the park when he shot Rosemont.

"The pair together had for years broken rules provided by the NCAA concerning the Proposition 48 athletes that came to Lookout Mountain State University hoping to play football. Their willful intent disregarding this rule, with monies that certainly would be a violation of tax laws, creates another web of unlawful complexities. This web became much wider in scope when Mr. Dwayne Price was murdered in his home, with an, if not complex, an expensive, plot to frame him as a drug dealer. This case is now considered closed with the death of one Jim Wheatley, an employee of Roberts, who attempted to murder or at least cause bodily harm to three other people: Max Milovich, Amber Duffy, and Ben Wright. Ms. Duffy shot and killed Wheatley with the weapon he apparently intended to use on her and Mr. Wright. Since again, Wheatley was a cog in Roberts' operation, this further widens the scope of unlawfulness to possibly accessory to murder, the proof of which would include hearsay and would increase the ramifications to Roberts 20-fold.

"I have to tell you ladies and gentlemen, this is all quite exhausting for me," Buffington said, momentarily taking his glasses down from his nose and pausing to awkwardly take another drink of water. "I remember a time not so long ago when college athletics were not so complex, when comparatively little money was involved, when athletes were willing to eat beans day after day and live in attics or basements for the privilege of participating. There weren't huge television contracts or potential multi-million dollar professional contracts at stake, with agents lurking, hoping to get the inside track on players. It was a simpler time - but I do not think that the experience of being part of a team, the joys of competition, the rewards of preparation, victories, and defeats, were any less. Society has put such value on sports that we as consumers - because of these astronomical

301

television contracts and advertising - pay more each and every time we purchase an item in a store. Now this attached value has also influenced the attitudes of parents when it comes to their children's participation in sports. Are they working only for the payoff at the end, the notoriety, the college scholarship, the pro contract? Have we become so blinded by the potential payoff, a payoff that is actually afforded the tiniest, most minuscule fraction of participants, that sportsmanship and the joy of competition – the fun - are archaic values? How is it that a parent blinded with rage could beat up a volunteer coach, that parents would fight other parents in the bleachers, that a father would make his son quit a team because his coach sat him out of one inning of *an entire season*, or a father as a coach could ruin his son's pitching arm, teach him to pitch with the other, ruin that one, with multiple operations, *before* he's 14-years-old? I have resided over such cases, heard such stories, and I can only ask myself, what example are we setting for the children?"

Buffington had continually looked about the courtroom as though an answer would appear in one of the faces of the members. He saw only attentive but blank stares. He scratched his silver hair, then cleared his throat.

"I apologize, ladies and gentlemen, perhaps I'm just an embittered, foolish, old man. Chap Roberts has fled the country, and should now be considered a fugitive from justice for the felony crime of attempted murder," Buffington said to a chorus of oohs and ahhs. "Quiet please. He has been quite tidy in his departure. I will give you the broad strokes, and they are the strokes of, again, a man with means.

"He has put in his wife's name, a woman he says didn't love him and wanted a divorce, their home and a bank account containing $5 million. He

302

has created, in conjunction with the business department at LMSU, The Sam Rosemont School of Business, a living laboratory of all his corporations – except apparently for three bars, which he sold. Undergraduates and post graduate students will get a hands-on opportunity to help run a real business in this program. Mr. Roberts has appointed or hired a, um, Leslie Workman, who will graduate from LMSU's current graduate school next month, to oversee the continued success of these vast businesses as well as the development of this program with University personnel. She will make the mint.

"He has also given $100,000 to the families of Betsy Parrish, Jennifer Newton, and to Ms. Duffy, to her, it says, for any pain and suffering now or in the future. He said he could not give anything to Ben Wright, because he is a college athlete and that it would be improper. He has elevated Mr. Max Milovich to CEO of Ridgecrest Insurance with a 40 percent increase in salary.

"Mr. North, am I to understand that you knew nothing of Mr. Roberts' plans to flee the country?"

"Sir, I attended only to matters concerning the businesses and Mrs. Roberts," North said, standing at the defense table. "He led me to believe he would stand trial and do his time if necessary… that these were arrangements made with prison in mind."

"And you, Mr. Jackson?"

"Your honor, we prepared for his defense up until 7 p.m. last night," Jackson said, also standing. "He was still battered and worn out from his wounds, but he seemed excited to get under way. I expected him here, just as you and Mr. Rinehart did. I'm obviously surprised at this turn of events."

"Well, apparently, without any investigation or forensic accounting, Mr. Roberts was shrewd enough concerning his finances to completely redistribute his wealth. I will read you this final paragraph from him," said Buffington, re-affixing his glasses.

"Judge Buffington, I am sorry for leaving in this manner, and not taking heed to your previous warning. As you may recognize from the events leading up to today, Sam Rosemont and I were on good terms when he died. I wish I'd died with him, Betsy Parrish, and Jennifer Newton. I've never before felt such guilt. Perhaps it's cowardly, but I saw no reason to have to bear it in prison. I have placed small amounts of money in accounts in just over 30 countries, and I, of course, have cash. I hired four separate and independent jets to fly me, or someone fitting my description, out of the country to four separate destinations. I know it won't, but I hope the half million dollars I forfeited for bail, and the gesture concerning the Rosemont School of Business, including corporations at an estimated value of $300 million give or take, will somehow lessen the perception of my wrongdoing, which by the way included years of quarterly payoffs of $25,000 – cash -- to LMSU President, Dr. William Everett, to turn a blind eye to the millions upon millions of dollars my businesses made fleecing our state supported school."

Buffington looked up from the letter and set it down, again looking over the faces of the court. "Pending the apprehension and return of Chap Roberts, at which time I will note, because I will not likely be around to sit, he should face charges not only of attempted murder but accessory to murder, and because peripheral matters are not the business of the day, as far as this court is concerned, this case is closed," said Buffington, with a firm rap of his gavel to its block.

Epilog

Among the Lookout Mountain State University contingency, the final rap of the gavel was followed by an awkward moment of stunned silence. People were standing, gathering their personal items, putting on their coats, as the knowledge that President William Everett had been taking payoffs from Chap Roberts sank in. What would the ramifications be for the boss? All while he tried to look inconspicuous and dignified.

Facing charges of extortion and looked upon on campus as suffering from a general moral irreverence – especially after Max Milovich brought to light the conversation between Everett and Coach Rosemont that took place in the hospital about firing Charles Nester, which ultimately set off Nester's murderous tirade – Everett was dismissed by the LMSU Board of Trustees. He came clean to authorities and spent a year in a minimum security prison, though he used the time to write a successful book about the state of Higher Education in America. Danny Smith didn't make it to New York, his Heisman bid falling short, possibly because of the demise of the program. He would go on to a great career in the NFL, as would Jerome Jones, Steve Lake, Aaron Wallace, and Ben Wright, who declared himself eligible for the Draft after New Year's Day, foregoing his senior year at LMSU.

Wright was taken in the first round. Because of his redshirt season, he took just 15 hours in spring, and graduated with a double major. He did his workouts and weight work with the Black Bears football team. The coaches could hardly blame him for moving on, as LMSU was starting a new and less glamorous era. Wright helped the upcoming quarterbacks as much as he could through spring and summer, traveling to mini-camps from Chattanooga when he needed to.

With the upcoming change of scenery and lifestyle, Ben and Amber also married that summer, back at The Biltmore. Amber ended her tenure at LMSU when the spring semester closed, and spent the next eight weeks joyfully planning the details of her wedding.

Chap Roberts had flown from Tennessee to Canada and then on to Paris that last evening. He kicked around Europe for a few years, living modestly, riding a bicycle for a while, never staying in one place for more than a few months, a concealed money belt a permanent fixture to his waistline. Sometimes the isolation and lack of being involved, of being the boss, of being connected, would overtake him, and he would drink in excess. More than anything, he longed for the rush that came with making command decisions for multiple corporations, of making the moves to turn a dying business into a money-maker. Eventually, he learned to appreciate and take satisfaction in the simplest of events, in beautiful scenery, a meadow or lake, or in architecture. Later he purchased a small pub in Switzerland, and eventually settled down with a much younger woman there. He longed for his buddy Sam Rosemont – just to share a laugh with someone who understood him. He looked back on the Jim Wheatley-Dwayne Price episode with sincere regret. He was never apprehended.

But before all that, the Black Bears buckled down, focused, kept their precision alive, and won their last four conference games under Bud Steel. It went in the record books as a 4-7* season. Never has an asterisk meant more. For LMSU, the players and coaches, the alumni, the fans, the community, it was remembered as a season of perfection under circumstances beyond trying, beyond insane, in fact, bordering on incomprehensible. On one hand, for the players it was a fantastic accomplishment and the rarest of feats. On the other, it was an example of the worst in men, what they will do to one another, the rules and laws they will break, their greed, their lack of respect, what they will do to rise above their peers, their decadence.

For those who understood its significance, the asterisk became a symbol that kept you grounded, that kept you working, reminding you constantly that anything can happen, that nothing is etched in stone. More than that, for all time, it was an asterisk that gave a warning. It also gave hope.

The End

Acknowledgements

Special thanks to: Coach Derek Christian; Coach Tony DeMeo, Coach Bob Pruett, Coach Tim Billings, Coach Gunter Brewer, Coach Mark Gale, Coach Jay Hopson, Coach Bill Legg, Coach Kevin Kelly, Coach Ernie Purnsley, Coach Bill Wilt, along with hundreds of coaches, assistant coaches, and players from the Southern, Southeastern, Mid-American, Big Ten, Big East Conferences; to Sports Information Directors Clark Haptonstall, Ricky Hazel, and Randy Burnside; to safety and security expert Jack Rinchich; to (the late) Barbara, Kyle, Sue, and Walter Hall for a place to write with a beautiful view; to teacher Tom Morgan for his Grade Saver Sheet; to Dr. Lillian Wilson for a single thought that endured years; Professor Dolly Withrow for advice and a humorous voice; to Pastors David Stauffer and Ross "Pepper" Harrison for any spiritual knowledge I've retained; to Coach Tex Williams for theories in athletic dedication and lifelong inspiration; to Dr. Alan and Nancy Morris for a beach house in which to write summer after summer, love and support; to Angie Woolum for hand-to-hand combat theory; to Jay Drumheller for humorous insights into various areas touched upon in the book; to friend Chip Ellis for helping me push boundaries and believe in more; to sportswriters Jack Bogaczyk, Don Hager, Chuck Landon, Tom Aluise, Chris Dickerson, and the late Mike Cherry for mentoring and writing guidance; to the late Jody Jividen for all of that plus so much more about writing, music, basketball and life; to Sam Hindman, friend and supporter who allowed me to meet so many of the above people by giving me my first shot at *The Charleston Daily Mail*. It was in his home, at 20, that I first said I wanted to write a novel; to Randy Oney for his graphics work; to my parents, Ruth and Alan Spradling for their love and support; to Chloe, Logan, and Chip Simmons for their enthusiasm after Chip's early read; to friend and former player John Humphreys for encouragement and reminding me of the long shadows; to my late sister Kelly Simmons for inspiration; to writer Andy Postman for a critical look; to writers (and SCR member) Joe Bird and Rebecca Goodwin for follow-ups to that; to founding member of the Shelton College Review Larry Ellis, a constant beacon of light; to Hall of Fame news correspondent Ed Rabel for opening doors; to my former agent, Diane Nine of Nine Speakers, for believing in the project through two failed contracts; to my three children, Evan, Audrey and Claire for love, support and a need for a dream; to my fantastic, loving, and wonderfully patient wife and partner, Mylissa Spradling, for believing in me; and to you, the reader, I sincerely thank you. I hope I provided an entertaining departure for a short time. And if so, please share with the other readers in your life so I may continue my pursuit of this dream. Next up will be *The Lost Lantern*. For more information or links to other projects, start at: andrewspradling.wordpress.com .

Accolades for *The Long Shadow Of Hope*

This is novel is a reflection, at least in part, of what this author, Andy Spradling, has experienced as an athlete, journalist, coach and college sports information employee...This book embodies what is the essence of a good read, e.g., strong story lines, character development, continuing twists and turns that accentuate the requisite research which is reflected in the attention to detail that is often absent in the works of even the most accomplished authors. Mr. Spradling has shown through this, his initial effort, that writing and story-telling are his forte. This is an exceptional sports book, but it is more than that - it is a darn good yarn. It's a quick, captivating read. Excellent – *Sam Hindman, former Executive, Thomson Newspapers and Publisher, The Charleston Daily Mail*

Read more reviews on Amazon.com

About The Author – It was Andrew Spradling's diverse path into his 50s that makes the characters of his books so rich. An athlete turned sportswriter, a college administrator, a musician and song writer, a restaurant owner who worked the establishments of Murrell's Inlet, South Carolina, in his youth, Spradling has interacted with people from all walks of life. And in doing so, he takes pride in having listened more than he spoke. West Virginia born and educated (WVSU), Spradling is a happy husband to Mylissa, and father of Evan, Audrey, and Claire. The 1999 West Virginia Sportswriter of the Year (National Sportscasters and Sportswriters Association), Spradling is the author of two books, *The Long Shadow of Hope,* and (coming soon) *The Lost Lantern.*

Made in the USA
Charleston, SC
21 July 2016